I0785343

NATALIA
HERNANDEZ

THE NAME-BEARER

NATALIA HERNANDEZ

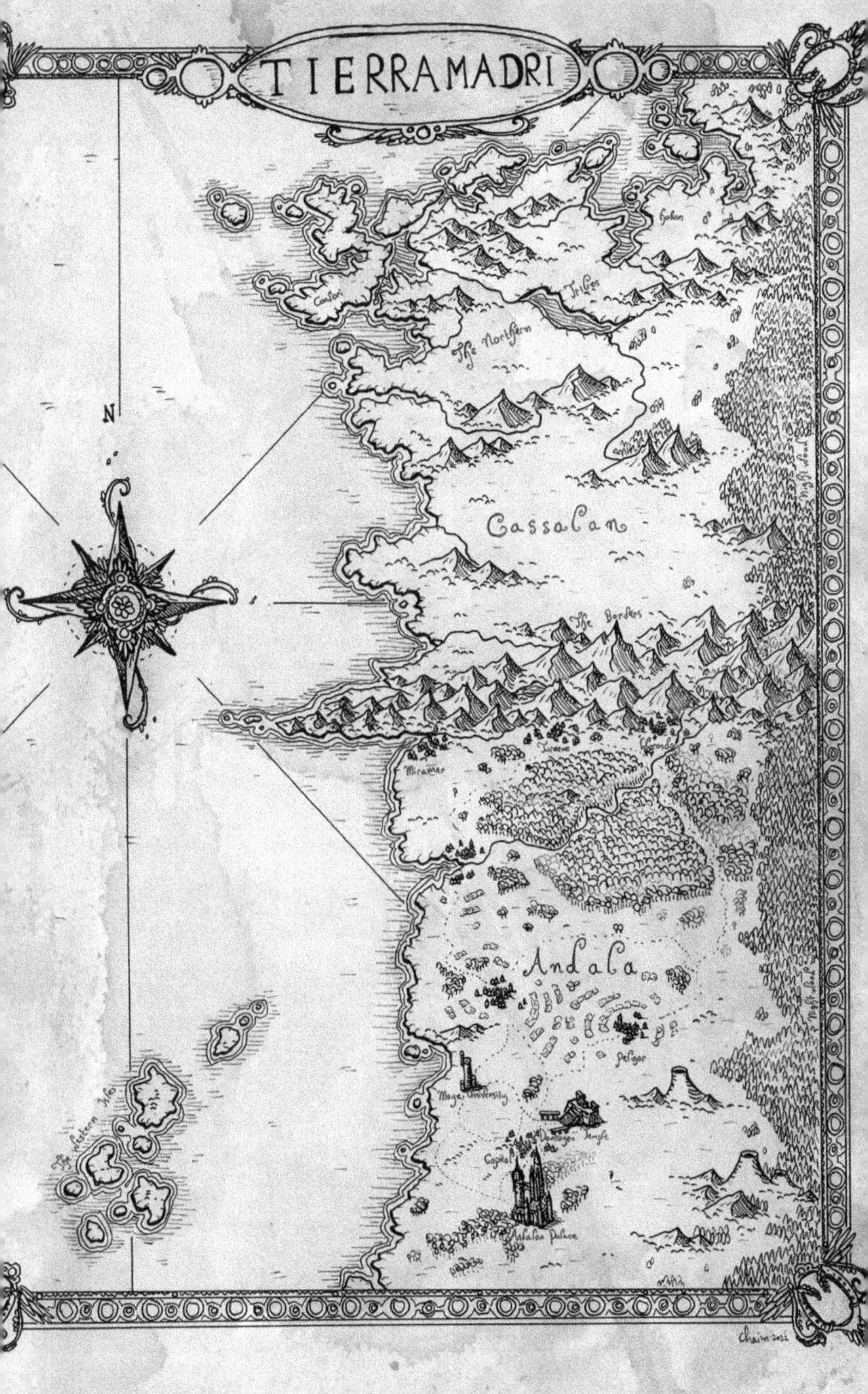

TIERRAMADRI
N
Gabor
Trilles
The Northern
Cassalan
Castori
Night Wood
The Borders
Sereen
Goraba
Miramar
Andala
Belgar
Night Wood
Mage University
Dominion Temple
Capital
The Western Isle
Antalon Palace

To each and every single one
of my TikTok followers,
who made this possible.

You make my dreams come true.

CONTENTS

ROYAL DECREE

Their Royal Majesties King Edwin of Thunder and Queen Myra the Morning Mist have decreed:

Upon the formal betrothal of two future monarchs, a Name-Bearer will be selected from the children of the land. The child may not be above the age of three.

When a Name-Bearer is needed, the Royal Bees will be informed. As messengers of the gods, they will find and make the correct selection.

Once chosen as the Name-Bearer, the child will be stripped of their name and serve as a vessel to receive the names of royal children from the great Flowers of Prophecy and deliver those names to the ruling king and queen.

Families of those chosen to be Name-Bearers will be rewarded with lodgings, land, and enough gold to comfortably live out the rest of their days.

(All is subject to forfeit should families try to contact their former child, now Name-Bearer.)

The Name-Bearer will live on the palace grounds and be trained to be the only living souls permitted and able to converse with the Flowers of Prophecy.

Once selected, the child is the lawful and rightful property of the monarchy and will have no ties, lawful or otherwise, to their birth parents.

So it is written, so shall it be.

CHAPTER 1

For the girl, the night had begun early, even before the great sun goddess Tz'ola bowed her flaming crown to dim its rays past the far western horizon. When the news had come, the girl had been shut in her room with strict instructions to remain there until it was all over. She didn't know how long these things were supposed to take, but it had been many hours.

It had been so long that the girl knew the exact number of stones making up the floor of her modest but clean palace room. They were of varying shapes, sizes, colors, and cuts, but they totaled 637. She knew there were 637 because she had counted each of them.

Twice.

There were only 116 panels of wood that made up her walls, but the one that was three panels down from the left side of her single bed had a stain on it that, if she squinted, resembled the long face of a vicuña.

The counting had been the first activity of the deliriously long, painfully slow, maddeningly quiet night.

After the stones and the panels, she counted the brightly colored borlas that hung on the edges of her bed covers. Twenty-five of the vibrant bundled tassels decorated each side of the colcha, except for the one nearest her pillow, which had lain undisturbed throughout the long night.

At some point in the middle of counting them she had grown hungry. Her stomach had cramped painfully from something other than anticipation and suddenly the borlas were more than just colorful decorations. The purple tuft of woolen string reminded her of fat kernels of purple corn, lightly salted and roasted over an open flame, drenched with green lime, the same shade as the tassel that neighbored it.

The next colors in the row: yellow, orange, and red, were a fruit salad of lucuma, granadilla and mango. If she leaned in just right, she could almost smell the pulpy, syrupy scent of them. Blue came next, crisp and clear as the freshwater lakes, quenching her burning throat, and then the pink as light and happy as the inside of a guava.

The girl had a fondness for sweet things.

Eventually even the borlas could no longer hold her imagination, and began irritating her for being mere threads rather than the food her mind promised. She also ran out of things to count. She would have attempted to count the stars in the night sky themselves, had the moisture in the air not blocked her view. It was always humid this time of the year.

So, instead, the girl began to pace. The floor beneath her should have been cold against her bare feet, but she had walked the straight path from her window to the door and back again so many times that the stones had warmed from the persistent friction.

She had just begun yet another lap when the abrupt rap of knuckles on wood pulled her up short, causing her heart to leap to her throat. The girl spun and stared wide-eyed at her door. It was time, she could feel it. With wobbling limbs she crossed her room slowly, deliberately, and pulled open the heavy barrier between herself and the fate which awaited her.

"The queen has given birth."

The child blinked heavy eyes at the messenger, her long lashes delicately brushing over the dark smudges under them. She was not surprised by his words. She had been expecting him, after all, and his message.

In a way, she had been waiting for his message for the greater part of ten years.

The girl squinted up at him, his silhouette made hazy by the thin veil of fatigue that shrouds children's eyes when they stay up long past their bedtimes. She blinked hard and shook her head slightly, both to accustom her gaze to the hallway light as well as against the vibrant colors painted on the man's face and brightly colored unqo.

The long piece of fabric hit just above his knees, the traditional tunic open on either side for his tan, veiny arms to come through. Geometric patterns and loud hues splashed the fabric, garish even by her people's standards, and they were known for their bright colors. It was then that she recognized him as the head palace steward, standing proud and pompously at her door, like an overpainted quetzal, the clear instigator of the noise which had startled her. Her shoulders relaxed ever so slightly. The familiar clash of his loud wardrobe suddenly made his looming frame seem much less imposing.

"The queen has given birth," he repeated, slower and louder than before, regarding her as if she had some sort of mental impediment that kept her from comprehending. But the girl had heard him the first time. She was aware that the queen had gone into labor in the early evening, and had been waiting for him ever since. She knew what his words meant.

A rush of icy fear cascaded through her, originating at the top of her head and rolling down her shoulders, cementing a heavy block of ice within her stomach before sending trembling ripples down her legs to her already cold feet. The entire sensation left her frozen in place, staring dumbly at the servant in front of her. His brows furrowed further at her in clear disapproval, creasing the skin between the heavily overgrown wires of hair.

"You must ask the Flowers to name him," he prompted her, frustration clipping his words. She flinched at the harshness of his tone, but she understood his irritability. This was, after all, why she had been chosen, so many years ago. Somehow, the girl managed an awkward nod at him, swallowing sharply against the sudden rush of bile that threatened to come up her throat.

Apparently, it was enough. "I will send for Rosa Maria to prepare you" he stated with a short bow, a tipping of his head, really, before he turned his long-legged stride down the corridor.

How long she stood in place, her hand gripping the edge of the wooden door, she could not tell. The initial fear that had overwhelmed her slowly gave way to a sliver of anticipation, which quickly transformed into something very near excitement. This was the moment that she had long waited for, her true life's purpose, the path laid out for her since she was a child. This was the culmination of nearly ten years of training.

It was the day she would speak to the Flowers of Prophecy.

Leaving her door open for light, she scurried to her only window and threw back the curtains to reveal the wispy tendrils of dawn floating like colorful feathers beyond the lush mountains. The top of their volcano, Andalango, was still shrouded with curling ringlets of mist, but they would soon give way and her verdant slopes would be clear. The kingdom, what could be seen from the girl's palace tower, was quite still. But soon the townspeople would awaken and the cobblestone streets would come alive with the noise and bustle of everyday life: the rolling carts of the men selling pescado y tamales, the grunts, cackles, and snorts of livestock, the discourse of women as they bartered in the market.

The smell of cafe would reach even her, high above them all, as would sometimes the chocolate caliente that others preferred. There would be outraged yells of those foolish enough to have their pockets picked by los ladroncitos - street urchins - and the children's pealing laughter as they expertly dodged and evaded the halfhearted grasps of soldiers. The sounds of Andala, her home.

The girl turned from the window, her gaze landing on the ornate trunk at the foot of her bed, the most beautiful and adorned piece in her small room. She crossed to it and knelt in front of it reverently, allowing her fingertips to dance over the intricate carvings on the polished and painted wood. Flowers. Beautiful, curling vines with elaborate blossoming flowers.

She had sat in this position countless times before, soaking in the beauty of the patterns and colors so often that she could recreate the entire thing from memory if asked. At the end of long days of studies and training, the chest was her only comfort, growing to be almost a friend over the years. Yet in all those years, she had never dared open the lid.

She had seen it open, of course, once a year. The best day of the year. The day when the palace seamstresses would come and measure her for the ceremonial dress. They would open the chest and remove the most beautiful piece of clothing the girl had ever seen. Living in the palace, she had been witness to all the latest fashions. She did not interact with the lords and ladies that so often frequented the events or balls, nor the people who seemed to live and work within the walls.

But she had glimpsed them often, in their finery: men's hose of deep blue silk and tunics of royal reds and ambers, with pure gold woven into the stitching.

Or the women, *oh the women.*

In their flowing gowns of gossamer and satin in the summer, or alpaca wool in the winter. They wore colorful fabrics that cinched tight at the waist with a chumpi, a long intricately woven piece of cloth that wrapped around their middle several times and served as a fashion piece as well as belt. The skirts tumbled out from their folds in pleats and layers that barely grazed the floor, wearing pollera on top of pollera, making them look like they were floating rather than walking. And the gems that dripped from their ears, their necks, their fingers... they sparkled so bright that she could see them dance with the catching light even from a great distance.

And yet, she had often thought, *none could compare to my ceremonial garb.*

It was her only personal possession, and the only thing of value that was truly hers. Even her friend, the wooden trunk, was only a means to keeping it safe and protected for the right moment. Every year she was measured, fitted, and alterations were made to keep it perfect and ready for the day it might be worn. The girl had waited for the day she could wear it longer than those few moments of fitting, when it would be hers alone. Once she had performed the Naming Ceremony and spoken to the Flowers, she would be allowed at court, a true Name-Bearer. Then perhaps she could make friends with real people and not simply inanimate objects.

She heard a noise at her open door and her head snapped to find its source. Her maidservant Rosa Maria was there, her own smudges under her eyes indicating an equally long night. Her hair, liberally streaked with gray, spilled from her usually severe bun, strands sagging limply by her face and plastered to her temples with old sweat. The girl wondered if she had been there at the birth of the new prince, and how long it had taken.

Rosa Maria noted the girl kneeling at the floor, and her gaze softened. The maidservant knew that others viewed the girl only as the Name-Bearer, holding one of the most important positions in the land, but she had known her since she was a babe. To her, the girl kneeling before her with rumpled and disheveled auburn hair, and a wild, almost panicked look in her eyes was simply a young and terrified child.

Rosa Maria forced herself to swallow her own nerves and smiled reassuringly at her, opening her plump arms wide. With a soft, grateful sigh the girl scrambled up off the floor and threw herself into the older woman's comforting embrace. It was rare for Rosa Maria to be physically affectionate, but other than being struck for failing in her studies or at the yearly fitting, they were the only times that the girl was ever touched. The girl noticed, absently, that she could now rest her chin on Rosa Maria's shoulder, and remembered that the last time they had hugged she had barely reached her bosom.

It had been after a particularly ugly illness had struck the palace, moving swiftly through the servants and killing one in four. The girl had fallen ill after a riding lesson. They later learned that one of the stable boys had been afflicted quite violently, and had infected several who had been in contact with him. She had survived; the boy had not. The first day Rosa Maria had seen her stand from her bed to use the latrine, tears had escaped the usually stoic woman's brown eyes and she had hauled the girl into her arms, nearly smothering the poor child in her weakened state.

Rosa Maria patted her back and pulled the reluctant girl away from her, holding her at arm's length.

"Estas lista, mija. You are ready for this," she murmured comfortingly, unexpected emotion making her voice thick. Thin lines crinkled at the corners of her eyes.

"You are ready," she said again with a sharp nod, smoothing a heavy hand over the girl's tangled hair. "I've ordered a bath, and the seamstresses are on their way."

Almost immediately two more servants entered her room, hauling a wooden tub. They left before more women came with pitchers of hot water to fill it, as the girl's room was too small to fit that many people at once. The last servant, a particularly busty young woman with bouncing gold curls and pleasant rosy cheeks walked in with a bowl of sweet-smelling petals and orange peels. She scattered them in the steaming tub and gave the girl a wink before flouncing out the door.

The girl briefly wondered what the Flowers of Prophecy would think of her bathing in petals, but as the palace kept fresh cuts of flowers in vases all around the grounds, she imagined that they did not mind.

Rosa Maria helped her strip off her simple night shift and held her hand as she stepped into the tub. A hiss escaped through her teeth as her cold, stiff limbs were submerged in the warm water, but as she settled in, she became quickly accustomed to the temperature and sighed at the rare pleasure of a hot bath.

Though sorely tempted, she did not dunk her head underwater, for there would have been no time to let her hair dry. Instead, she let her neck rest against the rim of the tub as Rosa Maria dragged a stool behind her, first gently coaxing out the tangled knots with patient fingers and comb, then twisting and braiding the dark red tendrils into an intricate pattern worthy of the Naming Ceremony.

From the corner of her eye the girl could see that Rosa Maria was also weaving long, colorful wraps in her hair in ceremonial fashion. The girl settled for lifting her hands, warm from the water, and pressing them against her cold cheeks and face. While Rosa Maria worked, the girl ran through her training in her mind, preparing herself for what was to come.

The position of the Name-Bearer is an important one in the realm. Upon the union of two monarchs, a prince and a princess, a king and a queen, heirs are expected. And thus, so is the Naming Rite.

The Flowers of Prophecy had named future rulers for as long as anyone could remember. There was no written record of where the Flowers came from, or when the rite began. It simply was so, and had been so, for all of Andala's history. The Flowers bestow the names of future rulers to only one person, a nameless one, existing solely to deliver names and never own one themselves. The Name-Bearer.

Those who are chosen are ripped from their mother's arms too young to even remember their faces. The girl had been chosen just before her third birthday. Or, so she had been told. She remembered little of her early days at the palace, and nothing at all of her life before it. But Princessa Issalia and Prince Enrique, only a few years older than she was at the time, had been promised to one another. Once their union was decided, their progeny was of course expected, and the realm was informed of their union. A Name-Bearer needed to be chosen.

A bustle in the corridor snapped the girl out of her reverie, and her door was suddenly blocked by three of the palace seamstresses. The three best, of course. They crowded into the small space, making the girl stand, shivering until they wrapped her in a drying cloth. The tub was taken away as the women flitted about the room, commending

Rosa Maria on the girl's hair, lighting oil lamps for added brightness, and opening the trunk to pull out the ceremonial dress.

As always, her breath caught in her throat when seeing it, the material slipping through the women's fingers like oil over water, nearly blinding with color and pattern and life. She still could not believe that she was not only allowed but *expected* to wear it.

The head seamstress, la señora Awaq slipped the dress over her head, being careful not to disrupt Rosa Maria's hard work. The fabric brushed her shoulders like butterfly wings, light and cool, making her shiver. La señora Awaq pinched her, not unkindly, a reminder to stay still, lest she be impaled by pins.

When not at fittings, the three women worked at the looms, training new generations of young girls in el arte del tejido; the art of the loom. The Andalan capital was well known for it's brightly colored fabrics and textiles, and none boasted finer wares than the Andalan palace.

Their expertise had the seamstresses working swiftly, in tandem, years of practice shifting their movements into a beautifully choreographed dance, their minds and motions as in tune as a flock of birds migrating south in the winter. In fact, the three women reminded the girl of birds, two young egrets tittering and flapping around la Señora Awaq, a proud and elegant swan.

The image almost made her smile, but she quickly suppressed it. This was a solemn day, an important day, and she was the Name-Bearer. It would not do to have anyone thinking she was merely a silly girl given over to silly thoughts.

Finally, the work was done. One of the egrets stepped into the hall and brought in a large standing mirror, propping it against one of the girl's bare wooden walls. The girl took a moment to smooth her hand over the skirts, letting the fabric slip in and out of her trembling fingers. With a fortifying breath, she lifted her head to view her reflection.

A gasp escaped her throat, and had it not been that the elegant young lady in front of her repeated the movement, she might not have recognized herself. The dress was long and heavy, and adorned with an almost overwhelming amount of delicate, intricately embroidered flowers in a myriad of dazzling colors. They curled and danced up from the hem, splashed boldly over the skirts, and rose to twine and stretch over her torso. It looked as if real flowers had found her and decided to use her as a base to grow, wrapping around her like ivy, but bursting with colorful buds and petals and leaves.

In each flower's center lay a precious stone, jade, opales, esmeraldas, even andalames were embedded into the hearts of each flower. The fabric rustled over her lithe body like gently flowing water from a mountain stream, rippling and glistening with her slightest move-ment. The bodice cinched tight against her torso, a chumpi of her own delicately embroidered and wrapped several times around her thin waist. Thinner, nearly translucent sleeves billowed out from just underneath her arms, and would have left her clavicle and chest ex-posed if not for her manta, which draped elegantly over her shoulders. The folded wrap mirrored the dress with flowers and gems and was held together in front of her breast by a solid gold tupu, a straight pin in the shape of yet another flower.

It felt impossibly smooth and soft against her skin, and she resisted the urge to rub her hands over her arms to luxuriate in the feeling. The skirts, composed of layers upon layers of polleras were heavy, and swished when she moved. The weight of the dress made her feel important, special, and older than her thirteen years.

She touched the threads reverently, luxuriating in each of the colors, the regal purple base peeking out from between the patterns. Purple was the royal color of Andala, the vibrant hue adorning the dress of most of the nobility. The dye came from the crushed shells of caracoles, which gathered only one time of the year when the tide was just right. They would cling to the rocky cliffs of the sea, waiting for those brave enough to risk falling into the perilous ocean to collect them. The nobles would have sopa de caracol that week, a hearty seafood stew to make use of every part of the snail.

One could always tell the upper nobility from the rest that week, as the soup would stain the lips and teeth of those lucky enough to eat it an inky purple. Rosa Maria told the girl that some of the nobility drank extra chicha morada that week, a drink made from sweetened purple corn, to simulate the dye of the snails and not lose face.

Once, a long time ago, sopa de caracol was a peasant stew that anyone could enjoy, but once the royals began dying their clothing purple the snails became a rare commodity and would fetch a higher price if sold to the palace rather than eaten by the poor.

Rosa Maria had also woven purple wraps and flowers into her braids, which had been swept back off her face. Her doe eyes, which had always tilted up just a touch at their ends, looked bigger in the mirror, wide with apprehension and excitement. She looked older, more dignified. Like a true member of the court.

The girl's vision suddenly became blurry, and she realized with horror that her eyes were swimming with tears at the beauty of the effort and craftsmanship of the women surrounding her.

The elder seamstress nodded approvingly. "Your reaction is not uncommon, child, and expected at the work of Señora Awaq." She chucked the girl under the chin. "Estas lista."

Silk shoes, instead of leather sandals, were slipped on her feet, adorned with their own flowers and gems. Had they been shown alone they would have been a marvel, but against the magnificence of the dress they seemed a simple accompaniment, nothing more.

At least they are comfortable, the girl thought.

It wouldn't do to have her tripping and falling in front of the Flowers of Prophecy! In fact, the thought alone turned her stomach and her little body began to tremble. Luckily the other women were too preoccupied with getting her ready to notice. She bit her lower lip and curled her hands into fists to steady herself. By the time the women were finished, she had her breathing mostly under control. Finally, with a final fuss of her hair from Rosa Maria, the girl was ushered into the hallway where the steward was once again waiting. He nodded at her and began moving briskly down the hall.

The girl risked one final look behind her, her heart beating heavy in her chest, to see Rosa Maria and the seamstresses watching her with what seemed like pride. Fortified, she lifted her head and followed the steward, determined to handle the ceremony with grace.

The walk to the interior palace garden was a long one, as her room was in a far tower, tucked out of sight from the royals. Soon that would change. Once she had completed the ceremony and spoken to the Flowers she would be accepted into high society and royal life, with rooms closer to the main body of the palace. She would be a true Name-Bearer, a position that held due respect and high acclaim. She would be able to speak to past Name-Bearers freely, not just once a month when the few that remained came to train her for the Ceremony.

She followed the steward around a corner and stopped at the head of an immensely long hallway that stretched towards the entrance to the Royal Gardens. It was clear that the entire palace was aware of the Naming Ceremony, because the space had been prepared for her arrival.

The entire hallway floor between herself and the two towering marble doors at the far end completely covered by alfombras de aserrín. The space smelled heavily of sawdust and pine, the long carpets made up of both materials, dyed in vibrant colors, as well as flower petals, seeds, palm leaves and feathers. There were three of the organic carpets between her and the garden entrance, each with a different geometric pattern framing its borders and a more complex image featured in the center.

The carpet closest to her was a visage of a bassinet, a young child's fist peeking over its side. A crown of pine needles, painted gold, hovered over their bed.

The second alfombra was clearly a depiction of the Flowers, green swirling vines and vibrant splashes of colored petals made from dyed seeds and fruit husks.

The third she was too far away to see.

The girl paused uncertainly, hesitant to step over such painstakingly difficult work. Palace servants must have toiled the many long hours of the night to prepare the walkway, it seemed such a shame to tread over such fine craftsmanship. Still, she knew it was what was expected of her, so with a deep, sawdust-filled breath, she stepped forward.

Leaves and petals crunched beneath her slippers, nuts and shells rolling away by her disruption. The smell of roses, pine, and wood grew stronger as she kicked up little clumps of the brightly colored dust. She was halfway across the second alfombra when she could finally see the third pattern.

It was her.

The carpet was a depiction of herself, the back of her head and shoulders as she gazed upwards towards a large, towering flower face that faded from one color to another. Her dark red hair had been fashioned out of hundreds, maybe thousands of small red feathers.

She nearly faltered. Her image had never before been captured, and certainly not in a way as grand and elaborate as this. Tears pricked at the backs of her eyes but she could not place the emotion that was summoning them. Was it pride? Anticipation? Fear? Perhaps a combination of the three, but it did not matter, as she could not give in to the luxury of gazing upon the artwork forever.

As she crossed over her own countenance she noted two guards stationed at the sides of the tall marble doors. It was clear that they were fresh to their posts as they were bare chested, save for the tattoos of royal glyphs which marked them as servants to the palace, stretching straight from their shoulders and down to their hips. Had they been the night guards they would have been allowed a covering of alpaca wool to stave off the brisk night air. In a few hours the Diosa Tz'ola would raise her head again and then their skin would be shimmering with sweat, droplets trickling down from their collarbones and behind their knees. But it was early yet and the girl could make out the small gooseflesh that raised their skin. The guard's lower bodies were covered with red and yellow checkered cloths fastened with bronze belts that held their weapons. In their hands farthest from the imposing doors they held long, pointed spears.

When the girl reached the guards, their eyes flickered quickly over her hair and dress before bowing to her deeply. She felt a special sort of thrill at the look and gesture. She was mostly ignored within the palace walls, but for the first time, with the alfombra which bore her image and the mark of respect from the soldiers, she felt the true significance of her position. *I am important,* she thought, jutting her chin forward with pride. In unison, the soldiers grasped the intricately adorned handles and pulled open the heavy doors, a gust of wind sweeping through the opening, lifting the multicolored aserrin which danced and sparkled around her, settling lightly on the hem of her skirts. They dragged the doors open only wide enough for a small person to squeeze through.

With a deep breath, she stepped forward and moved into the garden.

CHAPTER 2

There was an echoing grumble as the doors shut behind her. The garden air was heavy and thick, smelling of fresh florals and dirt. She knew the layout of the entire thing by heart, having studied its designs for years. This was, however, the first time that she had seen it in person.

The room itself stretched both far and high, and had large panels of glass welded together with heavy golden beams covering what would have otherwise been the roof. The rays of sun creeping up the sky glinted off the beam's shiny lengths, making light dance over the leaves and flowers. Towering trees and plants stretched out, some in orderly rows, others in brilliant splashes of twists and colors that looked like oddly organized chaos, the way only nature can be.

The memory of first learning of the Flowers of Prophecy was one of the clearest of the girl's youth. She had been sitting in the damp, musty library reserved for her lessons. Her instructor, Señor Alfredo, had been a paunchy middle-aged scholar that often smelled of sour berries, a scent that the girl would later recognize as fruit wine. He was balding at the temples, his eyes were sunken and deeply set in his skull and he had been missing a tooth right next to his top right incisor.

Even so, he had been kind to her, or not unkind, at least. Some of her instructors were quick to yell, and some to even strike her if they felt she was not paying enough attention. Past Name-Bearers were aloof and guarded, and she was not allowed to ask them questions. But Señor Alfredo was patient, and if he tended to doze off now and again, well, it simply gave her more time to read the old-world stories of heroes and dioses that were usually off limits to her.

He had, however, been uncharacteristically somber and alert the day he had told her about the Flowers. When he explained that the Flowers were sacred beings, ageless and wise, and the givers of royal names for centuries, she had been both incredulous and confused.

"Flowers do not talk," she had argued, a frown etched on her young brows.

"Not all flowers," her mentor had agreed. "Only the Flowers of Prophecy."

She had regarded him suspiciously. "But... they don't have mouths."

"No," he had replied, hiding a smile. "Pero hablan. And yet, they speak. We do not know how, only that every Name-Bearer, and no one *but* the Name-Bearer, has been able to hear them."

The rest of the lesson had been about the honor of being a Name-Bearer, and of the infallible nature of the Flowers, but she had still had nightmares that night, of giant flowers with gaping mouths and rows and rows of sharpened teeth.

The girl began making her way towards the center of the room, where the Flowers should be. The bright jewels on her shoes peeped out from under her skirts with every step, their colors matching the intricate designs of the mosaic tiles beneath her feet. She continued along, almost in a daze, making turns and following trails that others might have missed completely. Any outsider would have promptly gotten lost in the hedge mazes, or the nearly imperceptible paths carved out through the undergrowth, but she navigated the room as expertly as if she had been living there in the foliage her entire life. After a few minutes, when the girl was exactly where she needed to be to begin the ritual, she stopped and closed her eyes.

She could do this. She *would* do this. It was time.

The girl took five steps forward on the path and turned to her right, where according to her studies, a fountain should be. She knew it was there before she saw it. Even if she had doubted her training (which had been too well drilled into her to forget,) she would have heard its gentle gurgling. It was taller than she was, spilling crystalline clear water down three beautifully sculpted tiers. Each basin was shaped like the top of a flower, the petals bending backwards to tumble their contents down into the next. The small slivers of sun that hit the falling water in between each section created shimmering rainbows that reflected off the stiller pool of the bottom basin. Placing her hands lightly over one of the glistening arcs, she wet her palms with the cool water.

"Agua pura, purifica," she whispered, bowing her head. The water on her bare skin was strikingly cool, the sun not yet out long enough to warm it. She left her hands beneath the flowing stream, imagining her shortcomings, her faults, and all her earthly woes washing away with the cleansing and purifying touch of the water. When she could imagine the purity bathing her entire body like a white light, she cupped her palms, collecting some water between them.

"For that which nurtures us," she spoke clearly, making her way around the fountain, droplets rolling down her fingers and splashing delicately on the floor. She held her arms out in front of her as she walked, to keep from dampening her dress. Slowly and carefully she made her way down a walkway until the geometric tiles turned into a dirt path, which was lined by a row of tall trees. Their thick green foliage bowed elegantly towards each other on either end of the trail, shrouding her under their domed canopy.

She didn't realize that she had been holding her breath until she was well under their shade, and had to stop and suck in the humid air between her teeth. The smell of tree sap was strong, the oils within the trees' bark perfuming the space around her, making her sputter. Water sloshed in front of her and she stilled, standing motionless until her breath leveled out once more. Her hands trembled slightly but she didn't spill again, it was important that she had enough water for the next part.

The path ended and she stood before a small patch of brown dirt. It seemed harsh and out of place in the thickly populated garden teeming with growing, living things. But this was how all those living things began, and she understood that the soil was just as important as what grew above and beneath it. Deliberately she opened her palms in a wide arc, her arms swinging wide as if she were going to embrace a friend, the water falling from her hands and onto the bare field. Then she bowed deeply at the waist, her chumpi sliding up towards her ribs, and sank her fingers into a section of now-damp soil.

"Tierra mia, conectame," she murmured with a smile.

The girl imagined that same white energy that she had pictured at the fountain, but this time pouring from her fingers and into the ground beneath her. She visualized it traveling through the soil like roots, stretching far from her position and across the rest of the garden.

"For the homes that grow us," she continued, and with her hands still touching the ground, her nerves slowly began to dissipate. This ritual she understood, for she had practiced it for years. Straightening she lifted her arms above her head, making sure not to drop any clotting dirt onto her hair. She tilted her face up towards the glass window above her, the sun just high enough to pour a sliver of golden ray over her skin. Lingering for a moment, she allowed the light to warm her cheeks.

"Sol, que nos da vida." Instead of the white energy she let the sun rays fill her flesh, coursing through her veins like liquid gold, until she felt like a single, concentrated flame of power.

"For the love that warms us," she spoke, confident now.

Finally, she turned and faced the enormous hedge that separated her from the Flowers of Prophecy. She knew that they stretched in a perfect circle at the exact center of the garden, with no visible entrance or exit. She also knew the key to entering was in her hands. Crossing, she lifted her arms and pointed her palms, soaked with water, soil, and sun, out in front of her. With a last, trembling breath she grazed them over the shrubbery.

The hedge directly in front of her shivered, began twisting and furling into itself. The process was slow at first but then moved faster and faster until there was an arched entryway, perfectly molded for her shape and height. Without allowing herself the luxury of hesitation, the girl lifted her chin and stepped through. As the space was swallowed up behind her, she closed her eyes tight and gave herself a moment to adjust to the sacred area.

The air smelled slightly damp, earthy, wet, with an aroma almost like cinnamon. It was both sweet and spicy at the same time, and the girl felt just a hint of recognition in the notes, but the fragrance was just soft enough to not quite be able to define. There was a rustle of wind that swept the bottom of her skirts and moved tendrils of hair across her forehead, and the breeze carried with it the tinkling, melodic notes of music. It sounded like the faint chime of bells or the clinking of glass in the wind over an ethereal hum. The entire space seemed to vibrate around her.

Finally, she opened her eyes, and for the first time, came face to face with the Flowers of Prophecy.

No amount of training could have prepared her for seeing the Flowers in person. They looked nothing like anything she had ever seen or could even have dreamt of. They looked like flowers, and yet not at all like any flowers she had known. Their stalks were a deep, almost shimmering emerald and jutted out proudly from the ground, heavy and thick. If she had tried wrapping her arms around one, her hands would not have touched on the other end. They had two long leaves on either side, almost like arms or drooping wings. Equally thick and imposing roots undulated beneath the soil, their long tendrils rolling above and below the earth like a sea monster's tentacles. They shifted and tilted the ground beneath her feet, making her knees tremble with the effort of remaining upright.

And their petals - their petals were awe-inspiring.

Once, the girl had seen a glass blower work in the palace forge. The way the glass had rippled, stretched, and glistened had captivated her. It pulled like melted sugar, the man working quickly to shape the molten material. That was what she was reminded of when she saw the Flowers' faces. They were iridescent, shifting from one color to another, their very petals rippling and moving in constant waves and shudders. They were continually in motion, never stagnant, never still, and indescribably lovely.

Tears threatened to spill from her eyes once more, from her nerves, or their beauty, or an aching combination of both. She noticed that the hedges of their enclosure crept up to form a dome above the massive plants, effectively blocking the Flowers from outside view. Had their faces not been illuminated with whatever caused the rippling, shifting light within their petals, she would have been completely in the dark, with no sliver of sun to light her path. What flowers didn't need the sun to grow?

Had it not been for the years of training, the endless days of preparation, the rituals drilled into her head and the motions of the ritual practiced ceaselessly until her body would near collapse from exhaustion, the girl might have lost everything and simply stayed staring at the unbelievable and mesmerizing sight before her. But muscle memory kicked in, and she moved cautiously forward to take her place in the center ring, taking care not to accidentally step on any of the massive roots that continually rolled and shifted the ground beneath her feet.

She found her spot in the center, the floor thankfully devoid of any moving roots or vines and bowed her head, taking care not to let her gaze linger on any Flower in particular.

The girl pinched the sides of her dress with her least-dirty fingers and spread the skirts out far, sinking into a deep and well-practiced curtsy.

"I offer you greetings, Flowers of Prophecy," she began, head down and young voice wavering. She resisted the urge to clear her throat; she didn't think that would be very dignified.

"We humbly beseech your wisdom and generosity once more. Esta noche, Queen Issalia delivered a baby boy. As has been the way for centuries, we request you give us the name of the new prince and aid in beginning his long and prosperous reign."

The girl nearly sighed out loud in relief at the end of the speech but managed to hold it back. The hardest part was over, now she merely needed to hear the name and deliver it to the queen. Surely the queen could be no more frightening than the great Flowers of Prophecy!

The rustle of wind that had met her when she stepped inside the sacred space grew stronger, whispering through the stalks and branches of the Flowers. It was time! This was the moment the Flowers would deliver the Royal Name. Her heart thrummed with excitement, and she reached a hand up to clasp the tupu which held her manta in place. The cool sharpness of the gold helped steady her. The rustling became louder, and the Flower's stalks began moving, shifting, the roots rolling under the soil once more. The quiet movement began low towards the ground and made its way up, traveling in a circular motion around the ring of Flowers, finally wriggling and vibrating their petals. The music rose and the Flowers began to sway, almost as if dancing to the melodic chimes that swelled as their movement grew stronger. The girl only dared to peek through her eyelashes before lowering her gaze once more.

Then suddenly, without warning, all movement stopped, and the faces of the Flowers dimmed, plunging the girl into silent darkness.

A quiet gasp escaped her throat and she stumbled from the shock, her deep curtsy abandoned to fall softly on her knees instead. No one had warned her about this part; it was never in her studies. After experiencing the constant motion and the strange, beautiful melody of the Flowers, the stillness and quiet seemed unnatural, wrong. And enclosed in the dome as she was, she could not see anything without the Flower's illumination.

She knelt there, in the dark, the thrumming of her heart and her small, rasping breaths the only sounds in the eerie stillness. As the silence stretched, a trickle of apprehension made its way down her spine, lifting the tiny hairs on the back of her neck. Unconsciously, her body tensed. Was something wrong? Surely not. She had done everything right, performed the ceremony with precision. She had addressed he Flowers respectfully.

She hadn't erred.

Had she?

Her next breath erupted from her lips a little shakily, and her body responded in kind. But the girl pushed the thoughts away. She had never been told of anyone bungling the ceremony so thoroughly as to not receive a response. She certainly would not be the first! This was most likely just part of the ritual, perhaps the Flowers needed time to consider the correct name.

But why were they so quiet?

Suddenly, a single Flower, the one directly before her, began glowing once more. Slowly and softly at first, and then stronger, casting her in a small patch of light amongst the dark.

Then, it spoke.

"A future king was born this morn, but not unto the queen."

The words were not uttered with a single voice, but in a chorus of voices both masculine and feminine, sounds both high and low and overlapping with one another in a haunting lyrical tapestry.

Startled into forgetting her training, the girl lifted her head and stared at the Flower in front of her, where the voices seemed to originate.

"If found and brought to us to discover his true name, it will ring in a peace to this realm that will last for centuries."

When the Flower did not continue, the girl swallowed hard and whispered, "Que? Lo siento. I'm, I'm sorry, I do not understand."

The Flowers were quiet. Had she made a misstep, or perhaps misspoke?

"The queen, the queen's baby," she whispered more urgently. "The queen's baby needs a name."

The Flowers were still, save for the unnerving rippling movements from the petals of the single lit Flower in front of her. But they were softer, dimmer than they had been when she first entered. And all were quiet, silent, none speaking again. Dumbstruck, the girl stayed kneeling on the rippling ground, her head spinning and breaths coming now in panicked pants.

This had never happened.

Never in the history of any Name-Bearer's career had the Flowers refused the Naming. It was unheard of, and she could not fathom what would happen to her if she failed in her task, in the only thing that she was chosen to do.

"Please," she whispered again. "Please!" she repeated, louder. A small voice in the back of her mind despaired at the thought of her breaking protocol and speaking to the Flowers past the ritual, let alone raising her voice to them, but she was almost hysterical with desperation.

"Please, I must deliver a name," she pleaded.

But the Flowers did not answer.

CHAPTER 3

The girl did not know how long she remained kneeling in the dirt circle, surrounded by the silent Flowers. After some time, her eyes adjusted to the dim glow of the single, illuminated Flower and she could see that the rest had turned their petals to face away from her. It was shocking, and frightening, making her feel thoroughly discarded. Eventually the intense tingling in her left foot, full of pins and needles from having stayed still for too long managed to clear her head enough for her to stand.

She wobbled, and blinked at the Flowers, hoping beyond hope for a moment that her movement would somehow spur a response from them, but it was to no avail. They stayed quiet, the single Flower that still faced her shifting its petals from color to color in soft, undulating ripples but offering her nothing more. She forced her feet to move, shuffling and kicking up dust until she faced the hedge once more. She was in such a state of shock that she wasn't even surprised when the same archway immediately opened to let her pass once more.

The girl squinted at the sudden onslaught of sunlight once outside the hedged dome, her eyes adjusting to the change slowly. Almost mindlessly the girl began making the trek back to the garden doors. Her head felt light, detached, as if it were floating above her neck and connected by string. Numbly she found her way back through the path of trees and around the glistening fountain. Her feet stumbled when dirt ground turned back into tile but she didn't slow, continuing her dazed shuffle the way that she had come. After a few moments she stood back in front of the towering doors and stopped, uncertain about how to proceed.

What was she going to do?

Her training was very clear about the next steps, how she was to present the infant's new name to the royal family. Never once was it discussed what she should do if the Flowers refused the Naming. In fact, she was quite certain that no one had ever considered it even a remote possibility. Her instructors had been adamant about the importance of not giving offense, but it had never occurred to her to ask what to do if she inadvertently *did* offend, let alone what to do if the Flowers did not provide her with a name.

How was she going to explain it to the queen?

Perhaps she was dreaming. Perhaps it was all a nightmare, brought on by her apprehension and the long night. Soon there would be a knock at her door and she would realize she had dozed off and simply imagined the entire, terrible ordeal.

Absently, her eyes drifted to the artful etchings carved into the tall doors, portraying gnarled trees, squat plants, small birds and of course, flowers. Her hand lifted on its own, ready to trace the pattern the way that she did on her wooden chest, when she noticed the dried flakes of mud still coating her palms. She raised her other hand and stared at them in front of her, noting the way the dirt had settled into the fine lines of her brown skin. She could smell the faint, warm scent of the earth, feel the caked layer where soil and water had mixed, and in that moment she knew that it had been no dream. It was real, she had spoken to the Flowers, and they had denied her a name. Her muddy hands were too ordinary to be anything but proof.

Abruptly, almost angrily, she brushed them off on the sides of her skirts, an action she knew Señora Awaq would have despaired of, but the girl was beyond caring. Not knowing what else to do, she began pushing the doors open. One of the palace guards noticed their motion and aided her in dragging the marble far enough for her to squeeze through once more.

The steward was still there, waiting for her. Small beads of perspiration had begun peeking through his heavy face paint, creating small cracks on the symmetrical glyphs on his forehead and dampening his temples below his heavy black hair. He spared her a quick, curious glance, and turned to lead her down the corridors.

"Come," he called back to her. "The queen is waiting."

"Wonderful," the girl whispered under her breath, too quiet for anyone to hear.

With a dim sort of detachment she trailed behind him, noticing absently that the long hallway had been swept clean of the earlier alfombras. While the scent of sawdust lingered, she couldn't see even a stray nut or pebble on the well-polished stone floors. Her eyes stayed low, glued to the ground, her mind racing.

What was she going to tell the queen?

What could she say?

Would anyone believe that the Flowers had denied the new prince a name?

How would they react if she told them that somehow, another prince was born this day, and that they meant to name him instead?

Would they blame her?

That last question, at least, had an answer.

Yes. Yes, the blame would be cast solely and irrevocably on her. She was meant to be the speaker to the Flowers, if the Ceremony somehow went wrong, she would be to blame.

She was so engrossed in her lament that she did not notice the steward stopping, and nearly toppled him over by stumbling against his back. He glared at her, his cheeks flushed with embarrassment. Spinning forward once more the steward bowed deeply, far deeper than he had bowed for her, and addressed a looming shadow that had been obscured from her distracted gaze.

"My Lord."

It was then the girl realized that standing before them in the middle of the hall was none other than the Archwizard Auberon.

She had only glimpsed him from afar on select occasions, but she would know him from his look alone. He wore the traditional wizard robe in a deep mora, a bluer shade of purple more resembling black-berries. The robe was open at the top, woven strings dangling two amethyst beads interlacing from his neck down to mid chest. A pattern of wide diamonds was embroidered down the center of the robe down to his feet, alternating in hues of blues and cream.

Amulets and talismans hung from his neck, and rings, the likes of which she had never seen, adorned almost every finger. He was younger than she had thought, his hair black and slicked back, darker on top but liberally speckled with gray on the sides, and a crisp, tightly cropped mustache and beard framing a thin mouth. The bottom of his beard also boasted two streaks of gray, contrasting with the darkness of the rest of his features. His skin was a weathered olive, his eyes dark and dangerous under a heavy brow. In her shock at seeing him in person, the girl nearly forgot her current predicament.

"I will take her from here," he directed at the steward, his voice low and silken with a touch of an accent that she could not place.

"Por supuesto my lord," the steward replied with another deep bow, and then she was alone with one of the most powerful men in the realm. *What else could this day possibly bring?*

"Come," he told her, tilting his head and leading them through an entryway to his left. The door clicked shut as they crossed its threshold. Standing so near to him, she noted that he smelled lightly of smoke and palo santo, the heady aroma no doubt clinging to his clothing and hair. She was also shocked to find that he was not that much taller than she was. From a distance he always looked so imposing, and she was startled to find he wasn't the towering giant she had imagined. And yet, his stature in no way diminished the heavy aura of power that surrounded him.

"You're the wizard," she blurted out, staring at his bronzed face.

"Yes," he replied, arching a dark brow at her.

"You're the Palace Wizard!" She knew she was repeating herself, but somehow could not keep the words from escaping her.

"I am aware," he replied, smoothing his hand over his mouth and chin, a hint of impatience making his accent thicker.

"I'm sorry." The girl ducked her head. "I've just never seen you this close before." Curiosity, rather than fear, bubbled within her. Why had he taken her from the steward? What did he want from her? With dread, she realized the obvious answer. She had just met with the Flowers, their meeting was surely about the Naming. The Naming which had not happened.

"What did the Flowers tell you?" he asked her abruptly, instantly confirming her fears.

Her heart hammered so fiercely in her chest that she was surprised it didn't lift her skin with every beat. Slowly, she raised her chin.

"Perdon, my lord?" Her eyes darted away from his, stalling for time.

"The Flowers of Prophecy, what did they say?" his voice this time more demanding.

She was suddenly struck with the precariousness of her position. He was a stranger to her, and there were many ways in which he could respond. For the first time since his appearance, she began to feel frightened. If she angered him, she had no doubt that he could kill her on the spot.

The girl had heard some of the servants talking once about a young apprentice of his who had displeased him. In his anger, the Wizard Auberon had transformed the young man into a piglet and abandoned him on the palace grounds. This had resulted in the apprentice almost becoming a part of that evening's supper before he was transformed back into a human boy.

Once, when she was seven, lightning assailed the west tower of the palace, the wizard's tower, for three full days. Royals and townsfolk alike were terrified that the gods themselves had been displeased and were attacking the land, yet he had emerged unscathed. He explained, albeit belatedly, that it had only been an experiment he had been working on, which he had forgotten to warn the people about. There were countless other tales of his abilities, and although he was highly respected, that respect came with a heavy dose of fear. She simply could not tell him the truth.

"My lord," she started, widening her eyes in an attempt to look as innocent as possible. "Is this a test? I know I am to deliver the Name to the prince himself, and his royal highnesses. I would not betray my task or my training." She ducked her head demurely, quite proud of her performance. Everything she had said was true, no one could fault her for simply following her training.

"So, you would prefer me to take you to the queen?" he asked, and her eyes darted up to meet his. "Are you sure you would like to tell her?" he leaned forward. "Are you certain you know *what* you will tell her?"

The girl gulped. No. She didn't know what she was going to tell the queen. Dare she tell the truth? Worse, dare she lie? What would even be believable?

"Niña!" The wizard snapped, pulling her from her thoughts. "What did they say?"

"They said ... Jacobo." *Jacobo? Where had that come from?*

"Jacobo," the wizard repeated incredulously.

"Si." she continued, determined now. "They said 'name him Jaco bo.'"

A great rumbling sigh escaped his chest.

"His mother was named Issalia, Falcon of Frost. She grew to have a keen sight towards matters of state, and can always tell when an ally is turning cold. His father, the late king was Enrique the Tempest Storm. He was, until his unfortunate passing, one of the fiercest warriors and generals we have ever had. And you were going to tell the queen that the unerring Flowers of Prophecy in all their infallible wisdom bestowed upon their son the name ... Jacobo?"

She felt sweat bead above her upper lip, which trembled ever so slightly.

"You are the Name-Bearer. Pray tell, niñita, what does the name Jacobo mean?"

With horror, the girl realized her mistake. Even her subconscious, it seemed, was terrible at lying. From the look on the wizard's face, she knew that he was well aware of the answer.

He pinched her chin between long, cool fingers. "What does the name Jacobo mean?"

She shivered at the contact, too unaccustomed to casual touch.

"Supplanter," she whispered.

"What was that?"

"Supplanter," she repeated, a hot tear rolling down her right eye. She waited for his wrath, the sure retaliation due to her for lying not only to a member of the royal court, but a man of magia. So, she was shocked when instead the hand that gripped her chin raised to pat her on the head, almost comfortingly.

"Now that we have concluded that you are not one for misdirection, tell me what the Flowers actually told you."

Could she? Did she dare trust him?

"*Speak!*"

His voice boomed across the room like the sharp crack of a whip, the command reverberating in her skull with so much force that her mouth opened, and words began tumbling out, unrestrained.

"They said a prince was born today but *not* to the queen and if the child was found and brought to them they'd name *him* and there would be peace in the kingdom for centuries and they *wouldn't* name the queen's baby no matter how many times I asked and I don't know *why*, they wouldn't tell me, and I don't know why after ten years of training I blanked and said the name *Jacobo* and I don't know why I'm telling you this or why the bees even picked me to be the Name-Bearer in the first place!"

A curious shadow hooded the wizard's solemn gaze, and he spoke the words that would alter the course of her life forever.

"The bees didn't choose you, niña. I did."

The girl stared at the wizard, his words, at first, meaningless and absurd. *Of course* the bees had chosen her. She was "the Chosen", she was the Name-Bearer. The bees were messengers of the gods, they did not make mistakes. They were not influenced by earthly forces.

The dance of the bees is a joyous occasion in the realm. It foretells a union, a royal marriage, a celebration. When a royal match is decreed, even if the bride and groom are only children at the time and their marriage not for years to come, the kingdom rejoices with the promise of those good tidings.

Princessa Issalia and Prince Enrique were nine and ten years old, respectively, when their parents arranged the match, and would wed eight years later.

The only ones in the realm who do not rejoice at the dance of bees are the parents of children three years or younger. For to choose a Name-Bearer, a child must be young enough to forget their own name and be wiped clean. A vessel to deliver the names of others, but never hold a name themselves.

It is a high honor to be chosen. The parents are rewarded greatly for having given life to those children selected by the gods, the only ones that can speak to the Flowers of Prophecy. But those parents must forget that those children were ever theirs and live with the knowledge that they are no longer kin. They accept this, for it is the way it has been for hundreds of years. When the bees choose, a child becomes something more than just a babe.

But if the bees did not choose her, what then? What did that mean?

"What?" her voice was a whisper, a wisp of wind on the breeze.

He released another rumbling sigh, one that seemed to start in his very bones and shake its way free, clamoring up to his lips in a desperate escape. His eyes softened. Without the harsh creases of angry wrinkles, he appeared almost kind.

"Many years past, I was granted a vision, in a dream. The vision was ... beautiful." The corners of his mouth turned up, as if remembering. "It promised peace in our realm. I believed the vision to be one of prophecy ... so I went to the Flowers to seek guidance."

The girl jerked away from him as if she had been physically struck, stumbling against a small writing desk and banging her hip against the corner. It throbbed with the sudden assault, but she paid it no mind. The admission that *anyone* other than the Chosen, even one as powerful as the Archwizard Auberon, would *dare* attempt to speak to the Flowers was simply unfathomable.

His mouth tightened at her response, tension returning to his face.

"*You* tried to speak to the Flowers?" she whispered, shocked.

"Yes." His voice was stiff and cold once more. Had he been younger, and not a powerful wizard, the girl might have guessed he wanted to roll his eyes at her.

"That is *forbidden*!" she continued urgently, as if making him understand the absolute madness of his action could somehow erase it.

"Yes," he repeated impatiently.

"Only the Name-Bearer can speak to the Flowers! What if you had offended them?" The mere thought gave her a rush of nausea so potent she had to brace both of her hands against the desk and drop her head between her arms to steady herself. Her manta shifted over her shoulders, the sharp end of the tupu digging into her soft flesh.

"May I continue?" he asked, his tone sardonic. Somehow, in her contorted position, she managed a nod. As he drew in a breath to further explain, she couldn't help but mutter,

"I can't *believe* you tried to talk to the Flowers."

His fingers cracked as he tightened his hands, and the sound was enough to scare her into obsequience. Her instructors had always admonished her for speaking too much, and out of turn. But despite their best efforts she never could break the habit of speaking her mind, no matter how many times she was struck for it. But the Lord Auberon was a wizard, un hombre de magia, and he needn't strike her to instill fear. Weakly, she lifted one of her own hands and motioned for him to continue, not yet raising her head.

"The Flowers did not reply."

A small, hysterical snort escaped her. Had he truly expected them to address anyone but the Name-Bearer?

"But they gave me another vision. The face of a babe and where to find her."

At that, the girl straightened and turned to regard him solemnly. She understood what he was saying, but not what it meant.

"Me?"

He gave her a quick, sharp nod of confirmation. "I did not understand the vision until later that day when the union of Princessa Issalia and Prince Enrique was decreed. They were not much older than you were, barely babes themselves, but with a marriage to come,"

"They needed a Name-Bearer" she finished for him.

He nodded at her once again, and her brow furrowed.

"But the bees?"

"I placed an enchantment on the bees to find and choose you. They may be the messengers of the gods, but the Flower's prophecy was too important to risk intervention. I could not take the chance of them not choosing you."

She thought that nothing would surprise her after hearing that someone, *anyone* would have the gall to attempt to speak to the Flowers. But apparently there was still room for shock in her small frame, for the thought of anyone tampering with the will of the gods returned to her that rush of sickening giddiness. With it, however, came another emotion. It bubbled up inside of her, unbidden, but powerful, and a thought sprang to the forefront of her mind.

A thought that had been long buried, suppressed, compacted, a thought that she had shrunk into a tiny acorn seed and swallowed deep within her soul.

"*You* took me from my family, and the regular life I could have led?"

He said nothing, but she noted what appeared to be sorrow within his eyes. It wasn't enough.

"Why me?"

"I wasn't sure, until this day. Now I am certain. It is you who must find the unnamed prince." This time there truly was no more room, no more space for surprise within her already battered psyche. She gave way to the hysteria, and a bubbling laugh shook her chest.

"Me?" The laughs were choking her and turning into desperate hiccups. "I wouldn't even know where to start! I cannot traipse through the entire kingdom searching for random babies!"

"No one would expect you to." His voice was solemn. The laughter subsided. He wasn't completely mad, after all.

"Oh, thank the Goddess."

"The babe is too young; we must wait until at least his tenth year," he continued.

The girl felt the blood drain from her face. Perhaps he *was* mad. All men and women of magia had some sort of madness in their blood, after all.

"You cannot be serious. Who am I to find this child? I know not who he is, where he might be, or why the prince, right here and now in this very palace, is not worthy to be named! And you ask me to not only find this child, this unknown prince, but to wait ten years to do so? And what, bring him back to the Flowers for a Naming Rite? A decade later?"

"Yes," he answered simply. When she stayed staring at him, he continued, begrudgingly.

"The Flowers are never wrong. They name the royal line with whispers of prophecy as to what the child may become. If they will not name the queen's son, we must find the other. If finding this new child promises peace, we must attempt it. The fate of the realm is at hand. What if this peace means a cease to the fighting with Cassalan?"

She frowned. Andala had been at war with their northern neighbor, Cassalan, for decades, and the death of King Enrique behind their borders was a recent and devastating loss to the kingdom. The young prince would never have the chance to know his father.

"If the Flowers granted a vision of you, and spoke to you of this child now, then you are meant to find him. You cannot fight against fate, girl, and the Flowers are the foretellers of prophecy."

In her heart of hearts, the girl understood this to be true. The Flowers would not have spoken to her, was she not meant to hear their message, Name-Bearer or no. Terrified at the implications, but resigned to her fate, she faced the wizard once again.

"But ten years? Why wait ten years? What are we going to do for ten years? What am *I* going to do for ten years? What do I tell the queen to name her baby?"

The look he gave her was one reserved for foolish children, failing to comprehend the world around them.

"You cannot meet the queen. Clearly you are not sufficiently proficient at lying, and we will not invent a name to bring to her child. And we must wait at least ten years because I could not keep an infant safe here. I need time, and resources to circulate the Prophecy to those in power who need to hear it. We will need years to build our resources, and gather support and a following for the child. This cannot happen overnight."

Politics had never been her strongest subject, but even this the girl could understand. She nodded.

"It wouldn't be safe for the baby now."

"Nor is it safe for you, in the palace."

"What? Why me? It wasn't my fault that I am here, *you* brought me here! And it wasn't my fault that the Flowers wouldn't name her baby! You must tell them it is your doing,"

"*Think* niña!" he snapped at her. "Who would grow support for the child if I were imprisoned for treason?"

"But this isn't my fault," she whispered, tears threatening to spill once more.

"It will not matter, you must go."

In a flash, her despair gave way to hot, piercing anger. The tears burned up in her eyes and cold steel flashed in their stead.

"Go?" she shouted. "Go *where*? I have nowhere to go, no home, no family, no name!" Heavy accusation dripped from her words. "How am I going to survive for ten years?"

He regarded her for a moment, her arms tight by her sides, hands clenched into small fists, sprinkling bits of dried mud onto the carpet. Her slim shoulders moved up and down with the strength of her furious pants.

"I will send you to the Danrayens," he decided, in a tone that bore no argument. But argue she did.

"*The Danrayens*?" she all but shrieked.

His response was a curt nod, the matter, in his mind, already decided.

"You think to send me to the deadliest warrior women in the realm? To the most elite sect, training soldiers from children to be the walking weapons of the Goddess Danray?"

"I know the high priestess. She will train you."

"I'm 13! I'm too old to be trained! And more importantly, I'm not a warrior!"

"You must become one. Your path will be long and arduous, and the child will need your protection."

"But,"

"I will send you to her. She will train you. I will come for you in ten years' time, as it will not be safe to contact you until then. You will have many enemies, and the palace has many ears and many eyes."

CHAPTER 4

After the wizard made his decision, things began moving very quickly. In fact, the few hours since the prince's birth had been a marked contrast to the very long and lonely night prior to it. The girl had prepared for the moment for as long as she could remember, endured a sleepless night in anticipation, and yet in a few short hours her entire existence had been unraveled. It was no wonder she felt thin, fraying. She had no idea what to do, where she was going, what to expect. She didn't even truly know who she was.

The wizard appeared unaffected by her silence, in fact, he seemed relieved by it. His long, ring-adorned fingers scribbled a hasty note on a piece of parchment with an ornately feathered quill, the shiny wet ink disappearing the second the point hit the paper. More magia. Once he was finished, he rolled it up into a tight cylinder and sealed it with one of his many rings, bearing an insignia of a claw or talon pressed against wax that had not been there a moment before.

Despite the fact that her young life had been completely upended, the girl experienced a moment of brief awe. She had always been a curious and inquisitive child, despairing her instructors with her seemingly endless supply of questions. Had the wizard conjured wax out of thin air, or had the ring somehow produced it? If so, it was a practical bit of magia, which was surprising. She had little experience with magia, as mages were so rare, but the idea of it being used for anything other than extravagant party tricks or for strategic advantage in the war had never occurred to her.

As she pondered, the wizard pinched the parchment between two fingers and snapped, and there was nothing left but a small puff of curling smoke.

He turned his focus back to her. "We must get to the stables; my personal coachman will be waiting. You cannot be seen, especially not with me. It would bring up too many questions. Come this way."

A tremor of fear rippled through her body. She was expected to go straight to the queen after the Naming Rite, to present the name of the baby. They would be expecting her, and if she wasn't there soon, there would doubtlessly be an inquiry. Servants would be sent to find her, and if they weren't successful in locating her, soldiers would soon follow. If news of her departure reached the queen and her advisors, the girl would be hunted down, hauled in and questioned. They would believe that she had faltered, that she had erred, offended the Flowers somehow and caused them to refuse the Naming. If she confessed the truth about the Flower's strange prophecy, she would be labeled a traitor and imprisoned.

Or even killed.

Unfair as it was, she knew it to be true. It was that knowledge and the hopeless realization that she quite literally had no one else to turn to that drove her to place her temporary trust in the wizard. Or perhaps more of a begrudging, suspicious acquiescence than true trust. But in that moment, anything seemed like a better option than the palace dungeons, and the torture she was sure to receive. Even the absolutely terrifying proposition of hiding amongst the realm's most fearsome female fighters seemed preferable.

That is how she found herself following Lord Auberon out of the room and down the corridor, their footfalls soft and muffled on the colorful hand-woven carpet laid over the cold stone floor. After a few feet he pulled open a door on their left and she was roughly nudged inside. It was a chamber she had never been in before, and it had large, curving seats in radiant splashes of yellows, turquoises and oranges, with plush pillows in equally bright colors and green, blue and red geometric patterns. Footstools with dangling multi-colored tassels were placed before them, fashioned from hand carved wood and covered with vivid cojines.

There were several rolling food and ale carts, and a few musical instruments lay discarded haphazardly in the corner. But the most interesting part about the room was its walls. Every inch from floor to ceiling was covered by gloriously embroidered tapestries, hanging with the slightest overlap on one another. Each enormous piece of fabric depicted different scenes of people and animals, vistas and tableaus that at another time she would have delighted to study.

The girl caught a glimpse of three beautifully embroidered alligators in a tropical jungle scene, and she recognized them as Mamajove, Mamamedia and Mamavieja, the three Caiman sisters of the Andalan Rainforest. She wondered if all the tapestries depicted the gods and goddesses, but she didn't have time to investigate. In any case, although the girl had never been to a party before, she assumed it was one of the many rooms in the palace used for entertainment.

Her suspicions were quickly confirmed when the wizard lifted one of the heavy tapestries in the far right corner to reveal a hidden door. Rosa Maria had once mentioned that there were numerous hidden corridors and passageways in the very walls of the palace, but she had never been able to find one. She knew that they were often used to slip people to and from places unseen, and many lead to entertainment rooms like the one she was standing in now.

The wizard brought a long, tapered finger to his lips to indicate that she should be silent. The girl was far too nervous to attempt to speak, but she nodded to confirm that she understood. He eased the hidden door open, wincing slightly as it scraped the stone floor. They both paused breathlessly for a moment, but when it was clear that they had not attracted any attention, he motioned for her to follow him once more.

Together they began traveling through the palace walls, the wizard holding a gem in front of him that emitted a low, muted amber light, enough to allow them to see the path ahead of them but not much else. The twists and turns were too numerous to count and the girl knew that if she got lost, or missed a turn, she would certainly not be able to find her way out again. So she followed him as closely as she dared without stepping on his long robe or the backs of his feet.

After a few long minutes they began to descend a narrow flight of stairs, the railing slick with the damp that settles within the bones of old homes. Her feet slipped, twice, but she managed to hang on and right herself in time. She didn't think that the wizard would appreciate her barreling into him and knocking them both down in the process. By the time they reached the bottom a trickle of sweat was making its way down her back and her right hand was cramped from her nervous grip.

As she took a moment to flex and extend her fingers and shake out her wrist, she realized that they must be underground. The air held an earthen, musty smell, and there was an inexplicable pressure in the tunnel, like finding one's head under too many blankets on a warm night. The ground beneath her feet was dirt rather than the stone it had been before, the humid, moist environment making the path slick and slippery as they continued their journey onward. Eventually the muddy path turned to packed soil and they began to ascend once more, finally emerging behind the palace stables.

The wizard gripped her arm above the elbow and hurried her into the building, thrusting her behind a large pile of hay. She scowled at his retreating back. He hadn't hurt her, exactly, but he was certainly rougher with her than needed. Still, his absence gave her a moment to try to collect herself. Bracing her hands on her knees, she took a deep breath, the smell of horse sweat and dung instantly causing her to sneeze several times in a row.

She froze, lifting her head and wiping her streaming eyes as quietly as possible. Had she attracted anyone's attention? After everything, the last thing that she needed was to be caught so far from the main body of the palace. The girl strained her ears, focusing on the muted shuffles of hooves, and soft chuffs of horses and vicuñas. Pails clanged against wooden stalls, and she could just hear the murmured conversations of stable hands, but they were too far away for her to make out anything in particular. It all sounded perfectly normal until ... *there*. She tensed. Footsteps.

And they were heading towards her.

Frantically she darted her eyes around the room, looking for some-place to run, somewhere to hide. But there was nothing but hay, and the side door they had entered from was across from her and in plain sight of whomever was making their way towards her. What was she going to do?

The girl's eyes landed on a metal pitchfork, tufts of hay sticking to it's sharp points. She could pick it up, she could use it ...

How? How exactly will you use it? Are you going to stab whoever comes around the corner? Her head swam with the image. No. She didn't have it in her to hurt anyone, especially when the entire situation was very much not their fault. She wouldn't hurt some poor stable boy because of the mess she had gotten herself into.

Still, she thought, as the footsteps grew louder, *they didn't have to know that I don't intend to use it.* Maybe holding it would be enough to scare them.

She lunged sideways to scoop up the tool just as someone rounded the corner. Biting back a scream she grabbed the pitchfork ...

And almost toppled over in relief when she saw the bottom section of the wizard's robe round the corner.

He noted her on the floor, her left arm over the pitchfork, her wild hair liberally feathered with hay, and released an impatient sigh.

"Ven," he told her, motioning for her to follow him before moving back the way he came. She scrambled up off the ground and scurried after him gratefully, his earlier rough treatment of her momentarily forgiven. She spared the pitchfork one final glance and shuddered, relieved that she hadn't had to use it after all.

Lord Auberon led her to the side of the stable where the carriages were kept. There, a coachman was waiting next to a nondescript brown wagon. After living most of her life in the vibrant colors of the inner palace, the unremarkable vehicle was shocking in its simplicity. The coachman barely glanced at her before opening the door and helping her inside. The wizard said a few final quiet words to the man who nodded, swallowing hard, his Adam's apple bobbing up and down with the force of it. She had not realized until that moment that the wizard must have his own servants, loyal to him and not to the royal family.

Auberon spared her a final glance, not offering her any reassurances, or even bidding her farewell, merely jerking a curt nod in her direction before returning the way that they had come. She stared at the spot where his retreating back had been while the coachman quickly readied the horses, until he shut her door with an expert sweep of his arm and she was alone once more.

The girl collapsed against the padded back of the carriage bench as they began moving. Soft tremors began making their way through her body, creating little uncontrollable shivers. Soon her entire frame was trembling, and then she was shaking violently. She ripped out her tupu, shrugging off her manta and unwrapping her chumpi, which felt like it was suffocating her. Once half of her clothing littered the carriage floor she brought her feet up to her seat, knees pressed against her chest and wrapped her arms around herself. The tremors continued to wrack her body, as if an icy spirit had reached his hands within her skin, grabbed a hold of her bones and was rattling her from the inside out. Her teeth chattered and as she rocked herself back and forth. It was too much, it had all been too much.

It took the better part of an hour for her body to relax, and by then her muscles were stiff and cramped from the uncomfortable position and the tension. Once she began feeling more like herself, she realized that she must be further from the palace than she had ever been in her life. Nervous though she was about her situation, eventually her curiosity won out and she drew back the carriage curtains to peer out at the world which had been long denied to her.

The beauty of Andala momentarily distracted her from her woes. The land she had glimpsed from afar, high in her tower now surrounded her. Because she had spent the initial portion of the ride shivering in despair, she had missed the cobblestone streets, colorful marketplaces, textiles and city vendors, though that was probably for the best. She was not necessarily a recognizable figure to anyone outside the palace walls, however, a young girl with auburn hair and a flower dress would be fairly memorable to anyone later questioned.

But they were well outside the city now, in the rolling hills and plains of farmland country. Men and women alike worked the fields, their bare arms brown and glistening with sweat as they cut maize under the morning sun. Children ran through the crops, chasing one another with delighted shrieks. Eventually farmland turned to forest, not the dark foreboding Night Forest of the east that she had read about in her histories, but the lush and rich Great Andalan Rainforest, with towering ceiba trees, as tall as fifty men with smooth trunks that remained branchless until reaching the forest canopy, and then bursting into gnarled twists and spilling over with star-like leaf clusters. The land was green and flourishing, and the girl caught glimpses of swinging monkeys, large reptiles and multicolored birds. The sunlight filtered through the tree's wet fronds and created dazzling patterns on the dirt path, twinkling and dancing with each rustling of the leaves.

She wished that they were driving nearer to the coast, as she had always been fascinated by the ocean, but could only glimpse it from afar, and then only if she leaned her torso out of her tower window and twisted to the left. She had always thought that after the Naming, once she was a full member of court, that she could take a trip down to its shores. Now she wondered if she would ever get the chance.

As they rode, she contemplated what else would be denied to her, now that her life had changed so drastically. Would she ever see Rosa Maria again? Would she be able to read legends of the diosas y dioses in small, stolen moments between lessons? She had been so excited to be seen in her dress, to meet the queen, deliver the prince his name, and begin her new life at court. She wondered what her new rooms must look like; if things had gone differently she might have even been moving into her new quarters now.

She would have been very busy in the upcoming months, as there was no shortage of noble babies awaiting the prince's Naming so that they could be named themselves. The law decreed that any noble children without names could be brought to the palace for a Naming Rite, but only after the future king or queen was named first. Even then, they only qualified for a Naming Rite if they were born within five years of a royal birth. The Flowers always named future kings and queens, of course, but they could also name the children of nobility if their parents brought them forth. Only children named by the Great Flowers of Prophecy could be considered as a potential future match for the new prince or princess.

When the late King Enrique was born, fifty-three children were brought forward in the few years after his Naming to receive names themselves. Queen Issalia was, naturally, one of them.

Noble families with children born after the prince's naming could come forward and request the Name-Bearer's service, and some families even forwent naming children born months or even years prior to royal children's births in hopes that their own young ones could be considered as potential future monarchs. As the official Name-Bearer, she would probably have had noble families vying for her attention and favor, hoping she might decide to name their baby before the others, and therefore not have to wait the weeks or months it might take to get to them. She also couldn't just bring a list of unnamed children to the Flowers either; each child required their own Naming Rite, although the ceremony was much less complicated than when naming a prince or princess.

The previous Name-Bearer had explained it all to her in the last months. With the queen due to deliver soon, the girl had seen more of her predecessor in a few weeks than she had in her entire life combined.

The Name-Bearer before her was a woman of 33. She had been chosen by the bees at two-years-old, when the late King Enrique's royal parents had been betrothed, both but ten years old at the time. Nearly ten years after that, King Enrique the Tempest Storm was born and named. She lived as the Name-Bearer for nine more years, until he and Princessa Issalia were promised to one another, when the girl was chosen instead.

After retiring as a Name-Bearer, past Name-Bearers become known simply as "The Namers." They, on occasion, were needed to train new Name-Bearers, but they mostly enjoy their positions as members of the court, filling their days however they choose. The Namer's predecessor was a middle-aged man known as "The Nameless." And his predecessor? If he lived, no one spoke of him, and no one knew where he was. Perhaps he then was "The Forgotten."

El olvidado.

The shivering girl in the carriage would never ascend to The Namer, or The Nameless. She would be known as a traitor.

They drove the rest of the morning, afternoon and well into the evening, stopping only a few times to rest the horses. It was a long drive, and the girl both longed for it to be over, and yet wished it would never end. She knew not what was before her, and in her uncertainty would have preferred to brave the discomforts of a long trip far more eagerly than the unknown path that lay at her journey's end.

They stopped frequently, the thick canopy of the trees sheltering the horses from the fierce morning sun, but the sticky humidity caused them to perspire and tire quicker than they would have in the more arid areas of Andala. On one of those brief stops, the coachman offered the girl some water and a small, slightly shriveled apple. She realized, much later, that it had probably been intended as a snack for one of the horses, but at the time she was hungry and therefore appreciated the kindness.

At that moment she had asked for the man's name. She was trained as a Name-Bearer, after all, and names were always important to her.

But he had flushed red, stumbling backwards and shaking his head before leaving her alone once more. She realized then how much of a risk her mere presence was to others, and what an uncomfortable position she had put him in. Her already heavy heart wrung painfully in her chest, and she remained silent for the rest of the journey.

The girl knew that the Temple of Danray sat to the northeast of the palace, but still in Southern Andala. While full Danrayen warriors traveled throughout the realm, and beyond, initiates of the sisterhood were trained within the temple grounds by the Danrayen Priestesses. She also knew, from her studies, that it was at least a two-day ride from the palace to the temple. The wizard must have witched the carriage, or the horses, or both, to allow them to reach their destination much quicker. Once their party entered the solitary shade of the rainforest, away from the sight of people, they sped up, trees passing by the carriage windows in a blur. Eventually she drew the curtains, the speed and unfamiliar travel making her feel queasy.

Despite their haste, it was still well past nightfall when, with a quick, pitying glance the coachman finally left her, cold, alone, and frightened at the doorsteps of the Danrayen Temple. In that moment she knew not what was before her but understood with certainty that she could not go back.

The girl stared for a long time up at the temple before moving. She knew it was built up of several buildings and structures, but the front of the main entrance shot proudly up into the night sky, not quite the height of the Andalan Palace, but close. It was a long rectangle with the entry archway centered in the middle of two long stretches of stone, with a flight of steep, narrow steps leading the way in.

And all of it was cast in pure gold.

The sides of the temple were etched with Danrayen symbols and markings, depicting weapons, animals and geometric glyphs. Above the temple entrance, at the top of the long flight of stairs were long, spiked, golden triangles, forming a sort of sun-crown that perched on top of the entryway. Behind the main wall, in the distance, she could just make out the top of a towering sculpture of the goddess Danray.

Depictions of the goddess showed her with dark curling hair, but the statue carved in gold as it was glistened a pale yellow in the moonlight. The girl had always wanted to see that sculpture in person, since it was the largest image of the goddess in all the realms. She never thought that she would have the opportunity, and now she would be living with it. If she decided to go in, that is.

You could run. The thought was startling, and oh so tempting, but short lived. As exhilarating as the notion of freedom was to her, the idea was ultimately futile. It was true that her situation in the palace had changed drastically, but her situation in life remained the same. She had no one, and nowhere to turn to.

She stared down at her dress, fingering the brightly colored jewels embedded into the gown, realizing belatedly that she had left her manta and chumpi strewn about the wizard's carriage, along with her solid gold tupu which had pinned her wrap together in the front. She wondered if the coachman would deliver them back to the Wizard Auberon, or perhaps pawn the precious materials for himself? It would be dangerous to be caught with anything that hinted at contact with the Name-Bearer, but need often outweighed caution.

Still, it was early enough; her escape couldn't have reached this far out yet. Surely her clothing could fetch a good price, somewhere. She could sell them, and live...

Live where? she thought angrily. *And how?* She had only a mild notion of where she was, having studied maps of Andala and Cassalan in the past, but she had not paid too much attention as she never thought that map-reading would be a skill needed of her. She knew there were several villages near the Temple of Danray, the largest being Pelgar to the northeast, but in her state, she couldn't even be sure which way was north. And besides, she was more likely to get robbed, and stripped of her gown for its gems before managing to sell it. Then she would be worse off than she was now, still alone, still afraid, but naked and discarded.

And that was if she was lucky, and not assaulted, murdered, or sold to flesh peddlers. The wealthy never need worry about such things, of course. Should they find themselves without protection and captured by bandits, they would simply be held for ransom and released when their captors were paid. But those citizens of Andala without the coin to spare could be taken into servitude and sold as slaves. With the Andalan army preoccupied with the war in the north, there were precious few protectors within the realm to ward against evils within their own land.

In the palace, as a servant of the realm, she had been guarded, sheltered, considered valuable and special. She had had a purpose, a destiny. She was important. She was the Name-Bearer. Outside the palace walls, however, she was no one. She was alone and vulnerable. Just a child without a name.

Having no other options available to her, she resigned herself to seeing the wizard's plan through. The girl straightened her spine and began climbing the many, many steps to the temple. It was dark, but it was a cloudless night and both the moon and the multitude of stars in the midnight sky shone down and illuminated her path. The temple glimmered in their light, eerie and foreign and frightening, but the girl continued her ascent. When she finally crossed the threshold into the sacred Danrayen grounds, a woman waited to greet her.

She was the most beautiful woman that the girl had ever seen. She was tall, with russet brown skin and tightly curled black hair that reached just below her breasts. The darkness of her hair and brows contrasted sharply against her piercing amber eyes. She wore a striking yellow gown the color of the alstroemeria lily, that cut low and draped over a tight stomach and curved hips. The plunging neckline of the dress revealed a delicately complex phoenix tattoo, its head and body clearly visible between her breasts with wings unfurled and burning across her ribs until disappearing under the fabric. Her eyes were narrow, her mouth full and nose straight and proud. Her arms were toned and well formed, as was what else the girl could see. She radiated strength, power, and discipline. She was a warrior, through and through. And based on the intricate golden headdress she wore over her forehead and crown, a priestess.

Too exhausted and confused to remember her manners, the girl stared, lips parted and tired eyes wide.

"Are you her?" she finally asked, quietly. The woman's answer came in a voice as commanding as her appearance.

"I am the High Priestess Adira."

"Oh," was the girl's only reply.

The priestesses' sharp eyes examined the child, taking in her elaborate braids which were unraveling and twining down her shoulders, her satin slippers soiled and beyond salvaging, and the dirt streaked on the sides of her beautiful flower dress.

"We shall have to burn that." she stated. The girl's eyes filled with heavy tears. Surely she couldn't mean....

"Mi vestido?" she asked, fearing her response.

"Si."

Desperation clouded her voice. "But it's the only thing I've ever owned, the only thing that was ever truly mine!" Besides, it would be a crime to destroy a thing of such beauty, would it not? The priestess regarded her calmly.

"It is quite clearly made of fine riches known only to the palace. Most commoners have never even *seen* a gemstone, let alone owned one, and that dress has dozens. They will be donated for the temple upkeep. And most importantly, the designs mark it as a tribute to the Flowers of Prophecy; it cannot be kept."

Finally overwhelmed, the girl's knees gave out, and she crumpled to the ground, her beautiful skirts splayed out around her. She tucked her knees to her chest, and great choking sobs wracked her body.

"I waited my whole life to wear it. To be of service to the gods and speak to the Flowers. I was so excited to put it on... I knew the day I did would be the best of my life. How stupid I was!" she wailed, and wept, her tears soaking the fabric of her dress, swelling her eyes and making her nose bright red.

The High Priestess Adira waited, patiently, not interrupting her or commanding her to stop. She stood, still and with a compassionate expression until the child was spent. Only when the girl was quiet, soft hiccups escaping her throat, did she speak again.

"You will also need a name."

The girl jerked her head up in shock, her face streaked and splotchy.

"A name?" she asked, doubtfully. "It is forbidden."

"You are no longer the Name-Bearer, child, but deemed a traitor to the realm. You must become someone new. Like a young caterpillar who changes every aspect of themselves to become a butterfly, so must you transform."

The girl swiped the tears off of her face and inhaled deeply. Despite everything that she had been through since the morning, it was this moment that would ensure her status as a traitor; to the palace, to her queen, and to her position within the realm. The Name-Bearer is nameless, they are *forever* nameless. Everything that had happened to her up until this point had not been her choice, not really. Her actions were a result of fear and necessity. But if she was to give herself a name, that would be an irreversible decision, solidifying her defiance to the crown. Could she truly accept that there was no returning to the life she had known?

"Phanessa," the girl said, the name bubbling up from her chest and out her lips before she could stop it. She raised her gaze to Adira.

"Que?" the priestess asked her. A small blush crept up the girl's already flushed face.

"Phanessa means butterfly."

A small smile tugged at the warrior's mouth.

"Is that so?"

"I am the Name-Bearer." The girl lifted a shoulder in a small shrug. "I know the meaning of all names."

"You are the Name-Bearer no longer, *Phanessa*."

CHAPTER 5

It is well known throughout the realm, and beyond, that the Danrayens select only the strongest of young girls to join their ranks. Families who choose to do so may bring their daughters to be evaluated by the Danrayen Priestesses as early as five years old. Most children are selected and welcomed into the order between the ages of five and eight.

There are, of course, some exceptions. Some children whose families do not want to take them to the priestesses, for they do not want them joining the sisterhood. It is a difficult path, after all, and full of dangers more often than not. The training itself can be brutal, resulting in injury, and the final Trial is so arduous that not all survive. Understandably, many families do not want their girls deliberately putting themselves in harm's way.

Other families simply cannot afford to lose a single child, for they need the help within their homes. Girls who would have otherwise joined the path of Danray are forced to stay at home to take care of their younger siblings, learn the family trade, work the farms and fields, or are married off to wealthier suitors to help care for their families financially. Despite this, many of those girls still find their way to the temples on their own, despite their parents' wishes, for the path calls to them.

Other children find the priestesses or temples later in life, for they were born appearing male, but over the years come to embrace their inner goddess and transform to become their true selves. Many of these girls choose the Danrayen path, for the goddess Danray is the goddess of both battle and transition.

That is why both the butterfly and the phoenix are so prevalent in Danrayen culture. They are both creatures undone to become something more than they once were. Once a girl passes the Trials of Danray and is anointed as a full Danrayen warrior, they are allowed to adorn their mail, shields, weapons, and often even skin with the mark of the butterfly. Only Danrayen Riders, the highest order of Danray, and the priestesses can mark themselves with the image of the phoenix.

The night the girl arrived she had little chance to see anything past the temple's front facade, glinting in the moonlight. After her crying spell, the priestess Adira had taken her to a room full of clothing of which the colors, she would later realize, all mirrored the shades of the land around them.

She stripped off what remained of her Flower dress, feeling more and more vulnerable with each discarded layer. After Adira collected each scrap of fabric, and with them the last remaining ties to the girl's former life, the priestess handed her two sleep shirts, some underthings, and a cream and tan-colored sleeveless tunic with loose pants to wear the next day.

Priestess Adira led her to a clean, comfortable guest room where she was to rest. The priestess warned her that mornings began early in the temple, but that she would be given the luxury of remaining in her room until the noon meal, out of sympathy for the trial and journey she had just endured. This would be, she warned the girl, their only courtesy. She would be expected to adapt to the Danrayen life along with the rest of the trainees. The girl could do nothing more than nod dumbly before retreating into the room and shutting the door behind her.

She hadn't believed she would ever be able to sleep again, after the unbelievable series of events that she had been a part of within the last day. But she had not slept the night prior either, waiting for news of the queen's delivery and it had been a long, tiring day since. Ultimately exhaustion won out and sleep claimed her quickly, her small body giving in to the weariness that enveloped her the moment her head hit the pillow. She slept well into the next morning, waking to the bustle and conversation of young women drifting through her window. The unexpected sounds, as well as the unfamiliar room served to fully disorient her until she remembered where she was, and what had happened to bring her there.

Hot tears burned a path from the outer corners of her eyes, down her temples and into her hair, as she lay in a strange place feeling more alone than she had ever been in her life. She wanted to scream *"It's not fair!"* to anyone, to everyone, but she had learned long ago that no one would listen. No one would care. She was in her situation whether or not it was fair, and no amount of screaming or crying would change it. The only thing that she could do was make a choice. Her next steps were her own, she only needed to decide what path to take. Bending her elbows behind her she sat up and swiped away the moisture on her face.

Again she considered leaving, running away to somewhere, any-where else. But the same obstacles that she had come up against the night before were still as insurmountable in the light of day. She had nowhere to go, and nothing to her name that would aid her journey. She was penniless, defenseless, and nameless.

Well, she considered. *Perhaps not nameless anymore.*

A foreign feeling unfurled just behind her sternum, and a tiny smile tugged at the corner of her lips, the unused muscles quivering slightly after being inactive for so long. The feeling blossomed as she remembered answering the Priestess Adira the night before. *Phanessa,* she thought with a wild, reckless thrill. Perhaps she could become Phanessa. A Danrayen initiate, a trainee, destined to become a warrior.

She could learn, couldn't she? She was clever, after all, all of her instructors had said so, though some admitted it begrudgingly. She could hold her secret close to her heart, shrink it, fold it, tuck it away behind her ribs and never speak of her past again. She could leave the Name-Bearer behind, and adopt this foreign girl, Phanessa, as her new self.

It was as good a plan as any. It was, in fact, her only plan.

With grim resignation she decided then and there that if this was to be her home for the next ten years of her life, she would do everything in her power to survive it, and never give anyone cause to doubt that she was not a true initiate.

Swinging her legs off the bed she scooped up the tunic and pants Priestess Adira had given her and pulled them both on, wincing as the fabric scratched up her legs. In the palace all her clothing was silky, gentle and soft. Nothing ever rubbed her flesh abrasively, or pinched, or had to be held up by long scraps of hide like the pants she was wearing. The clothing also smelled ... strange. Not bad, and the fabric was certainly clean, but it smelled earthen, and maybe just a tad musty. It didn't help the unfamiliar, unpleasant experience of donning on this new identity.

Trading the finer cloths for stiff burlap, itchy wool and tanned leather was going to be a difficult transition, and yet ... she had never worn pants before, and it gave her a small, rebellious thrill to do so now. The unrestricting clothing may have felt awkward, hanging off her narrow hips and rubbing together between the insides of her legs, but it also offered her a sort of freedom and mobility the likes of which she had never known.

She refused to feel self-conscious about her wardrobe, knowing that many women wore pants, especially warriors and soldiers. Even some women in the palace preferred them, though their versions were made from flowing silks and perfectly tailored to fit their frames. Still, she gathered up all the tattered scraps of her courage and finally emerged, following her nose and the moving tide of young women heading in a single direction, assuming that both would lead her to the meal hall.

On her way she took note of her surroundings for the first time and was in awe of just how different her days would be for her here. Her former life of the brilliant textiles, vibrant patterns and vivid colors of the palace would be replaced with the less radiant but warmer tones and hues of her new home. Where the palace was eye-catching and flamboyant, the Temple of Danray was warm and homey, bursting with the muted colors of the earth.

The training fields were weather-beaten and rich, and the buildings full of coppers, bronzes and golds. She noted that the Danrayen warriors and trainees all wore outfits in hues of fawn, mushroom, sage, and nut-brown that helped them blend in with their surroundings, and she was glad for the new wardrobe that helped her to look like she belonged, regardless of how scratchy and stiff she might find the fabric.

The temple grounds were much larger once inside the interior walls than they had appeared on the outside. The compound was shaped like a rough horseshoe, with the main building, the long stone rectangle at the bottom holding the entrance, library, and study halls. On the other side of that long building, in the center of the horseshoe sat the training grounds, large fields with strange wooden contraptions used for practicing strategy, endurance, and building muscle. Weapons of all kinds were on display, if they were not properly placed on their stands and racks then they littered the ground and fields instead. There were swords, staffs and bows on mounts, an archery field with various targets (some moving) and a lifted arena for public duels and exhibitions.

There were young girls everywhere.

They were short, tall, slender, muscular, round. Some were missing limbs, or an eye, or had other outward disfigurations. It seemed that any young woman was given an equal opportunity to become a warrior, they were each fiercer than the next and all devastatingly beautiful in their strength and resilience.

Two long rows of smaller buildings made up the sides of the horseshoe, and consisted of the barracks that the girls shared, the bath houses, and the mess hall on one side, and the stables, an armory, and the indoor training facilities on the other. At the open top of the crescent shape was the Temple Garden with the massive statue of the Goddess Danray. She was the most impressive thing that the girl had ever seen, carved in pure gold with painstaking attention to detail and glorious down to each individual eyelash. She towered over the surrounding land, casting great shadows over the grounds depending on the time of day. In the hot midday sun, some of the girls could be seen seeking refuge under her watchful shade, sprawled in small groups, their conversations drifting with the gentle breeze that did little to assuage the humidity.

She noticed that if crossing through the center of the temple grounds, the girls would turn to greet the goddess's figure, raising a clenched fist and pressing their thumbs to their necks, in the hollow of their collarbones. It was the spot where the great goddess' arrows met her enemies' flesh, and it was in that way that they honored her.

The girl quickly adopted the gesture, but felt a twinge of guilt in doing so. She was an imposter and had no business repeating such a sacred symbol. Despite the guilt, she longed to see the statue closer, and wondered when she would have the opportunity to do so. But as quickly as the thought sprung to her mind, the sweet smell of flowers drifted into the yards and she was hit with a deep, twisting pain within her chest, the scent reminding her of inarguably the worst day of her young life.

Of course, she thought ruefully. The statue was in the center of the temple gardens, and she had had enough of gardens, and flowers, to last her a lifetime. Just like that, her excitement to see the sculpture withered within her.

When she finally made it to the meal hall she stood in line with girls of various ages and sizes. Her presence was a cause for speculation and curiosity, as she was far older than most initiates to the temple and the Danrayen way of life, and she received many stares and whispers which made her cheeks and the back of her neck burn. Surprisingly, however, it seemed that she was quickly accepted. No one went out of their way to speak to or try to befriend her, but the whispers and stares died out in favor of more interesting conversation and gossip. After all, any girl can choose the path of Danray, at any time, if the priestesses accept her. To the others, she must have been deemed as someone strong enough to pursue the warrior's path, as if not, she would not have been allowed within the temple. The girl resolved that the truth never be discovered.

She decided once again that she would accept the path that the Archwizard Auberon and High Priestess Adira had set her on. *Phanessa*, this new, strange girl that she had been forced to become, would do her best to fit in as a trainee. If this was to be her life, then she would embrace it. No good would come of it otherwise. And if the wizard was in earnest, and in ten short years she would be forced to journey throughout the kingdom to find the unnamed prince, then she would indeed need to learn how to fend for and protect herself if needed. She was clever, she reminded herself again. Surely, she could learn how to blend in and adapt to the new life she would call her own.

Over the next few days, the girl threw herself into her new life with abandon. She rose early and joined the ranks of initiates, making her way to training and lessons and training again, with breaks only to eat, bathe, and sleep. Then she would wake and repeat the process all over again.

However, she quickly learned that the Danrayen life did not come easily to her. It seemed that mere conviction was not enough to magically transform herself into the new young woman that she had decided to be. First of all, she was weak, her physical exercise having been limited to occasional walks through the palace grounds and a riding lesson once a week. Her arms could not push the weight of her own body up from the floor when attempting the morning exercises that the other girls breezed through, nor could they pull her weight up to vault over walls or barriers that the others maneuvered so easily. Every muscle in her body became stiff and sore.

On her second day she could not lower herself into a seated position, her legs would give way halfway to sitting and plop her down abruptly, her thighs burning with exertion. Though she had never believed herself to be clumsy, the careful and delicate nature which had been ingrained in her by her palace training made her attacks awkward and half-hearted. She stumbled over her own feet, backed away when she needed to attack, and often dropped both her guard and her weapons.

It was clear, at least to her, that she was no warrior.

She spent her first few days terrified that her secret would be all too apparent, and that in no time she would be found out, betrayed, arrested for treason and dragged back to the palace in shame for punishment. She dared not think about the punishment. So, she pushed herself harder, ignoring her exhaustion, her screaming muscles, and the many, many bruises that formed in spatters and splotches over her battered body. No matter how hard she tried, however, it seemed she would never catch up to the strength and skill of the others. Even so, she did her best to adapt to her new home.

It was the beginning of her second week of training, when bone-weary and spent, she sat on the dirt field of the training yards panting, rivulets of sweat streaming down her face and neck.

"Wow," came a young, feminine voice behind her. She twisted her body to see its owner.

"You're not very good at this." The voice belonged to a girl about her age, standing in a leather jerkin, with her small fists propped against her hips.

Everything about her was sharp. Her eyes were thin slits, her eyebrows slashing upward towards her temples. Her cheekbones were high and pronounced, her nose straight and pert. Her jawline was strong and ended in a keen, pointed chin. All her bones and limbs and the muscles that covered them seemed angular, her collarbones jutting out strongly, protruding from her deep brown skin. Even her hair, which was an explosion of tightly wound curls bursting from her scalp was sharply cut, hitting just below her jaw. Her hair was a surprisingly light color, an almost white that contrasted against the richness of her skin. It wasn't the first time that she had noticed the fierce Danrayen, she was hard to miss.

"No," she answered her, simply. There was no use in denying it, after all, she wasn't any good at any of it.

"How old are you?" the young warrior asked.

"Thirteen."

"And you *just* decided to join the Danrayens?" The other girl's eyes widened, abandoning the cat-like squint for a moment. "Wow. It's no wonder you're terrible."

The girl glared angrily at her, wiping her brow with her shirt. It didn't matter that the Danrayen was correct, she didn't have to be so rude about it.

"I'm fourteen and I've been here since I was five. I'm going to be the best warrior Danray has ever seen. She will smile down at me with pride." The statement was not delivered haughtily, but with an unwavering self-assurance that she couldn't help but envy. She also didn't doubt it. She had seen her in the training yards on several occasions, and she was spectacular, easily the most talented of all the trainees in their age range. Perhaps even better than some of the older girls as well.

"That's lovely for you," she managed, through gritted teeth. The two stared at each other for a tense moment. The young Danrayen cocked her head, consideringly. Then she seemed to come to a decision, and gave her a determined nod.

"I'll help you," she declared.

"What?"

"I'll help you train."

The younger girl blinked at her, bewildered. "Why would you do that?"

The other girl shrugged. "That's what friends do."

Friends. The word knocked the breath out of her faster than the combat lesson had. She had never had a friend, and scarcely dared to hope.

"I -" she started, and was appalled to hear her voice crack. Clearing her throat, she continued. "Thank you."

The girl smiled, and extended a strong, calloused hand down to her. "Come on. I'm Damika."

A grin broke through her sweat-soaked face, and for the first time in her life, she replied, "Phanessa. My name is Phanessa."

CHAPTER 6

The day she offered her tutelage, Damika took Phanessa fully under her wing, making sure that she sat next to her in classrooms, accompanied her on excursions, and joined her at meals. That first evening Phanessa trailed behind her new mentor in the meal hall gratefully, her tray an exact replica of what Damika had served herself, a hefty spoonful of aji de gallina -a spicy chicken dish, a few small, narrow potatoes cooked with butter and herbs, wild greens, and sweet plantains. Instead of sitting at one of the small outer tables as Phanessa was used to, the older girl had led her to a larger one in the middle of the room and sat them down next to a short, stocky girl with light hair cropped close to her head and brilliant eyes that could not decide their color.

"This is Petra," Damika yelled to her over the loud voices of the room while sliding on to one of the long benches. She motioned for Phanessa to join them, nodding at Petra with a smile. "This is Phanessa. She's new."

Petra eyed her curiously. "I've seen you in the yards," she told Phanessa, her voice surprisingly sweet for someone who appeared so intense. "How old are you?"

Phanessa flushed. She thought that she had done a good job of going by unnoticed in the last weeks, blending in with the myriad of other girls at the temple. She hadn't counted on being so abysmal at the physical trials of the warrior's path that she was being recognized by others. If Petra had noticed her in the yards, it was only because she was terrible. Shame twisted in her belly.

As if reading her thoughts, Damika clasped a companionable hand on her shoulder and grinned at Petra. "She's thirteen, and brand new. She's not very good yet, but she'll get better." Relief crashed through Phanessa and she shot a timid but grateful smile at her new mentor. Satisfied, Petra began telling them about her day, who had won in an archery competition, about an unfortunate accident that landed an older girl in the infirmary, and how a particularly mischievous donkey nicknamed Travieso had managed to sink his teeth into a trainee's pants, ripping it mostly off and exposing her bottom. She had shrieked, Petra informed them with a playful glint in her eye, and had tried to shield herself from her unexpected exposure for precisely two seconds before abandoning modesty completely and sprinting ass-out after the beast, leaving a trail of very colorful language in her wake.

Soon Phanessa was laughing along with the two of them. Before their meal was finished they were joined by two other young trainees. First was Taruka, or Taru as they called her, who was notably tall, with long dark hair and equally long lithe limbs that were still gangly in her youth. She was soft spoken and exuded a quiet sweetness that immediately put Phanessa at ease. It was clear that she and Petra had a special bond, their conversation so quick and effortless and laden with so many private jokes that the two almost seemed to speak in their own language.

A while later another girl joined their group, arriving to their meal late, her square face and chubby cheeks flushed and her tumbling honey-colored curls in disarray. Her figure was plump, all soft rounded flesh and gentle curves. Damika narrowed her eyes at the girl as she plopped down next to them, her tray untouched.

"Where have you been?" Damika asked her, but the girl only flashed her teeth in a little smirk, punctuating it by sticking out her tongue. Damika just rolled her eyes.

"This is Raidea," she informed Phanessa, and as the other girl's mouth was currently being stuffed with food, she merely offered Phanessa a hearty wink. Damika shook her head.

"Careful of this one," she joked to Phanessa. "Es una sinvergüenza, forever causing mischief!"

At the accusation, Raidea's already impish eyes twinkled brighter with merriment.

"If you must know," she told the group when she had finally swallowed her mouthful. "I had to go to the temple seamstress for some breast bands. She arched her back slightly, and sure enough, where the other girls were still mostly flat, she had two small, but visible slopes. Raidea looked down at herself proudly.

"They've been growing for a while now, and I finally thought it time to do something about them."

"Don't they get in the way?" Petra asked her, openly staring at the shirt that was stretched tightly across her chest. Her voice was a mixture of horror and amazement.

Raidea laughed. "Not really," she replied. "Besides, as most of our enemies will likely be men, I'm sure they'll prove to be a good distraction." She bounced a bit, and her chest bounced with her. They all burst into laughter, Phanessa's cheeks growing hot with embarrassment. She knew about the ways to womanhood, of course, her palace training had taught her the basics. But she never thought she would be talking so openly about it with other girls her age. Was this what friendship would be like?

Friendship. It was a foreign concept to her that made her heart squeeze and head hurt, just a little.

After eating, Damika took her on a proper tour of the temple. They passed by the open fields where a woman with flaming red hair and an equally red face was brushing a black and white llama.

"That's Priestess Ovidia." Damika told her. "She is in charge of all the wildlife here at the temple. She's also the head trainer of the Danrayen mares; all horses that are sent into war with Danrayen Warriors are personally trained by her and her team. Even some of the palace generals come to have their mounts trained by her as well."

They looped around the far right side of the temple grounds and made their way towards a clearing near the forest glen. There, tucked out of sight was a small but homey looking cottage made of deep red clay and surrounded by what appeared to be a small vegetable garden. It was circled by a wooden fence, probably to keep the llamas and burros from eating the crops. But the door to the house was open, and there was a tell-tale ringlet of smoke slow-dancing from the chimney to indicate that someone was home. As they approached, Damika broke into an easy grin and her posture relaxed.

"Come," she said. "You should meet Mamá"

Phanessa's eyes widened, and her eyebrows shot so far up that they were almost lost in her hair.

"Your mamá lives here?" she asked in disbelief. Damika merely laughed.

"Not *mi* mamá ... just Mamá. You'll see."

The girls reached the garden gate, Damika vaulting over it easily while Phanessa lifted the hatch and swung the small wooden door inwards. She made sure that the lock engaged behind her once she entered. She wasn't sure who this Mamá was, but she didn't want her first impression to be the girl who let the animals eat the woman's vegetables!

Inside the cottage there was a large open cocina with a heavy pot hanging over a crackling fire, and a long wooden table with six fat stools surrounding it. The roof was high, and from it hung many multi-colored bundles of different drying plants, herbs and flowers. The windows were open as well as the front door, and the smell of hojas de laurel, aji, oak, citrus and countless other odors tickled Phanessa's nose, along with the heady aroma of cooking meat, hot peppers and coriander of the seco de cabra in the pot. And in the middle of it all, in a brightly colored huipil was a very short, beaming woman.

She seemed to be about the Priestess Adira's age, but where Adira was hard, and severe, this woman was soft and warm. She enveloped Damika in a fierce hug which the young girl sunk into with a soft, contented sigh. They rocked together for a moment before Damika pulled back, motioning for her to step forward.

"Mamá, this is Phanessa. She's new."

Mamá directed her welcoming smile to Phanessa and shuffled across the space with her arms wide. Before she could react, she too was swept into a warm embrace that smelt of honey and hierbabuena. After the disastrous last few weeks, she couldn't say that she minded it at all. As if sensing her emotions, the woman gave her an extra squeeze, patting a heavy hand on her upper back. Somehow the motion felt like it dislodged a sliver of the tightened knot stuck within her torso, and suddenly the girl could breathe a little easier. But that was silly. It was probably just due to inhaling the hierbabuena. Mamá released her.

"Welcome, welcome chiquita! How lucky you are to have made such a good friend as Damika already!" she said as she puttered about, her small steps leading her to the fireplace where she gave the pot a good stir.

"Han comido?" she directed at Damika, who nodded.

"Si, we just ate, gracias Mamá."

"Then sit, sit. Tell me all the chisme." The girls sat at the table while Mamá continued to move about the space, pulling plants from their stalks and grinding them into paste, sweeping the ground, pouring limonada, and periodically stirring the pot. As she worked, Damika talked about her latest classes, the newest weapons she was training with, and retold the story of Travieso that Petra had just recounted to them.

Mamá laughed so hard that she finally had to stop moving to remove a cloth from within her sleeve and wipe her streaming eyes. Phanessa couldn't help but grin with them. But then, Mamá turned her attention to her.

"Y tu, chiquita? How has it been for you?

Phanessa swallowed hard, glancing between Mamá and Damika, uncomfortable with the sudden attention. Finally, she lifted her left shoulder in a half-hearted shrug.

"It's been ... fine," she answered, unconvincingly. Damika and Mamá shared a look.

"Mmhmm," Mamá murmured. "And how has it *really* been?"

The woman's golden eyes settled on Phanessa's own, and a foreign tingle swept across her skin. She felt her flesh tighten in on itself, as if to make her smaller, to shield her from the woman's penetrating gaze. She saw too much, and Phanessa worried that any second she would guess her secret. That she was not who she claimed to be, that there was in fact no Phanessa, that she was an imposter, an intruder, even worse, a traitor, that she was the missing Name-Bearer and she didn't belong there at all. Mamá was going to see it all, in her eyes, so to keep the woman from discovering her she needed to say *something, anything*.

"I think this was a mistake," she blurted out. "I'm clearly no warrior!"

That was definitely not the kind of "something, anything" she had in mind. Even if it was the truth. *Especially* because it was the truth. Mortification flooded her. She couldn't believe she had admitted to something so dangerous! Mamá or Damika would tell the priestesses about her doubts, she would be kicked out of the temple and then what would she do? Where would she go, who would she be? She squeezed her eyes tight in shame.

And snapped them right back open again when, to her shock, both Mamá and Damika began laughing! Her jaw dropped in confusion.

"Everyone feels that way when they first start," Damika told her. Mamá nodded.

"With birth there is always pain," she explained kindly. "And you are being born anew. It will take some time to find your feet again."

"But —" Phanessa started, too stunned to hold back. "I'm terrible!" she confessed. "I can't fight, or use weapons. I haven't once hit anyone, or anything. I'm useless!"

Damika laughed again. "You just need practice. And I already told you I'd help you with that!"

"And more importantly," Mamá interjected, "there is more to becoming a warrior than weaponry and fighting. Spend time with your new friends, and you will learn how much more. And come see me anytime you need."

Phanessa left Mamá's home feeling exposed, and more than a little confused, and yet somehow more resolved than ever to prove, at least to herself, that if she could never be a true Danrayen warrior, she would at least try her very best.

Over the next few weeks, Phanessa began getting to know each of the girls that Damika had introduced her to, all of them accepting her into their fold as easily as her new friend had. From the moment that Damika had pulled her into their group, the other girls began going out of their way to help her in classes as well, especially when Damika was otherwise engaged As all of their training overlapped in certain areas, there was hardly a session where at least one of them wasn't present. Except, of course, at her basic training. Phanessa was still grouped in with the newest initiates, most of whom were between five and ten-years-old, much to her perpetual embarrassment. Still, she saw the others in some basic weaponry, the non-physical classes where she was excelling, and bunked with them in the evening as the sleeping arrangements were organized by age group.

Petra, by far the most talkative of the group, was the first to open up to her. Phanessa learned she was the daughter of a prosperous farmer in the village of Tureene, near the Cassalain border. She had lived on their farm with her father and six brothers, as her mother had died giving birth to the youngest of them. She had joined the sisterhood at seven-years-old.

"I always wanted to be a great warrior," she told Phanessa one day while they were both assigned stable duties. Phanessa found the brushing of the horse's manes calming and soothing, and could have spent the entire time lost in her own thoughts, but Petra was never quiet for long. Not that Phanessa minded, as she enjoyed listening to the other girl talk. She had been given so little opportunity for conversation in the palace.

"With four older brothers and two younger, we were always getting into scraps. By the time I was six I could already beat Adan, who was ten!" Phanessa smiled at the unrestrained pride in her voice.

"When I was seven, I found an enormous hammer. It was some sort of tool for breaking stone under the soil, a farming tool. But I thought it was a great weapon. I dragged it from the shed to my father and brothers and demanded that they take me to the priestesses for consideration." She whooped with laughter. "The way my father tells it, that hammer was at least half my weight! They couldn't believe I had managed to move it that far. I was pretty little back then." Phanessa suppressed a giggle. Petra was "pretty little" still! But she could clearly picture her as a small, blonde child, cheeks pink with exertion, demanding to be taken to the Danrayens. Luckily her father had assented, and she had been accepted into the sisterhood.

According to Petra, her grandfather had been a soldier in the Andalan army, but he her father had fallen in love with Petra's mother and had chosen the life of a farmer instead of following in those footsteps.

"I never met him," Petra confided to her. "My grandfather, I mean. But my father thinks that he would have been as proud of me as he is." A quick pang of jealousy struck Phanessa. She had never had a family, let alone one that was proud, supportive, and loving. *Petra is very lucky.* Looking at the easy grin on her new friend's face she couldn't help but smile with her. *At least she knows it.*

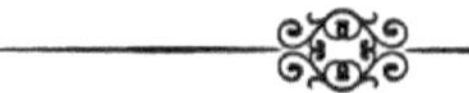

On a particularly hot spring day the girls all found themselves indoors, fanning themselves with makeshift palms twisted in on themselves to catch the wind. It was the kind of day when everyone's hair was perpetually plastered to the back of their necks and at the edges of their brows, and when one would idly swat at the sensation of flies on their legs only to find droplets of sweat instead, rolling from behind their knees and tickling their skin. The air was so thick and murky that it seemed almost impossible to catch one's breath, feeling instead like you could drown on dry land from the humidity itself.

As a result the History of War class was fuller than usual, the girls abandoning their outdoor pursuits in favor of some small amount of shade. On any other day it was not a particularly popular class, after all, Andala had been at war with Cassalan for generations. No one could remember precisely when it had begun or why, all they knew was that Cassalan and its cruel and brutal people were most thoroughly to blame.

After the lesson and the tales of all the horrors inflicted on Andalans at the hands of their enemies, the girls lingered in the classroom, both the heat and their anger boiling the blood beneath their skin. Damika bubbled over first.

"They should just leave us be, *monstros,*" she hissed. "When we are full warriors, we will end their terror once and for all."

Phanessa nodded aggressively, shaking a few droplets of sweat loose from her hair. She knew she wouldn't be a warrior like the rest of them, but she fully supported the cause. It was the Cassalains and their endless war that had taken their king Enrique from them. She remembered the chaos in the palace when news of his death had arrived. Queen Issalia mourned so deeply that the palace shamanes worried she would lose her unborn child. The grief had been palpable, seeping into the very palace walls. Phanessa had cried herself to sleep for more than a week.

Sprawled on the floor, which she claimed was cooler, Raidea made a slashing motion with her arm.

"We will cut them down and be rid of them all at last. None would dare cross our borders again!"

Petra whooped and kicked her, rather ungently, in the leg. An action that no doubt would have led to a tussle if not a full-out brawl had the weather not been so abysmal. Instead, Raidea merely grunted. Taruka was oddly quiet.

"What do you think Taru?" Petra asked her, when she realized that Raidea wasn't taking her bait. "How shall we end them all?"

Taruka shrugged a slender shoulder. "They can't *all* be bad."

A heavy hush fell upon the group, Raidea pushing herself up to look at Taru with incredulity, Phanessa sharing a shocked glance with Damika. *Of course* all Cassalains were bad. They were terrible, horrible, *monstros*. They weren't like them, they weren't the kind, decent, hard-working people of Andala. They were the enemy.

"How can you not think they're horrific?" Damika asked her sharply. "They've been at war with us for decades, for centuries, maybe!"

Taru was too graceful to squirm, but under their confused scrutiny her face scrunched up with a mixture of embarrassment and indecision. Finally, she smoothed out her expression and spoke.

"You know my ancestors were from the Hakhan tribe, one of the small factions that live above the Cassalain borders?" The girls all nodded, even Phanessa. She was palace-educated after all, and Taru always wore her dark hair in the traditional Hakhan braids and lined her eyes with kohl in the way of their people.

"Did you ever wonder how we came to live in Andala, all the way from the North?" Phanessa snuck a glance at the other girls. Based on the blank look on their faces, they had not. Even Petra, who was closest to Taru, seemed confused. Taruka sighed.

"My people, my family, migrated down the mountains, through Cassalan and into Andala, hoping to escape the many wars that plagued the northern tribes."

As the girls settled, Taru told them of their journey. How it had been a dangerous trek, not simply due to the battles between tribes, or even the war between Cassalan and Andala. The borders between the two realms are clearly divided by a large span of mountains that stretched from the western coast to the eastern boundary of the Night Wood, which of course no one would dare to enter. The expanse of mountains is simply known as "The Borders" and are some of the most dangerous areas in both Andala and Cassalan. The paths through the few passages underneath the mountains are costly, and safe passage is never guaranteed.

Paying the inflated price was still preferable than attempting the treacherous climb over their precipitous slopes, which were rocky, slick with ice and snow, and dangerously steep. Because of their sacrifice, Taru's family disapproved of her warrior's path, distressed that she would choose a life of hardship after all they had endured to provide her and her cousins a better life. But when a priestess came to assess the girls in their village when she was a child, Taru had left with her, unrepentantly.

"But I remember the stories that my abuelitos used to tell me. During their journey they were in constant danger, and people were violent and cruel. But they also found help, and even friendship ... on both sides of the border. By Andalans and Cassalains. I just — I just can't imagine that they are all as bad as we say."

The last part was delivered softly. Though it was not technically treasonous to sympathize with their northern enemy, it certainly wasn't something anyone would want overheard.

The rest of the girls fidgeted, uncomfortably. It was Petra who finally broke the silence.

"I don't know Taru. My family's farm is right on the border. Our village has been plagued by Cassalain raids since I was a babe. They've killed just as many people on our land as the real monstros from the Night Wood do on their borders ... I can't imagine any good in Cassalains when they kill just as easily as shadow-jumpers or orcuyos. Maybe you remember their stories wrong"

Taruka merely shrugged again, but looked upset.

"Could you write to your abuelos?" Phanessa asked her softly. "Maybe they could clear things up?"

Taruka shook her head. "No. I haven't spoken to my family since I left for the temple. Their disapproval was ... strong. They gave the priestesses the money and jewels that would have been my dowry when I came of age, and then cut off all ties."

The heavy silence crept back into the room once more. Finally, Raidea nudged Taru's shoulder with her own, too hot to offer any more physical comfort.

"Well, I wish I knew what to say to you to make you feel better, but you all know I don't have parents or grandparents to miss."

"How did you — " Phanessa began, and then immediately shut her mouth with a flush. How could she dare to ask Raidea's path to the Danrayens when she was unwilling and unable to share her own story? It wasn't right. But Raidea knew where her thoughts lay anyway.

"How did I come to the Warrior's Path?" she asked with a grin. "Well, that is a good story, in fact. Probably better than Taru's ancestor's story!" The last bit was delivered with an air kiss in the direction of Taruka, who smiled and rolled her eyes. The mood lifted a bit with the action.

"Well, you all know I'm an orphan. Don't know who my parents were, y que? I don't care. I don't remember anything about them anyway. I grew up with a small gang, of sorts, ladroncitos in the Andalan capitol."

Unbidden, Phanessa's eyebrows had raised. They had grown up not far from one another, then. And yet, they couldn't have been further apart. While Phanessa was learning society arts, the meaning of names, and practicing for the Naming Rite high above the city in the palace, her friend was learning to beg and steal on the streets below. According to Raidea, she had been an accomplished pickpocket, even at an early age, and was discovered by the High Priestess Adira herself on one of her visits to the city.

"I was around eight, best we can figure. I never really had a birthday, so we can't be sure."

Raidea had been in the middle of lifting a nobleman's coin purse when a guard had grabbed her by the arm. The way she struggled, clawed and spat at the guard with all her scrawny eight-year-old might had made Adira smile, reminding her of a cornered jungle cat. She had petitioned the guard to allow her to speak with the child and proceeded to explain to her the ways of Danray. It was not an easy path, she had warned Raidea, but so long as she was within the temple walls she would not lack for food or shelter. And she would learn to defend herself, and others. Raidea had agreed on the spot.

Phanessa was still chuckling from Raidea's wild story when Petra swung around to face her.

"Ok new girl," she said. "Your turn!"

The smile instantly dropped from Phanessa's face.

"Uh, que?" she stammered. "What do you mean?"

"What brought you to the Danrayens? And so late in life?"

As close as she was becoming to the other girls, it was still Damika who Phanessa remained closest to. They spent much of their time together, training and studying of course, but also playing games and having long conversations. Up until that point, Damika had never offered any information about her life prior to the Temple of Danray, and had never asked it of Phanessa either. Phanessa hadn't minded it; in fact, it was a relief. With a simple question, however, she was reminded that the safety and comfort of her current position was simply an illusion. It would be dangerous to let her guard down, even within their little group.

Phanessa would have to think of a lie, and though she had had much time to prepare one, she hadn't been able to commit to anything. Mostly because she didn't *want* to lie. She couldn't tell anyone the truth, of course, but she also didn't want to deceive the young women who were so quickly becoming her friends.

"Oh," she stammered, fidgeting on the wooden bench. "I, — it's ..." anxiety crawled up her chest and tightened around her throat like the fingers of an invisible spirit, cutting off her ability to speak. She found it difficult to swallow, and her breath was coming in tiny puffs, unable to penetrate the vice grip that held her silent. Just when she thought she might crack from the pressure, Damika came to her rescue once again.

"What does it matter?" she asked, casually flipping a small dagger in the air and catching it with unfailing precision. "She's here now."

Petra and Taruka exchanged a look, and Raidea rolled her eyes.

"You two are a lot alike," Petra said finally, and the rest of the girls abandoned their questions in favor of a table game. The idea that she could share similarities with Damika brought her a small rush of delight, but mostly Phanessa felt relieved. And grateful to her friend. Because of Damika she didn't have to invent some sort of half-hearted lie. They didn't try to pry again, and she could breathe easier knowing that, at least for now, her secret was still safe.

CHAPTER 7

Months passed, and then years. Phanessa grew accustomed to the way of life in the temple, the tutelage of the priestesses and the companionship of women. Her days became filled with learning the ancient arts of Danray. She took combat classes, lessons in blade battle, archery, and different styles of defense and attack. She ran, in the sweltering sun, the pouring rain, and through the mountainous country that had greeted her after her journey through the Great Andalan Rainforest. She learned battle tactics in the classrooms, how to use terrain and weather to her advantage, and developed the mathematical, organizational and logistical skills needed to maintain an army through war. The temple healers taught her how to stitch cuts, bandage wounds, and how to create salves and potions to restore depleted energy or encourage healing.

She learned how to be strong and steadfast, loyal and decisive, but also that earning those qualities did not make her any less of a woman. She witnessed firsthand how femininity was not exclusive to soft spoken words and fancy dress, and that embracing more traditional "feminine things" in no way made anyone weaker. She hiked and explored the neighboring hillsides, learned to climb trees, pick mangoes and limones, and forage for edible fungi and greens.

In time, her aversion to the Danrayen garden dissipated, (though she was still not an admirer of flowers) and she would spend time under the statue of the goddess. In class, which was mostly held outdoors, they were taught to create snares for small prey, light fires from even damp wood, and find their way by the light of the stars. Despite having been confined within palace walls her entire life, Phanessa was pleased to find that at those tasks, at least, she surpassed expectations.

In those classes she could finally return the favors of her friends, helping them instead of them helping her. She explained how to spot small tufts of fur caught on briars when tracking prey, the best grass for starting fires, or what logs would grow the fattest mushrooms. But her instructors despaired at her lack of ability with any classic Danrayen blade or bow. And though her fighting improved immensely, she unfortunately never did develop the full fluidity and grace of movement that her Danrayen sisters so clearly embodied.

And none more so than Damika.

From Damika her training continued. Long after the training yards were empty, Damika would be there, forcing Phanessa to repeat a certain strike, or parry, or roll, until her muscles trembled and her body felt like pressed parchment, thin and brittle. Damika seemed to never tire, never falter, and Phanessa sometimes wondered if she wasn't the great Goddess Danray herself, reborn. It was a blasphemous thought, of course, which she would never give voice to, and one that Damika would have been horrified to hear. But though she may have been a mere mortal, she was an extraordinary teacher, with a calming, unfaltering patience for Phanessa's errors.

And she made many errors.

But over time her body strengthened, her muscles hardened, and her movements became easier and more practiced from repetition alone. When Damika realized that throwing knives were the easiest weapon for Phanessa to wield, she had her practice with them for hours on end. She would even blindfold her with thick leather straps, spin her slender body around and have her attempt to hit targets from instinct and sound alone, with mixed results. But Damika was undeterred, as were the other girls, all determined to make a warrior of her yet. But more so, and somehow just as importantly, Damika and the others did not just teach her how to better swing a blade, dodge a weapon, or block a blow.

They also taught her the simple and quiet luxuries of friendship.

When Phanessa pushed her body beyond its ability and her legs seized in twisted knots of agony, Taruka was there to massage out the spasming muscles with homemade salve made from arnica leaves and chuchuhuasi. When oozing blisters formed on Phanessa's palms from her endless practice with the throwing knives, Petra showed her how to fashion makeshift gloves out of strips of softened leather. When Phanessa's mind and soul was worn down, beaten, and as weary as her body, when she wanted nothing more than to scream her secret from the top of the Goddess Danray's statue, to wail that she was *not one of them* and to *please make it stop*, for surely the torture that awaited her in the palace dungeons could be no worse than the daily torment she endured at the temple, Raidea was there with a hug, a stolen cookie, or a dirty joke to ease her heavy heart and troubled mind.

And when her long, thick russet hair kept escaping its ties and falling over her eyes at the most inopportune moments, blinding her, making her sweat, slowing her down, it was Mamá she went to. In a rare moment of fierce resolve, she found her way back to the comfortable cottage and asked the woman to cut her waist-length auburn hair into a practical, chin-length cut. Mamá, seeing the resolute set of Phanessa's eyes and mouth said nothing, but sat her down on a short stool and fetched her scissors. Phanessa only cried a little, thinking of the times Rosa Maria had spent brushing and braiding all her fine hair. But Mamá hummed a soothing tune as she cut, slipping her fingers comfortingly through Phanessa's locks as they fell around her like the falling ash of a volcano. Afterwards, they shared a bowl of hilachas and black corn tortillas, and by the time Phanessa headed back to her dormitory she was feeling stronger.

Those small moments of kindness and friendship, given freely without conditions were something that she had never experienced before. Rosa Maria had been kind to her, but she would not have called the woman a friend. Nor had she been motherly in the way that Mamá was. Damika and the others taught her what it was to confide in someone, to share dreams and secrets and idle gossip. There were more girls, of course, training and learning the ways of Danray. But the five of them, Phanessa, Damika, Petra, Taruka and Raidea grew to form a merry band that Phanessa gave thanks for daily. For the first time in her life, she stayed up too late, not from nerves or cold or bitter loneliness, but giggling into the night telling stories and sharing silly gossip.

They were the best years of her life, and yet, there was an ever-present cloud looming over her, shadowing her happiness. Deep down, she could not escape the guilt she felt over her deception. Every time someone called out "Phanessa," or whenever those outside of her group asked about her time before joining the sisterhood, she became quiet, reticent, and secretive. The rumor grew that she had been in an abusive situation, dishonorable parents, perhaps, and that she had run away to join the Danrayens as soon as she could muster up the courage. She didn't attempt to disprove the story, as it kept people from asking her too many questions. She continued to be comforted by the fact that Damika never spoke of her past either, or what had brought her to the Danrayen Temple so young. She just knew that because of it, the older girl never insisted that Phanessa share her own story, for which she was grateful. But she didn't like lying, to her teachers whom she respected so highly, to her friends that she treasured dearly, and especially not to Damika, who was the closest person to her that she had ever had.

Together the girls began stumbling into adulthood, sharing in the many changes that come with growing older. Phanessa's girlhood figure began to harden, slowly, building small muscles underneath her slender frame, though she never caught up to the strength and stamina of Damika. She also never grew quite as tall as Damika did, and neither of them ever caught up to Taruka, who grew out of her clothes at almost a monthly rate, much to the temple seamstresses despair. Despite her rapid growth spurt Taruka remained graceful and elegant as ever, and improved with her bow every day. She became quite spectacular with it.

Petra too developed an affinity for a particular weapon, and abandoned most others to hone her expertise. She was a natural with a Morningstar and often joked that it was her "Mourning Star" because *'it would leave her enemy's family in mourning.'* Every time she made this boast the other girls would roll their eyes at her over the bad pun, groan in protest and throw things at her, but she would laugh good-naturedly.

Like Petra, Raidea remained on the shorter side, though Petra was all compacted, solid stone compared to Raidea's voluptuous and rounded figure. Underneath her comfortable layer of flesh that made men and women alike want to be near her, she was as strong as the rest of them, but enjoyed that others underestimated her due to her softer features.

Damika continued to be a finely tuned weapon, with her ascent into young-adulthood simply honing her already exceptional skills. Her added height gave her an added advantage against her enemies, and any untrained muscle was developed and sharpened to near perfection.

In their own, individual ways each young girl grew towards the woman, and warrior, that they would one day become.

Once Phanessa turned fifteen, she began receiving a small, weekly stipend from the priestesses and was allowed to join the older girls on day trips to Pelgar. There she was able to explore the marketplaces, taste her first sips of ron in the local cantina, and converse with the locals should she so choose. The townspeople were used to Danrayen visitors, and the young men often dared each other to speak to the girls, flirting with them shamelessly.

Raidea was the most brazen of their lot, and spared the others no detail of her encounters, whether they wanted to hear about them or not. Damika had a few suitors of her own, brief as they might be, but Phanessa was far too shy to want to speak to the young men, and preferred to stay back with Petra and Taruka, who seemed content to enjoy each other's company. After so much time inside palace walls, and then within temple grounds, those visits were a rare and special treat for her, a glimpse of what she imagined normal life to be. So much did she enjoy her life with the Danrayens that there were moments when she almost forgot that she was not truly one of them.

Almost.

The knowledge, however, that her time with them was brief (as the years were passing much quicker than she had thought they would) and that she would have to leave them someday weighed heavily on her mind. Had she truly considered the repercussions of her presence in the temple, perhaps she would have tried harder to stay apart from the other initiates, to blend into the background. But the promise of friendship, companionship, warmth and acceptance from people her own age was too strong of a temptation, and she could not pull away from any of them if she tried.

It was a cool afternoon in the fall a few years into her time at the temple when Raidea approached the group with a proposition.

"Absolutely not," Damika's lip curled up in disdain. "That's not happening."

Petra snorted loudly. "I'm with Dami on this one. No gracias."

Taruka rolled her eyes at them. "Vamos, it's not that bad!"

"It's ridiculous!" Damika argued.

"It's tradition!" Raidea yelled.

"It's a waste of time!" Petra interjected hotly.

"Um ..." Phanessa's voice was quiet, but broke through the yelling. She had heard Raidea's proposal, but wasn't sure of what it meant. Or why it was causing such division amongst her friends. "What exactly *is* the 'Dance of Danray?'"

Raidea's eyes lit up as both Damika and Petra groaned.

"Oh, it's *wonderful*! It started as a way to teach discipline and control, but now it's sort of a lost art, though some Danrayens still attempt it. Haven't you seen some of the older girls practicing? They all stand in a circle with their weapons, and start moving, swinging and jumping and striking as they make their way forward in rotation. The point of the dance is to strike the person in front of you while avoiding the blows of the person behind you. Someone outside the circle is playing music and the beat starts off slow, at first, then gets faster and faster. The faster the beat gets, the quicker you have to move, making sure to continue attacking the person ahead of you but not letting the girl behind you have any advantage. Your movements get faster and faster until suddenly, everything stops!"

"It takes great trust in your team, you have to believe that everyone will stop when the music does. Not just that, but no step or movement is preplanned, you adapt in the moment with the women around you. You must trust that you can strike and fight to the best of your ability and that the girl ahead of you will match you, blow for blow. You need to have a lot of faith in one another." Taruka added.

Phanessa *had* seen some of the Danrayen initiates practicing something similar. She thought that it had looked beautiful, and was about to say so, when she remembered something.

"Wait, isn't that how Valentina almost lost a finger?"

"Yes!" Damika and Petra shouted while Raidea rolled her eyes.

"But she didn't, did she? Dami I'm surprised you don't want to try it, you're always on about us getting more practice."

"That's not practice," Damika argued. "It's a dance."

"A dance with *weapons*. A *dangerous* dance with weapons!"

"I'd like to try it." Taruka interrupted, crossing to Raidea with a smile. "My culture has different warrior dances, but I never got the chance to learn any of them. I think it would be nice to learn one with my new family." She delivered the last sentence with a sweet smile towards Petra, who groaned.

"Fine!" she conceded, standing and crossing to the two of them. "How am I supposed to say no to that?" Phanessa heard her grumble under her breath as she crossed in front of her. She ducked her head to hide the smile that rose over her friend's exasperation.

When she looked up again the three girls were staring at her and Damika expectantly.

Phanessa shrugged. "No se, I probably won't be very good at it." When it looked like her friends were about to argue with her she threw up her hands in mock surrender. "Alright!" she laughed. "It won't hurt to try, right?"

Raidea and Taruka cheered, but Damika groaned again. Phanessa felt a bit insulted; she wasn't used to Damika's disapproval.

"You don't have to join us," she mumbled, drawing her shoulders up to her ears. Immediately the derision fell from Damika's expression and she sprung up to throw an arm around her. Phanessa relaxed against her friend.

"No seas tonta, of course I'll join you. Who knows, we might be incredible at it, and end up becoming traveling performers instead of warriors! We will paint our faces and join a group of singers and actors and illusionists. Our grace and beauty and skill will be the talk of the realm. Y sabes, we'll be so marvelously skilled at it that we'll end up dancing at the palace for the queen herself!"

The other girls laughed as they began moving to the practice fields, but Phanessa stiffened once more as she choked on a fake chuckle. She knew that Damika had been joking, of course, but the mention of the queen and the palace had been an unwelcome reminder of her past. The idea of standing before the queen wasn't a joke to her, but something straight from her nightmares. Luckily, she didn't have too much time to dwell over it, as the girls reached their destination and began gathering their weapons.

Damika and Raidea chose practice Danrayen blades, Petra stuck with her Morningstar and Phanessa held two small daggers, one gripped in each fist. As the dance wouldn't work with a bow, Taruka traded hers for a long wooden staff instead. Then, they took their places, facing outwards in a circle. Phanessa would have to avoid the strikes from Damika to her left, and attempt to deliver them to Raidea on her right. Raidea had already roped some poor new initiate to play the drums for them, and at her signal, they began.

The dance started off well, the girls taking small, measured steps, their swings and blows calculated and deliberate. Phanessa deflected a slow swing of Damika's sword on her left while lunging forward with her right-hand dagger, an action that Raidea easily avoided. From the corner of her eye Phanessa could see Taruka bringing her staff parallel to her body, pointing straight ahead of her and then twisting her torso so that it cut a wide arc in front of her. The movement effectively blocked Raidea's blade on her left, while aiming directly at Petra's face on her right. Petra ducked under the wood with a small spin, twisting the chains of her weapon at the same time and directing the spiked ball towards Damika's ankles, which she easily hopped over. They began giggling, each trying to knock their opponents off of their stride while avoiding the efforts of the girls behind them.

This is fun, Phanessa had a moment to think.

Then, the beat of the drum began to speed up.

Sweat began tickling Phanessa's temples as she struggled to keep up with the pace. The girl's movements became less fluid and more clumsy, each struggling to keep up with the tempo while both delivering and avoiding blows. When the beat picked up yet again Raidea stumbled, and Phanessa had to quickly pull back her blade before it was embedded within her friend's flesh. But her sudden movement had Damika cursing behind her and she turned her head just quickly enough to see the tip of Damika's sword a mere inch from her neck. She shrieked and stumbled into Raidea, who reached out to keep from falling. Unfortunately the only thing close to her was Taruka, whose shirt was ripped from collarbone to stomach by Raidea's grasping fist. As she tried to reach up to cover herself, her staff somehow ended up between Petra's legs and she too began to topple.

The five of them ended up in a heap of knees, elbows and weapons, their twisted limbs tangled together on the hard ground.

"Is everyone," Phanessa started,

"Weapons! Check your weapons!" Damika yelled.

"Did anyone get hurt?" Taruka asked, still trying to cover herself. Petra was frantically patting her own body, and Raidea lay half on Phanessa, half on Taruka, stunned. Then, she began to laugh. One by one, as they all realized that everyone was fine, and that miraculously no one had been impaled by any sharp object, the other young women began to laugh with her. The new initiate on the drums very cleverly decided to make her escape at that moment, shaking her head as she scurried away. The girls laughed until there were tears streaming down their faces.

"I don't think we'll be joining any traveling troupes," Petra shot to Damika, who just laughed harder.

Wiping her eyes, Taruka sat up carefully, making sure not to disrupt any of the weapons.

"We'll practice."

CHAPTER 8

Not all of Phanessa's time in the sisterhood was pleasant. Although she made many friends throughout those years, she also had the misfortune of making an enemy. It was not something that she had ever considered. Phanessa was not particularly accustomed to being accepted, but she had never fathomed herself important enough to be hated. She had been so consumed with the fear of being discovered and deemed a traitor to the realm that she had never imagined that there could be other dangers within the Danrayen walls, but she was mistaken.

There will always be those who covet what others have. Even the Danrayens were no exception, and housed a few young women who were power-hungry and greedy. As ill-skilled as Phanessa was, she might have been ignored by them completely, had it not been for her friendship with Damika.

Damika was well-liked, respected, and admired. Through her natural ability in combat and leadership abilities, the priestesses kept a close eye on her. She was clearly being considered for the Danrayen Riders, the highest order within the sisterhood. Only the most elite fighters were chosen for their sect, and they were often seen on the front lines of battle, or guarding upper royalty, protecting towns and people too weak and defenseless to defend themselves. Only a Danrayen Rider could ascend to priestesshood and become members of state, conferring in foreign diplomacy and prominent matters to the kingdom. Due to this, the priestesses were the most highly trained, skilled, and powerful members of the Danrayens. Because of their superior knowledge and ability, all Danrayen Riders must return to the temple in mid-life to ascend to priestesshood and continue training the next generation of Danrayen warriors. Only Riders and priestesses wore headdresses and could bear the marking of the Phoenix to show their rank.

It was a highly coveted position.

The knowledge that Damika was almost assured this path was a matter of envy and resentment to some. But as she was too strong and self-assured to be touched, the young women with envy in their hearts turned their resentment towards the weakest of the pack, the most vulnerable of the friend group. Phanessa.

Most of their barbs and traps were easily avoided. They liked to try to trip her, or give her a quick poke on the fields with the sharp ends of their blades or spears. They spoke in "whispers" loud enough for her to hear, openly questioned her heritage and wove cruel stories about why she would join the Danrayens so late in life. They were mean, petty girls, but more of an annoyance than any real threat. And if, in moments when she found herself alone, Phanessa let a few tears fall over their hurtful words, she never told anyone. She had to become a warrior, after all, and warriors did not cry over mean-spirited children.

Not all the torment was that easy to endure, however. The worst of her critics was a stunningly beautiful raven-haired daughter of nobility named Kichka. All women have their beauty, and Danrayens more so than most, with their strength, confidence and warrior's hearts, but Kichka was beautiful in the way that the oceans, or a storm, or the endless night was beautiful. The kind of beauty that draws one in with its wonder but is also somehow frightening in its mystery. A mystery that was aided by the fact that Kichka had magia. The first time that Phanessa saw the tell-tale sapphire sparks crackling around the girl's fingertips, she had been amazed.

"She's a Danrayen *and* a mage?" she asked Petra, awed. There were so few gifted with magia that she had not been aware that any of them might choose a path other than becoming mages, healers or shamanes.

"Si, and she won't let you forget it," Petra snorted. "She thinks it makes her special."

"Doesn't it?" Phanessa imagined that it would be a great benefit in battle, but Petra shrugged dismissively.

"Not in the eyes of Danray. A warrior's heart is far more important than a warrior's skill," she replied, tweaking Phanessa's nose. "Never forget that, little one." Phanessa scoffed. She may have been on the shorter side, but Petra was clearly the smallest!

"And her heart?" she asked her, curiously.

"Well, I would never want to speak ill of my sister," Petra tried to send a Raidea-like wink in her direction, but only managed a clumsy squint. "But she has to earn her place here, so do we all, magia or no."

Phanessa had her first run in with Kichka not long after that conversation. It was evening, and most girls had retired to their rooms for the night. But Damika had suggested that Phanessa run a few miles on the yards to build up her stamina. Phanessa hated running, but she hated disappointing Damika even more. Once she had run a distance Damika would have approved of, or at least, not been completely disappointed by, she made her way to the baths, soaked in sweat and dreaming of her soft bed. Phanessa's training had made her much better at gauging her surroundings, but as exhausted and sore as she was, she didn't notice that she had company until Kichka stepped out from the shadows and into her path.

Phanessa halted abruptly, uneasy and worried about what she must smell like after a long day of work and a night run, and crossed her arms tightly across her chest. Kichka smiled at her, but there was no warmth behind the action.

"Phanessa, isn't it?" her voice flowed like slow dripping honey. Unnerved, Phanessa simply nodded.

"You're Damika's partner in the training yards." It was not a question, but Phanessa nodded again.

"You two are close friends, aren't you? At least, she is a very dear friend to *you*. You, on the other hand," she sighed, her face twisting into a practiced look of pity. "Honestly, it's just such a shame that you force Damika to cater to you as you do. She is far more skilled than you; do you not worry that you are holding her back in her training? Do you not think that you do her a disservice by making her stoop to your level?"

Phanessa's eyes widened at the words and the tone in which they were delivered. Guilt and regret flooded her system, because although cruelly spoken, the words were no worse than what she had told herself time and again. Despite the embarrassment that was squeezing her throat like a vice, she made herself meet Kichka's dark gaze to respond.

"Damika also trains with General Alessia, privately." She hated the soft, timid timbre of her voice. Defiantly, she lifted her chin. "*And* we switch partners often, so she does not *only* train with me." It was true. Someone as talented as Damika wouldn't simply train with a single, inexperienced girl. She sparred with older initiates, dueled often with other girls proficient in weapons other than her preferred Danrayen blade, and took personal lessons with General Alessia, a master at swordplay and battle tactics. Helping Phanessa was simply another form of exercise, and more a kindness than anything else.

Kichka's syrupy smile fell, her eyes narrowing.

"If you were truly her friend, you would insist that she stop debasing herself by training you. She should seek out those on her level. I would be happy to offer myself for practice. I am, after all, a far more suitable partner than you."

Phanessa shifted, uncomfortable, guilt-ridden, but also a bit angry. The emotion was startling, and new. She hadn't had much practice standing up for herself, but she imagined what Damika, or Petra would say in her place. So she jerked her chin up and met Kichka's disdainful gaze in defiance.

"It is Damika's decision. If she wants to train me, then that is what we shall do. I am her partner."

"You will not be any longer. You will say you wish to train with someone else and suggest that I would better aid her in becoming the best warrior that she can be."

Utterly disgusted with the entire conversation and tired of standing in the dark exhausted and smelling of sweat, Phanessa let out an undignified snort and resumed her journey to the baths. Kichka stepped in front of her with a hiss. The hair on the back of Phanessa's head began to stand on end, and a small shiver trickled down her spine.

A ripple of blue light crackled around Kichka. Calmly, as if she hadn't just hissed like a wild creature not a moment ago, she lifted her hand and examined her fingertips, small electric lines interweaving between her fingers. Phanessa stared at them in fascination.

"The priestesses are *always* watching Damika." The blue wave rippled more forcefully. "How is anyone else to gain their favor if they will not watch our progress as well?" The magia was beginning to hum, an uncomfortable deep buzz that made Phanessa's teeth hurt. "I need to train with Damika if I am to ever receive their attentions. You will do as I say, or I can make life very unpleasant for you." Without warning a spark of blue power shot out from Kichka's outstretched hand and struck Phanessa square in the stomach. She doubled over, grunting from the shock of it. Any guilt or remorse evaporated with the pain.

"You aren't allowed to use magia outside of your studies!" Phanessa gasped out, incredulously, before another wave of electrifying blue pain shook her to her core. Her body trembled violently and she landed on her knees in the dirt.

"Mañana." Kichka whispered, leaning over her, her dark hair casting an ominous shroud over Phanessa's face. "Tomorrow you will excuse yourself from Damika." With that, she turned and was gone as quickly as she had appeared.

Magia. She couldn't believe Kichka would actually dare to use magia against a fellow trainee, and within temple grounds. When Phanessa lifted her shirt, she found a spider web of blue markings spread across her lower belly and hip. Furious, she picked herself up and thought about what to do.

Kichka was breaking all the rules of the Danrayen code. She had threatened her, attacked her unprovoked, unarmed, and used her magia against her. Something that was strictly forbidden during training and should only be reserved for true enemies. But she couldn't report her to the priestesses, for the last thing she wanted was to earn the reputation of a snitch. Giving in to her was not an option either. Though she may not be much of a warrior, she certainly wasn't a coward. Besides, even if she did decide to go through with it, Damika would never allow it.

Somehow, she would have to find a way to handle it herself.

Phanessa dragged herself to the baths, suddenly grateful for the late hour which meant fewer people and darker rooms. When she made it, she was relieved to find that she was the only one there, and should anyone come in, the candlelight was low enough that the magical injury would appear as a bruise like any other. Examining her wound more closely she realized that the strange spiderweb patterns actually resembled the ancient, forgotten glyphs of magia users, and rippled with blue underneath her skin, marking her flesh with crackles of blue light that gave her pins and needles as they moved.

There were no shortage of injuries in the Danrayen Temple, and a large mark over flesh would be nothing noteworthy among warriors in training, but this? This was very obviously a magical injury. She assumed the strange and uncomfortable rippling would fade as her injuries improved, and refused to imagine the alternative. Weary, Phanessa washed up quickly and was relieved that no one came in to disrupt her.

She dragged her heavy body up the stairs and quietly sought out her bed, sinking into her pillow gratefully. But sleep was hard won, as Kichka's words echoed nastily in her head, her injuries resonating a low dull throb of pain with each beat of her heavy heart. Luckily the blue light was not visible through her clothing. On the bed beside her, Damika rolled over and blinked sleepy eyes at her.

"You're back late," she whispered, her jaw cracking with an enormous yawn. It almost made Phanessa smile, but worry ate away at her. Gingerly, to not upset her wound, she rolled over to her side to face Damika. Instead of meeting her eyes, she traced patterns on her bed sheets.

"Damika," she whispered back. "Why do you help me train?"

"What do you mean?" the older girl asked her.

"Do you think, pues, don't you ever think that you are wasting your time? That maybe you could be a better warrior if you spent more time training with people who are better than me?" Afraid to look up, she steeled herself and asked, "Am I ... am I holding you back?"

Holding her breath, Phanessa nearly choked when she heard Damika chuckle. She had just bared her soul, voiced her deepest insecurities, and Damika was laughing at her?

"Don't be so silly," Damika replied, her voice thick with fatigue. The words came out forcefully, Damika's breath tickling Phanessa's lips and making her inhale sharply. A strange feeling left pinpricks over her skin and she felt more electricity, but this time not over her injuries. Instead of burning it tickled, squeezing around her heart and tugging in her belly. Before she could examine the emotion further, Damika reached across the small space between them and dragged her thumb over Phanessa's forehead, smoothing out the wrinkles from her frown and making Phanessa swallow hard. Then she rolled onto her back and shut her eyes. "Go to sleep, Nessa." she managed to mumble, before taking her own advice. Phanessa stared at her sleeping form, watching the steady rise and fall of her friend's chest.

Nessa. She had never had a nickname before. A slow smile creeped up the sides of her lips.

Damika called me Nessa, she thought with a giddy rush that swept through her flesh, before sleep claimed her as well.

Despite her fears being mostly assuaged, she still spent a fitful night, tossing and turning with troublesome dreams. When the sun began creeping up the horizon she rose with the others, tired and nervous.

On their way to the mess hall for breakfast, Taruka pulled on her sleeve to lead her away from the others.

"Are you alright?" she asked her softly, concern etched on her bronzed face. Phanessa wasn't surprised. Taruka was almost as quiet as she was, but while Phanessa's silence was due more to shyness and worry that she would say the wrong thing and be discovered as an imposter, Taruka's quiet way was because she listened intently and observed everything. Phanessa forced a smile.

"Just tired," she replied. "I didn't get much sleep."

"Even after all that running Damika made you do?" Taruka nudged her with a smile. Phanessa's dislike of running was no secret. She smiled again, this time less forced.

"I was afraid Damika would find me in my dreams and make me run some more!"

"If anyone could manage it, it'd be Damika!" Petra interjected, having joined them at the back of the pack. Damika and Raidea waited for them both at the food line, trays in hand. Phanessa's heart lightened at the sight. *Mis amigas.* Who cared that a few girls disliked her, when she had the company of such fine women?

Her confidence lasted until about midday, when they were all assembled in the practice yards. Kichka approached their group confidently, tossing her long hair back over her shoulder. It rippled like spilling ink down to her lower back. Damika spared her a quick glance and then turned away dismissively, her mind on the day's lesson. Petra and Taruka didn't notice her at all until Raidea loudly asked,

"Something we can do for you Kichka?"

They all halted, eyes turning towards her. Kichka smiled and cocked her head at Phanessa expectantly, but she simply jutted out her jaw and repeated her exercise on her wooden practice sword as before. Kichka's eyes flashed with anger, but she merely smiled at the others and murmured a quick "no" before moving along. The rest forgot her presence almost instantly, but the ugly, nasty feeling that had kept Phanessa awake all night returned. She knew she would pay for her defiance later.

She did not have to wait long. After lunch she and some other girls went on a long ride through the neighboring forest, an exercise she always looked forward to. Despite her awkwardness when it came to weapons and bows, she had yet to fall off a horse, thanks to her palace training. Content and a bit lazy after having been out in the sun for so long, she lingered in brushing the lovely chestnut mare that she had used for her ride that day.

Her name was Azucar, she was as sweet as the sugar she was named after, and she was Phanessa' favorite. Whenever she could, she would arrive at the stables early to claim her, feeding her clumps of her namesake smuggled within her pockets. She took extra time brushing out some burrs stuck in her coat, taking care not to pull too roughly. Distracted by her task and the crooning praises she was delivering to the sweet animal for her patience, she found herself alone in the stables.

She was completely unaware of her solitude until a shadow quickly blocked the afternoon sun, causing Azucar to toss her head in surprise. Instantly Phanessa realized her mistake, and instinctively knew that the figure entering the stable behind her must be Kichka. She jumped away from Azucar, afraid that she would get kicked or trampled if she was startled further, or worse, that the poor mare would get caught in Kichka's wrath.

Phanessa vaulted out of the stall, and not a moment too soon, before her feet even hit the ground white hot lightning shot through the back of her neck and traveled down her spine. She slammed into the hard mud, unable to gain her footing. Azucar whinnied and swayed, pawing the ground nervously. Phanessa looked up, tears of pain streaming from her eyes, and she saw Kichka blocking her exit.

"You think you're clever?" Kichka hissed at her, the hot shocks of power striking out at Phanessa again, her body convulsing from the painful magia. Kichka, her body emitting a pulsing blue aura stalked forward, contempt etched on her face.

"You really think you can defy me?" she shot down at Phanessa, struggling to stand. "You are weak. Powerless. No one, insignificant, tiny." She struck her again and Phanessa convulsed, groaning in pain. Kichka crouched and through the pain-induced fog that veiled her sight, Phanessa could see the girl's black eyes ablaze with blue sparks. *Mad*, she thought. *She's mad.* In that moment none of the young woman's beauty was apparent; she appeared more like a rabid animal than a Danrayen girl.

"You will do as I say," Kichka declared, spittle striking Phanessa on the cheek. She was too weak to brush it off. "You will convince Damika to train with me, or I will make sure you suffer every day that my wish remains unfulfilled." The electrifying pain hit her once more before Kichka left her, panting and sweating on the straw-covered ground.

Once Phanessa was sure that she would not return, she pushed herself up with shaky limbs, leaning against Azucar's stall until she felt certain that her legs could carry her to her next lessons. Fortunately, the remainder of her day was to be spent learning battle tactics in different terrain, an indoor lesson that she usually dreaded. Today, she was grateful, for at least she would be seated, and could allow her aching body some small respite. Azucar nipped at her hair, nuzzling into her shoulder. Phanessa allowed herself a brief moment to press her face into the horse's mane before gingerly making her way outside.

In the following weeks, Phanessa's worry and anxiety grew to a never-ending sense of fear and foreboding. She was on edge, nervous and easily startled. Some days she could escape unscathed, having not strayed too far from her group for too long. Other days she would be careless or get caught unaware and be rewarded with new blue markings on her skin. Kichka took care to focus her onslaughts on parts of her body that would not be seen outside of her clothing, and Phanessa took to bathing when the other girls were not around to avoid awkward questions and accusations. It was easier to pretend nothing was wrong when she was around them, as they gave her a feeling of safety that she had never appreciated more.

She knew, of course, that things could not continue the way they were. But she had no idea how to battle against magia. Perhaps if it were a fair fight ... but even then, Kichka was a Danrayen warrior with or without her magia. Either way, something had to change.

Twice she was able to throw something at Kichka and break her focus before fleeing. Once, she even managed to hit her. Her aim had improved immensely through Damika's training, and it gave her a grim satisfaction to see the welt on her forehead the morning after pelting her with a small rock. But she paid for it terribly later that day and limped with fresh new bruising all over her right ribs and hip. It was then that Damika noticed.

"Why are you limping?" she demanded with a frown. "I didn't see you injured on the fields, what happened?"

She couldn't tell her. "I fell and landed on my side on my run," she lied. "It's nothing."

"You're lying to me," Damika accused, eyes narrowing. "Why are you lying? You're terrible at it, by the way." *If she only knew!*

"It's nothing."

"Show me if it's nothing then."

"What's going on?" Petra had heard the commotion and joined them, Taruka following quickly after.

"Can't I get any privacy here? Any at all?" Phanessa yelled. She was mortified of being found out, as if the girls didn't already think her weak enough! The last thing she wanted was for them to learn that she couldn't even handle a simple bully on her own. "It's bad enough we have to see each other every second of every day, we must bathe together and sleep in the same quarters, can I not have a simple moment to myself?"

Ignoring her outburst, Petra looked at Damika, who shrugged. "She hurt herself and won't show me."

"I didn't! I'm fine!"

"Aw, let's see it then!" Somehow, Raidea had joined the group.

"Leave her be." Taruka interjected. "She need not show us if she does not want to!"

"Hell with that!" Damika said, pouncing on Phanessa, who struggled wildly.

"Stop! I don't have to show you anything, maldita!"

Petra whooped, dodging one of Phanessa's elbows and jumped into the fray. "Here Damika, I'll hold her down! Stubborn burra!"

Taruka and Raidea laughed on the side, the scene an outrageous, innocent tussle among friends. But as soon as Phanessa's shirt was raised, a collective gasp quieted the group. They stared at her with horror in their eyes. Unable to stand it, Phanessa shut hers. The bruising was bright, and ugly, the same blue spiderweb pattern of glyphs that had etched itself all over her body over the last weeks. The marks faded in time, but fresh as the latest ones were, they were a horrible sight. Old bruising and new crisscrossed their way over her body, some still flickering with power underneath her flesh.

"What is this?" Damika whispered, softening her hold on her friend. "Oh Phanessa, que paso?" she was shocked to see tears glisten in the older girl's eyes. She couldn't speak, she didn't know what to say.

"Kichka."

They all turned to look at Taruka. Clever, sharp-eyed Taruka. "Those are magical markings, in the same color as Kichka's magia, and I've seen how she's been looking at Phanessa."

"Why didn't you say something?" Damika accused both Phanessa and Taruka. It was Taruka's turn to grow misty eyed.

"I didn't know!" she whispered, horrified. "If I had known —"

"This isn't your fault!" Finally, Phanessa had found her voice. She sat up, smoothing her shirt back down. "I should have been able to handle it myself."

"Why?" Damika asked. "Why wouldn't you tell us? Why wouldn't you tell *me*?" Phanessa looked away in shame. Damika's jaw set in an angry, hard line.

"Vamos," she said, hauling her to her feet. "We're going to Priestess Adira *now*."

"No!" Phanessa cried, jerking away. "No! I'm not a snitch, or a crybaby! I won't!"

"Don't be stupid!" Damika yelled at her. She stared in shock. She had seen Damika angry, but she had never yelled at her! "For someone so clever you can be so stupid!"

"This isn't a matter of snitching!" Raidea interjected. "She's broken the code, terribly. The priestesses need to know."

"You aren't weak for reporting her or asking for help" Taruka told her softly. "That's what you're worried about, isn't it?" Phanessa couldn't answer.

"You're so stupid." Damika repeated to her, without the anger in her voice this time. She pulled Phanessa in for a fierce hug, carefully avoiding her injuries. "Silly, silly girl. You have more strength than the lot of us, you work twice as hard, you complain half as much, and you never give up. There isn't any part of you that doesn't have a warrior's heart."

It was too much. Phanessa burst into tears, burying her head in Damika's shirt. The others surrounded them, embracing them both together, a tangle of arms. Phanessa had never felt so warm, or so loved.

Together they went to the High Priestess Adira, and with the strength and support of her friends, Phanessa told her everything. From Kichka's demands, her refusal, and the abuse she had suffered since. Hearing the whole story for the first time, the other girls grew stiff, fury rolling off of them in waves, but they stayed by her side, shaking with indignation on her behalf.

The Temple Shaman was summoned, and through her testing she verified that the cause of her injuries was, in fact, magical in nature, and furthermore could attest that the particular signature left behind belonged to Kichka. After that, Adira's verdict and sentence was quickly executed. Kichka was to be expelled from the sisterhood and removed from Danrayen grounds immediately.

The group watched from the top of the stairs as two priestesses led Kichka out of the temple. Damika and the others viewed her departure with deep satisfaction, Phanessa with lingering embarrassment about the whole ordeal.

Never had she been more aware that she was not a true Danrayen. No matter what her friends said, the fact that they needed to intervene to save her was mortifying. Surely now they would guess that she was not meant to be there. And how was she expected to travel out to the real world she had never known, to find a strange child and somehow deliver him to the royal palace as the new prince, if she couldn't even handle a simple bully?

She watched, sick with guilt as Kichka, beautiful, angry Kichka flipped her dark hair to meet her gaze, eyes filled with rage and pure, unadulterated hatred. As she faded from view, Phanessa couldn't escape the sticky fear that this would not be the last time she saw her, or her magia.

CHAPTER 9

After that ugly incident life in the Danrayen Temple mostly went back to normal, or as normal as the home for an elite sect of warrior women in training could be. The other meaner young women began leaving Phanessa alone, having lost their leader, and life went on.

The greatest difference was the fact that Damika was readying for the Trial of Danray.

Once passed she would be a full Danrayen Warrior, with all the due honor and respect that went with it. Girls who walked the path of Danray could take the Trial at any time, and at any age, whenever they and the priestesses deemed them to be ready, but most did so between 20 and 25. They needed to specialize in at least one weapon and one skill, such as sword fighting and battle tactics, archery and tracking, or battle axes and healing.

No matter how skilled and accomplished a Danrayen student, they were only considered a full Weapon of Danray after passing the Trial. Only then could they bear a butterfly marking on their armor, jewelry or bodies.

Damika began training harder and longer than she ever had before. The only way to spend more time with her was to join her on the training fields, which Phanessa did, often. Not being around her friend was painful, and she much preferred the dull pain of the outer bumps and bruises Damika left on her flesh, rather than the inner, throbbing ache in her soul whenever she imagined life in the temple without her.

"Damika, let's go in!" Phanessa yelled across the field to her friend on a particularly rainy afternoon a few months before the Trial. The setting sun was already well concealed behind dark gray rain clouds and what had started out as a sprinkle was turning into a real shower. The dirt underneath their feet was already turning slick and most of the girls had abandoned their outdoor activities to warm up inside by a fire. But Damika shook her head, flinging droplets of water from her hair with the movement.

"Not yet!" she called back to her. "But you go, Nessa, I'll be in soon!"

Phanessa didn't believe that for a moment. She knew if no one pushed her, Damika would run herself into the ground. She crossed the training yard, her shoes squelching in the growing mud. A crackle of lightning shot through the sky with a rumble of thunder not far behind. Damika barely noticed.

"Vamos, Dami!" she insisted over the rain. Using both hands she shoved her own soaked hair off her face. Damika paused at the gesture, angling her body towards her friend.

"Let's go in together," Phanessa said again with her most winning smile.

Damika's gaze dipped down to her mouth for a fraction of a second, and then her own lips pulled up into an answering grin.

"If you manage to flip me, we'll go in," Damika called out to her.

"Que?"

Damika threw her blade on the muddy ground, and braced her legs apart, lifting her hands in a defensive pose in front of her.

"Vamos, Nessa," she teased, parroting Phanessa's earlier words. "Flip me and I will go in with you."

Rolling her eyes, Nessa copied Damika's stance. She wasn't nearly as strong or skilled as her tireless friend and was under no illusion that she would manage to flip her, but she knew better than to argue with her when she had that reckless glint in her eyes.

"Fi — *ine!*"

Before the word had fully left her lips, Damika charged at her, changing the word into a startled shriek. They collided, hands gripping each other's upper arms, legs snaking out trying to trip the other's. Giggles erupted from both of them as their feet kept slipping from under them, sliding and sticking in the slimy mud. One misstep had Damika launching sideways and Nessa pressed the advantage, twisting to slam her back against Damika's chest and using her body's own momentum to flip her onto the field. But Damika managed to kick her leg between Phanessa's at the last second, sweeping one from under her and toppling them both on to the wet ground.

Nessa's breath was knocked from her lungs as she landed half on Damika and half in the mud. Before she could recover Damika rolled her onto her back, pinning her body down with her own and immobilizing her arms over her head.

They both laughed, Phanessa's giggle coming out a little breathlessly from both the fall and Damika's weight on her chest. Rain poured over them freely, plastering their clothes to their bodies and surrounding them in white noise as the heavy droplets splashed the mud around them. Then Damika's gaze met Nessa's and their laughter died away.

The rain was cold but Damika was warm, so warm above her that Nessa was surprised the water wasn't hissing into steam when landing on her flesh. Damika loosened the grip she had on Phanessa's forearms and let her thumbs sweep back and forth on the inside of her wrists, slowly, almost idly, her eyes never leaving hers. Nessa shivered. They shifted slightly on the mud and then they were much closer, Nessa finding it hard to breathe again. Damika's nose brushed against hers and suddenly time slowed, droplets of rain suspending in the heightened air around them. Nessa's eyelids fluttered shut —

Then the entire field was lit up like it was midday, for a flash, for a second, and a roaring crack and grumble shook the very ground beneath them. The girls startled, scrambling up from their position, braced and ready to fight, then stared in wide-eyed shock at one another. Thunder. It had only been lightning and thunder. Wordlessly Damika offered her hand to Phanessa and they ran off the field together, the storm too close to be safe in the open, and the moment, whatever it was, was lost. It was only later, lying in her bed freshly bathed and changed, that Nessa allowed herself to wonder what it was, exactly, the storm had interrupted, and whether she was relieved or disappointed that it had.

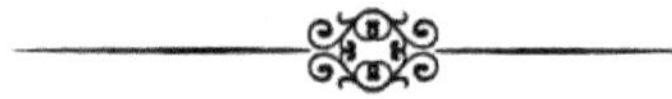

At 18, Damika would not only be the youngest initiate to ever earn the distinction of full Danrayen Warrior, but be one of a very small group to have earned her place before 20. In celebration of the upcoming honor, the girls ventured out to spend some time in Pelgar a few months before Damika's Trial, knowing that their friend's time would be scarce in the upcoming weeks with her preparations.

It was a bittersweet outing, for after the Trial full Danrayen Warriors were expected to spend years serving different positions in the realm, as soldiers in the war, as guards within the palace, and aiding in security for tradespeople on water and by land. Only once they had experienced many roles and walks of life could they choose and forge their own path.

They were also not allowed back within the temple walls until that moment, so it would likely be years before Damika could return to see any of her friends.

The thought alone made Phanessa's heart constrict in her chest. For days she had felt panicky and short of breath, distracted in her training and studies. There was the chance that she herself would be gone before Damika returned, and what if she never got to see her again? Or worse still, upon learning her secret, what if Damika never forgave her for her deception?

She made herself take a few deep breaths in through her nose and out through her mouth, as her instructors had taught her. Slowly, the vice on her chest relaxed a little, and she shoved her worries aside. It was a day for celebration, not sorrow.

The girls made their way into town, ignoring, this time, the advances of young men and the promise of distraction from the vendor stalls. Before reaching the cantina, Raidea pulled back, grabbing Phanessa by the arm and slowing them behind the rest of their group. Phanessa tilted her head at her in surprise. Raidea waited until the other girls were out of hearing range, and then winked at her.

"So," she told her. "You were chosen!" The words slammed into Phanessa like a staff to the gut. She gaped at her in horror. How had she found out? No one but the Archwizard Auberon and the High Priestess Adira knew her secret, and she had never even spoken the words "the Name-Bearer" since that fateful night so many years before. The instinct to escape flooded Phanessa's system, her legs tensed, demanding that she go, run, flee! They had made it to the outskirts of Pelgar by then, people crowding the narrow alleyways and flooding the main square to which they were headed. Was the other girl going to deliver her to the local authorities?

What could she do?

"I'm, I'm not! I don't know what you think you know, or what you've heard, but I," at her raised voice, more townsfolk turned to look at them. She gulped, and softened her tone. Raidea was her friend, perhaps she could plead with her?

"Please —" she choked out.

"No, no," Raidea interrupted her. "No use in trying to get out of it, the rest of us voted, and it has to be you!" Phanessa's brows shot up, her heartbeat still pounding inside her head.

"What?" she asked the other girl, confused. Was she not talking about being chosen by the bees? Raidea smiled widely at her, and Phanessa heard a townsboy sigh near them, lustily. Tense, her shoulders were raised to just below her ears and her hands were clenched into trembling fists. But Raidea seemed relaxed, and not angry at all. She leaned in conspiratorially.

"You're going to ask Damika if the priestesses have asked her to become a Danrayen Rider!" Her eyes sparkled with glee and Phanessa almost collapsed from relief. They had all been curious to know if the priestesses had approached Damika about being a Rider, but their stubborn friend had not mentioned anything to any of them. She hadn't even confided in Phanessa, and part of her was glad to have an excuse to broach the subject. Still, her body remained rigid with the fear that she had been discovered. She forced herself to relax, her shoulders dropping, inch by inch.

Raidea, oblivious to the terrible scare she had just inflicted on her friend, marched them into the cantina and to the bar top where she looked at Phanessa expectantly. Out of the corner of her eye, she could see the other girls already sitting with various drinks. She hesitated, chewing on her lower lip. She was thirsty, and the tavern served a cold, rosa de jamaica drink with sweetened ron that she enjoyed, but...

The small stipend that the priestesses gave her only went so far. Petra was sent coin by her father every year, and when Taruka left her family they had disowned her, but allowed her to take the trunk that would have served as her future dowry. Damika always seemed to have coin and was always happy to share with Phanessa, but she had never asked where it came from. It was one of the unspoken rules of their friendship, neither asked about each other's past.

Now, with Damika's Trial and departure fast approaching, Nessa had been carefully saving her coins to purchase her a parting gift. Something for her friend to remember her by. So as tempted as she was to join the others, she shook her head at Raidea with a smile. Raidea rolled her eyes and shooed her away, turning to the barkeep with a flirtatious grin. Chuckling to herself, Phanessa crossed the crowded room to her friends, who cleared a space next to Damika for her.

Across the table Petra caught her eye and raised her eyebrows, the unspoken question on her face. Nessa nodded as inconspicuously as she could. She would ask the question that had been on all their minds. Before she could open her mouth, however, a tall red glass was slammed down in front of her, Raidea squeezing in beside her, holding her own drink. Nessa grinned at her gratefully, lifting her cup to take a sip. It was the rosa ron, her favorite.

"Thank you," she whispered, but Raidea brushed her words off with a wave, gulping down several large sips from her own tankard.

The five young women sat with their drinks, speaking about everything and nothing at all, until an uneasy silence fell upon their group. One by one, pairs of eyes landed on Nessa, expectantly. She swallowed the final droplets of ron and cleared her throat, turning to face Damika more fully, only to be roughly elbowed by Raidea in the ribs. Phanessa glared at her. She was going to ask!

"Damika." She regarded her friend seriously. "Have the priestesses approached you about becoming a Danrayen Rider?" The others held their breath.

Damika took a long pull of her drink and wiped the foam off her upper lip with the back of her hand. She stared down at the table, not meeting their eyes.

"They have."

The girls all looked at each other, more in awe than surprise. The women knew that it was bound to happen, and had expected it, but to be chosen as a member of the Danrayen Riders was such an enormous honor!

"I said no."

At first, the words didn't register. They all looked at each other, blinking, a small frown etched on Taruka's delicate brow.

"Que?" Petra shrieked, slamming her open palms on the table between them and jumping up, causing half of the cantina to turn and stare. Taru grabbed her arm and forcibly tugged her back down, where she stared open-mouthed at Damika. The other girls waited quietly until most of the patrons had turned back to their own business.

"Why would you say no?" Phanessa finally asked her.

Damika sighed heavily and ran a frustrated hand across the back of her neck. Her gaze was serious, and troubled.

"I don't want to be a member of the state, or a priestess," she told them, pursing her lips with determination. The rest gaped at her at the admission. "I don't want to give the queen or prince advice on a war waging miles to the north," she continued hurriedly, her words pouring out of her mouth in a jumble, as if once given voice to her innermost feelings, she couldn't stop.

"I don't even want to join that battle, to join the war, as a fighter or politician. I want to help our people *here*, in Andala. Our home! We have plenty to fight on our own land, ghouls and shadow-jumpers from the Night Forest. Cassalains that sneak past our borders and raid our farms. Flesh peddlers and bandits that steal from hard working commoners."

Her voice grew hard and determined. "We should be helping our own people," she told them, looking each of them in the eye. Phanessa shivered.

"Together. The five of us will travel throughout the kingdom and do great deeds, saving those weaker, the poor, the innocent. Bards will sing songs of we warriors, the Daughters of Danray!"

"Eso!" Petra cheered, slamming her tankard down, cerveza sloshing over the rim and over her hand. She licked it off, a motion that Phanessa noticed drew Taruka's eye. When she saw that Phanessa had caught her staring, she blushed and raised her own cup to her lips.

Interesting, Phanessa thought. It was something to ponder later.

"¿Qué dices, Nessa?" Damika asked, slinging a companionable arm around her. "Shall we be the stuff of great stories?"

Guilt gnawed at her insides. There was nothing she wanted more than to join her friends on grand adventures and live her life for her alone. But her fate had been sealed long ago, and there was no denying the will of the gods. Sometime soon, the wizard would come for her.

"I fear I would just hold you back," she said, smiling sadly at the amazing women before her. How she would miss them! "We all know I'm not much of a warrior."

"No seas tonta!" Damika declared, giving her a shake. "Danray would not have chosen you otherwise."

"Maybe she made a mistake?"

Damika dismissed this with a snort, and Taruka gave her a quiet look. But Petra and Raidea gasped at her, scandalized.

"The Great Goddess Danray would *not* make a mistake!" Raidea insisted.

"Besides," Petra cut in "there are different types of warriors. You may not be natural at combat, but you are the best tracker here, a wonderful rider, and you've gotten quite good with throwing daggers." Phanessa's eyebrows raised in surprise.

"We will return for your Trial, and ceremony" Damika told her. "And then we will ride together."

From there the conversation turned to the induction ceremony and feast that would follow Damika's Trial. Several young women had passed their own Trials in the years since Phanessa had joined the Danrayens, but the girls had only been allowed to attend the ceremonies once they turned fifteen. The first year that they had attended the girls were put to work, serving drinks and clearing plates. Phanessa had been petrified of tripping or spilling a beverage on someone of great importance. However, her palace training had emerged and she had made it through the entire evening without a single mishap.

Afterwards, their little group had stolen a few bottles of alcohol and watched the sunrise, giggling and dizzy from mixing the fizzy drinks with vino y cerveza. Of course they had each woken up with a terrible headache and sworn never to drink again. An oath that they promptly broke the following weekend in Pelgar, all memory of past discomfort well forgotten.

Each ceremony since had been a joyous celebration full of food, dancing, and good cheer. The priestesses invited past Danrayens, soldiers, members of state and others to join them in the revelry. It was the only time that men were allowed on the Danrayen grounds, unless specifically invited by a priestess. As Damika was the youngest trainee to ever attempt the Trial, *and* fully expected to pass it, her celebration promised to be even more grand than the ones before. People were coming from all over Andala to witness it.

"What is everyone wearing?" Taruka asked suddenly, and Phanessa's head jerked up at the question.

"What do you mean?" she asked, a small frown crinkling the skin between her brows. "Won't we wear what we normally do?"

The other girls laughed, Damika dropping her arm around her shoulders once again.

"You can wear whatever you want, Nessa," she told her with a squeeze. But Petra was not having it.

"Of course we have to wear something special! Our Dami is going to be a full Weapon of Danray! She will no doubt be looking spectacular, and we cannot shame her by looking ordinary by her side!" her grin was wide, her eyes a bit glassy from the ale. But the words were delivered earnestly as she beamed at Damika with love and pride.

Phanessa felt her stomach plummet. If she could barely scrape together her meager stipend to afford a gift for her best friend, how was she going to afford an entire new outfit? Damika glanced at her curiously and Phanessa quickly shifted her expression, not wanting to alarm her friend. The others began discussing gowns versus armor, what weapons they would display, as well as color and fabric options while Phanessa stared at the bottom of her empty glass. In her periphery she saw Raidea lean towards her and she shifted, plastering a fake smile on her face.

"Meet me in the kitchens tomorrow, an hour before dawn," she whispered with her signature wink.

"What?" Phanessa asked her, confused.

"Just trust me" she replied, shifting away once more. "Before dawn."

The next morning, Phanessa dragged herself out of bed with a soft groan. With the physical, mental, and emotional demands of the Danrayen path, sleep was a luxury, and to give up even an hour seemed like a grand sacrifice. But Raidea had never asked anything of her before, and she was curious as to why she would request her presence now.

Stifling a yawn she pulled on her britches, tucking her shirt into them before lacing the ties in the front. Her clothing reminded her of the conversation of the day before, and nerves tightened her belly. What was she going to do about the ceremony? If she was the only one who didn't arrive to Damika's celebration in a new outfit she would die of shame.

Maybe one of the older girls has something they could lend me, she thought as she slipped out of the room and down the stairs.

Her ears burned with embarrassment at the prospect of having to ask, but anything was better than shaming Damika on the most important day of her life. Perhaps the coin that she had saved for her gift should be used for a new outfit instead … Phanessa pursed her lips, a small frown pulling down her brows. She had so wanted to give her a gift, but a choice must be made.

If only High Priestess Adira had allowed me to keep even one jewel of my flower gown!

It was impossible, of course, there was no reason why a "regular" girl like herself would have such a gem. And the Danrayens were taking a great risk harboring her amongst them, even the price of her ceremonial gown fell short in comparison to the prospect of safety and security within their walls. Trotting towards the kitchens, Phanessa couldn't help but grin ruefully. A few short years ago her greatest problems were being discovered as a traitor to the realm, captured and tortured and potentially killed. The fact that now she was worried about what she was going to wear to a party was laughable in comparison.

But the fact was, it mattered to her.

A blast of heat hit her as she made it into the kitchens, the stone ovens roaring and chasing away the morning chill. Several women were there, bustling about with various ingredients and dishes. Raidea was stationed towards the back at a long table, her strong arms busy kneading dough. When she saw Phanessa she lifted an arm, covered in flour up to her elbow, and beckoned her forward.

"Buenos dias cariño," she greeted her with a happy smile. Phanessa smiled back at her. Of their group, Raidea, Taruka and Phanessa were the most cheerful in the morning, with Damika quieter than usual when first waking. And Petra? No one dared speak to her before her morning meal.

"Buenos dias," she managed to choke out in between a wide yawn. What was she doing there?

As if reading her mind, Raidea shot her another grin. "I know that you have been worried about coin," she told her. Phanessa stiffened, but didn't deny it. She supposed it was fairly obvious after their inter-action at the tavern.

"Do you ever wonder," Raidea continued, "how an orphan without a moneda to her name can afford to buy everyone the occasional round at the tavern? Or commission a new outfit for Damika's ceremony?"

Phanessa started, considering. The truth was that she had never given much thought to where or how Raidea was able to pay for her things, but now that she mentioned it …

"There are plenty of things within the temple that our priestesses could use some help with," Raidea continued, separating the dough in front of her and twisting them into shapes that Phanessa recognized as the rolls that were served at breakfast -pan dulce. "And if you should find your day open for a few hours here and there, you can earn a fair bit of coin for yourself."

Phanessa's brows raised in surprise. There were tasks that the Danrayen initiates were expected to do, of course. Over the years they had all mucked out stables, cleaned and polished weapons, and organized scrolls and documents in the library. But she hadn't considered that she could volunteer for more duties, or be paid to do so! Eyes alight with promise, she launched herself at Raidea, wrapping her arms around her and burying her wide smile against her shoulder.

Raidea was motionless for a moment, Phanessa had never been overly physically affectionate with any of them, and Raidea's throat constricted with emotion at the rare event. But the surprise was quickly brushed away and she hugged her in return, covering Phanessa's back with white streaks of flour.

"I already asked High Priestess Adira for you," she told her with a chuckle and Phanessa pulled back to look her in the eye.

"When did you have time?" Phanessa asked her. They had been together all evening, and the morning had not even started!

"I saw her on my way to the kitchens this morning," she replied.

"Doesn't anyone sleep around here?" Phanessa grumbled.

"Some more than others," Raidea replied with a pointed look. Phanessa grabbed a scrap of dough and threw it at her friend, but Raidea deflected it easily.

"She said it was fine, and gave me a list of priestesses with extra work they could use help with. You'll earn enough for a pretty dress in no time. For now, help me with the pan."

"Thank you Raidea, truly."

Raidea merely blew her a kiss in response. The silly grin remained on her face as she crossed to wash her hands at the water pump. She was truly blessed in her friendships.

For the next few weeks Phanessa worked herself to exhaustion. She continued aiding in the kitchen with Raidea some days, on others waking equally early to help Priestess Ovidia feed the animals. She helped with washing the bedding during any free times in the afternoons, returning to the kitchens after supper to wash dishes. She transcribed notes for classes, scrubbed floors, and learned to make candles. Any extra chore or task that she could claim, she did, the exception being weeding the temple gardens. Though her aversion to flowers had lessened, she still didn't want to spend more time than necessary in their presence.

CHAPTER 10

D amika's Trial was conducted on the second day of spring, in Phanessa's fourth year at the Temple of Danray. It was a beautiful day, of course. Phanessa thought that even the gods themselves must be watching in support of her friend. Damika rose at dawn, and the others with her in a show of quiet solidarity. Together they walked to the Altar of Danray, where Damika sat between the Goddess' feet to meditate.

They stayed with her for a while, quietly absorbed in their own thoughts, until Petra's loudly rumbling stomach interrupted them. Grinning at one another, the mood broken, they left Damika and went in search of breakfast. Phanessa could only stomach a bit of fruit, too nervous for her friend to have much of an appetite. When they emerged from the dining hall a while later, Damika was still at the altar, and would be, until midday.

As Tz'ola's sun crown inched its way up the morning sky, the priestesses began making their way into the inner sanctum of the temple grounds, housed beyond the great Goddess statue. None of the girls had ever crossed the Goddess' feet and into the sanctum, and wouldn't until their own Trials. No initiates would be allowed inside to view the tasks and challenges Damika would face, as she would have to pass them on her own.

When two of the instructors finally roused Damika from her contemplation, Phanessa gnawed on her lower lip anxiously. Damika was undoubtedly the best student in the order, but the Trial was meant to challenge even the most fierce.

But Damika rose with conviction, her spine straight, her face resolute. She didn't meet her friend's eyes as she crossed to the sanctum and climbed the steps to its interior.

The doors shut with a reverberating clang behind her.

There was stillness in the garden, the young women waiting in near silence. Only a few hesitant whispers could be made out, and the rustle of fabrics when some inevitably rose to relieve themselves and return in a rush, not wanting to miss anything.

Not all the Danrayen trainees pass the Trial. Some emerge from the inner sanctum refusing to continue, others need to be carried out from exhaustion or injury,

A few have even died.

Those who do not pass the Trial cannot be Danrayen Warriors, and they usually leave the temple to pursue other paths, elsewhere.

But not all.

The most well-known example of a Danrayen who had not passed the Trial was a favorite among the trainees.

Mamá.

Mamá had been at the Danrayen Temple for as long as any of the girls could remember. It was whispered that though she had failed in the Trial, she had somehow not failed the Goddess and was still in her favor. The Goddess Danray saw that she had a warrior's heart but not a fighting spirit, and had allowed her to stay at the temple, not as a priestess, but in a role no less important. Mamá had warmth and wisdom, comfort and kindness to give them all. For the Goddess knew that young women need more than just training; they also need love.

Mamá had been the only person Phanessa had confided in when she was being targeted by Kichka. Not that she told the woman the extent of her torment, of course ... she knew that Mamá would have reported Kichka right away for her abuse. She had merely allowed herself a few moments of vulnerability, crying in the woman's arms.

"The other girls are so much stronger, so much better than I will ever be," she had confessed, wiping her eyes and nose on the handkerchief Mamá had passed to her quietly. "I don't belong here. I will never be a true warrior."

"And what is it that you believe makes a true warrior?" Mamá had asked her with a small smile.

Phanessa had thought of her friends, the truest warriors she had ever known. "Someone who can fight. Who can handle any weapon and battle any opponent," she answered, thinking of Damika. "Someone loyal and quick to action, defending those who cannot defend themselves," she continued, picturing Petra. "A warrior is someone who does the right thing, who rights wrongs and sees what others do not." That was Taruka, through and through. "And someone who gives people the benefit of the doubt, never jumps to conclusions, but uses every advantage they have when they need to." Raidea.

"How about someone who cares about the wellbeing of others besides themselves? Someone who finds the missing, feeds the hungry, mends the wounded, heals the sick, and comforts the grieving? Are they not heroes as well? Are those not heroic acts?"

Phanessa had frowned, thinking about it.

"Of course those are heroic acts," she admitted. "But all the girls have skills in those things. In tracking, and healing, and hunting. I am no more skilled than any of them."

"I have heard you have quite the skill in hunting and tracking, as a matter of fact. But that is beside the point. You have training that regular folk will never have. It is a great responsibility and burden to bear. Even the weakest Danrayen is more skilled than most regular people, and whether or not you choose to believe it, you are in no way weak, mija."

She had left Mamá feeling confused, but somewhat comforted. Perhaps she would never be the pride of the Danrayens, but perhaps she would not be a disappointment either.

A grating sound from the direction of the sanctum snapped her from her memory and her head flew up, her gaze drawn towards the doors. The sun indicated that a few hours had passed, and they finally swung open once again. Phanessa sprang up, straining her eyes to see …

And there was Damika. Sweat-soaked, obviously exhausted, with a long nasty gash stretching from her left shoulder down to her wrist. All the girls ran towards her, but she and Petra reached her first. They helped to steady her, leading her down the stairs and towards the infirmary. At first, Phanessa thought the roaring in her ears was the blood rushing back to her head from pure relief at seeing her friend alive. Then she realized that it was cheering.

Damika had passed. She was a full Danrayen Warrior.

Inside the infirmary, color was returning to her friend's pale face. She lay on a bed, the Priestess Ianuaria calmly sewing her injury. Petra, Taruka, Raidea and Phanessa all crowded around her.

"How was it?" Raidea asked, almost reverently.

"You know I can't talk about it," was Damika's only response.

It was forbidden to discuss the Trial with those who hadn't undergone it. For a moment Phanessa's heart sank, knowing that she would never undergo the Trial to become a true Danrayen Warrior, and therefore would never know what challenges her friends would face within the sanctum. For a moment she was sorry that she couldn't go through it. But the lingering pain and fear in Damika's eyes was enough to dissuade her of that notion.

Perhaps it's better this way.

"Let her rest," Priestess Ianuaria said with a gentle pat on Damika's newly bandaged arm. "There will be much to celebrate this evening, and she will need her energy."

Damika smiled at them as they trickled out of the room, Phanessa last. She wanted to say something to her, anything that might chase the shadows away from her friend's eyes, but all she could manage was a half-hearted wave. By the time she was out the door, Damika was asleep.

Having the entire day off, the girls split to spend the time as they pleased. Petra and Taruka decided to go for a ride before getting ready for the evening's festivities. Raidea and Phanessa, however, had both volunteered to assist with the preparations for the celebration, having negotiated with the priestesses to be paid ahead of time, allowing them to purchase their outfits for the evening.

For Phanessa, this consisted of fawn-colored wool breeches with leather laces that criss-crossed up each side, from calf to hip. Her tunic was the same color of fawn with cream stitching, which hit just above mid-thigh and sported more leather straps to create an open corset effect on each side. Her hair had long since grown out of the short cut from years past, and it hung unadorned to her shoulders in lazy red waves. Sturdy leather boots completed her outfit, and Phanessa was in absolute awe of the effect. She had not worn anything so fine since her flower dress, and her heart cramped painfully at the memory.

She had visited the village tailor at every chance for measurements and fittings. As it was the largest amount she had ever paid for anything in her life, Phanessa had never even considered the fact that the tailor, being a gentle-hearted sort, charged her half of what the garments were worth. It covered the cost of materials, but not the many hours of labor that went into fashioning it.

Pobrecita la nena, the woman had thought. *Warrior's work is hard enough for these chiquitas and anyone could see this one works harder than most.*

Phanessa would have despaired at the woman's thoughts, and the kindness would have furthered her feelings of guilt and fraud. But she was thankfully unaware, and very much pleased with her purchase. With one last tug of her tunic and lacing of her left boot, she left the girl's common room and stopped to regard herself in the floor length mirror in the hall.

I look strong, she thought, surprised. *Almost as if I truly belong here.* She quickly brushed that thought aside. It was Damika's day, a time for celebration, not regret.

That evening the temple was a bustle of music, food, and festivity. For once, the space was full of vibrant colors. The training yards, usually a mess of trampled dirt and mud, had been covered instead by long planks of wood with brightly painted geometric designs, creating a large open floor with an area for dancing and long tables full of food and drink.

The tables were covered by multicolored woven runners, their colors blending into beautifully symmetric patterns. Sprigs of leaves and flowers decorated their surface between plates of meats, cheeses, beans and pastries.

Nessa and Raidea had spent hours shaping the tamales, frying the plantains and tostones, and patting the black corn tortillas into the perfect shape. Hanging oil lanterns illuminated it all, each suspended on thick ropes that crossed from one side of the inner buildings to the other, colored tassels hanging with puffy string balls between them. Danray's sculpture watched from a distance, moonlight highlighting her strong face.

Danrayen Warriors who had long since passed their Trials and had been close enough to make the journey came to partake in the revelry. There were even some men in attendance, soldiers, ambassadors, and mages. As men were not permitted on Danrayen soil unless invited by the priestesses themselves, it was always a rare and interesting development for some of the young women. Those who had an interest in men were careful to position themselves near them, awaiting an opportunity to approach or be approached.

Everyone wore their finest attire, whatever that meant to them. Some came in full armor, others in cured leather. Some wore lovely dresses, like the High Priestess Adira, who arrived in a fire-red gown that was cut high on both thighs, showcasing glinting daggers strapped to each. Raidea also wore a dress, but hers was in a stunning cobalt blue and cut low on the top instead, drawing attention to her ample bosom.

"I see you've decided to display your weapons tonight," Petra remarked, raising her eyebrow and jutting her chin in the direction of Raidea's chest.

"Y que bueno, I'm glad that I did." Raidea replied, casting her gaze at a small group of soldiers who were sneaking glances at them in interest.

"You look beautiful." Taruka smiled at the two of them. "Both of you. Bellas."

"So do you," Phanessa replied honestly. Taruka wore a long hunter green cloak over a simple white and fern colored gown. The arms were tight on her toned biceps, a result of all her archery practice, and flared at the elbow. Her hair bore more braids than usual, and she had taken more care in applying her kohl and face paints.

"You look like the Lady of the Green," Phanessa continued, referring to the jungle goddess most favored in small villages surrounding the Great Andalan Rainforest. Taruka's responding laugh was light and airy, like the tinkling of wind chimes, and Phanessa noticed once again how Petra watched Taru, with a small smile on her lips. Phanessa covered a smile of her own behind her hand, wondering if her friends knew their feelings for one another.

Then again, what do I know about such things?

A hush descended over the party, and instinctively everyone turned to the great steps where Adira stood, arms held high to command their attention. When she was satisfied she had it, they lowered slowly, and she announced loudly and clearly enough for all to hear;

"The Goddess Danray smiles upon us all today. For on this night, we welcome our newest sister and Weapon of Danray to our circle. Welcome, Sister Damika, Daughter of Danray!"

From the sides of the temple, off the very rooftops of the buildings, enormous resplendent figures launched into the sky in perfect unison. They were barriletes gigantes - giant kites. There was a collective gasp from the crowd as more and more of the multicolored circles blazed into the sky, their soft tissue-paper figures lit from within by temple magia. They swayed and danced on the night breeze, each shuddering shake spilling bright flecks of rainbow sparkles from their faces and down on to the party below.

The beat of drums echoed around them, an urgent pounding that rumbled low and then sped up to a frantic beat, chasing something, an apex, a crescendo, the culmination to their wild song. Just as they struck their final, reverberating note, Damika emerged.

She stepped out from the temple doors, high above them and paused at the top plateau before making her way down the many steps. There was a shocked pause, and then a thunderous applause.

Damika looked glorious.

The front of her hair was pinned back from her face, showcasing her high cheekbones, full mouth and strong jaw. Her eyes were framed by her heavy lashes, carefully brushed with just the slightest bit of paint to accentuate their length. The old leather jerkin she often favored was replaced by full leather armor, top to bottom, and polished to shine.

La Espada de Danray was strapped to her back, a dagger at her waist, and she no doubt concealed even more weapons on her person than could be seen by the naked eye. She looked every bit like a Danrayen Warrior, and tears blurred Phanessa's sight at the realization that her childhood friend had been replaced with an accomplished woman, too soon leaving in chase of adventure.

It took quite a long time for Damika to make her way through the crowd and to her friends. It seemed everyone wanted to stop her, congratulate her, and ask her about her plans for the future. Men and women alike brought her drinks and asked her to dance. As their group waited for her to make their way to them, Phanessa passed the time by watching the crowd. Many of her sisters wore new outfits of their own, some danced while others ate and drank, but most took advantage of the rare occurrence of men in their presence to practice their flirting.

Phanessa even spotted the Priestess Adira chatting to a particularly handsome soldier and almost smiled, but then caught the tightness in the priestesses' posture. With a small frown she watched them, their heads bowed closely together, talking in urgent, hushed tones before the priestess grasped the soldier by his arm and led him away from the festivities. Despite their obvious tension Phanessa wasn't worried about the priestess; she was more than capable of handling herself. Besides, something in the way that they spoke made her believe that they were not strangers. Before she could ponder it any further, however, Raidea nudged her. Damika was making her way towards them.

By the time she reached the group, the corners of her mouth were tight, and her hands trembled ever so slightly with repressed irritation at the many well-wishes from the crowd. Damika wasn't the best with strangers. With each hug and good-natured slap on her back from her friends, however, the stress began visibly leaving her body.

"Cerveza?" Petra asked, passing Damika a tall glass.

"Thank you" she replied, gulping down half of it at once, which elicited an impressed nod from Petra. "The nobles keep passing me small glasses of mixed liqueur." She scrunched up her nose. "You'd like them, Phanessa, they're sweet."

"How are you?" Phanessa asked her, ignoring the remark. There was nothing wrong with liking sweet drinks after all. Cerveza was bitter. Damika patted her injured arm lightly. "Priestess Ianuaria did wonders," she replied. "I can hardly feel it." At the movement Phanessa's eye was caught by a flickering of light.

"What is that?" she pointed and was surprised to see her friend blush.

"A gift from the High Priestess," Damika confessed, twisting her shoulder to show off a new leather armband adorned with overlapping mixed metals. "It seems that they are still trying to convince me to join the Riders."

"Seems a bit sentimental for Priestess Adira." Raidea remarked, tracing a finger along a braided pattern along the band. Damika grinned and slipped a fingernail under a notch of a longer metal piece, prying it up. From there she slipped out a small, slender spike.

"The tip is meant to be dipped in poison, which you can then mix in an enemy's drink, or simply prick an opponent if all else fails. No me gusta the thought of poison; I'd rather defeat them hand to hand … but I can't say it wouldn't be useful in a pinch." Smiling, she slipped it back into its holding place.

"Now *that* sounds more like the High Priestess!" Raidea remarked with a grin. "Now, Dami mi amor, you know I am unbearably proud of you and am happy to stay with you lot for the rest of the night celebrating …"

"Go on," Damika laughed, all traces of earlier discomfort finally disappearing, softening her face. "I wouldn't be much of a Weapon of Danray if I hadn't noticed the three soldiers guapos taking your measure." Her chin jutted in the direction of the men in question, who were indeed continuing to sneak glances at the group. "Please, don't let me keep you."

Raidea grabbed Damika's face and kissed her square on the mouth, surprising another chuckle from the girl.

"I really *am* so proud of you," she repeated, releasing her and turning towards her targets. "Any of you ladies care to join me?"

Taruka and Petra glanced quickly at one another and shook their heads. When Raidea slid her eyes over to Phanessa, expectantly, she repeated the motion. If she had no idea what to talk about to the village boys closer to her age, what could she possibly have to say to full grown men and soldiers?

"But which one will you choose?" she asked Raidea. The older girl laughed and tossed her head, her shining curls bouncing with the movement.

"Oh mija … who said I had to choose?" and sauntered off in the direction of the men. Cool fingers touched the underside of Phanessa's chin.

"Lift that jaw off the floor," Damika told her, her eyes twinkling with amusement. "She was joking ... probably."

Beet red, Phanessa realized that she had in fact been left with her mouth hanging open. But who could blame her? Raidea couldn't help but be scandalous. When the heat began fading from her cheeks, she noticed that Petra and Taruka had disappeared together, leaving her and Damika alone at the edge of the party. There was so much she wanted to say but didn't know how to begin. She fingered the small, wrapped packet in her pocket, suddenly feeling very foolish to have bought it. Stealing her nerves, she drew in a breath and took it out. It was wrapped in a bronze-gold fabric, tied with a white ribbon.

"I got you something," she told her, hesitantly. Damika's face lit up.

"You didn't have to get me anything!" Despite the words, she sprang upon the gift with glee. Phanessa's face ignited into a heated blush.

"It's really nothing, not much, really. Nothing quite so fine as what Priestess Adira gave you ..."

"Oh Nessa! It's wonderful! I love it!"

Damika cradled the delicate butterfly pin in her cupped hands. The outsides of the wings and body were constructed with fine gold wire, twisted meticulously to preserve the grace and intricacy of the creature. Inside the wire were amber stones, solidifying the inner shape of the butterfly in the same golds and browns of the wrapping. Colors that reminded Phanessa of Damika.

She looked up and was shocked to see Damika beaming at her, misty eyed. Before she could say anything, Damika crushed her in a fierce hug. The hard armor and protruding weapons hidden on her person jabbed at her, but Phanessa didn't care. She threw her arms around her friend, holding back tears of her own. After a moment, she was released.

"Come on, let's take a walk in the gardens." Damika set down her now empty glass and began heading that direction, Phanessa in tow.

They crossed the training yards in silence, moving quietly over the fields and into the temple gardens. It had become one of Phanessa's favorite places, despite the multi-colored flowers and their painful reminder of her past. Or, perhaps, because of it. Sometimes she wondered if she didn't enjoy that painful memory, as it kept her anchored to her fate. Sometimes the urge to forget, and forever play as a true Danrayen was overwhelming. But not in the garden. There, she was forced to remember.

In wordless agreement the girls made their way to the Statue of Danray, and towards one of the marble benches surrounding the goddess' courtyard. They sat on its cold surface.

There was so much to say, and yet neither of them spoke. In Phanessa's mind, and heart, Damika had saved her life. Through her patience and guidance she had shaped her into someone almost resembling a warrior, something she would have thought impossible years ago. Damika had been kind to her, a true friend and companion. Now she would be leaving soon, and Phanessa had never really thanked her for it, never truly spoken her feelings. If not now, in the quiet of this night, then when?

Phanessa opened her mouth to speak.

"I've decided to take an assignment," Damika blurted out, suddenly. Surprised, Phanessa twisted to better see her friend.

"You have? I thought ... I thought you wanted to go looking for adventure first."

"Well, that's just it, this seems like quite an adventure. It was explained to me this afternoon, after the Trial. And I know that the priestesses are trying to convince me to join the Riders, and that they think a taste of this sort of mission would change my mind, but I don't know." She was twisting a leather strap from her tunic between her fingers nervously. "It seems worthy."

Phanessa was quiet, watching the night sky.

"Can you tell me about it?" She asked as Damika's hand slipped under hers on the bench.

"No," she whispered. Phanessa nodded. She assumed that would be the case.

"When would you leave?" There was a long pause, and Damika's fingers interlaced with hers.

"Tomorrow."

"Tomorrow?" Phanessa jumped up, whirling to face her straight on. "Tomorrow? You can't leave tomorrow, that's far too soon! You can stay in the temple for a full month before you must leave, why would you go tomorrow?"

Damika had stood as well, and she grabbed her hands again.

"I have to, Nessa!" she pleaded. "The mission, it's important, and it's urgent. They would have had me go today if skipping the Ceremony wouldn't have been viewed as strange, and suspicious. No one can guess where I'm going or what I am about to do."

Phanessa trembled with suppressed tears, her hands limp under Damika's grip.

"When will you return?" Even in the dark, she could see a light dim in Damika's eyes.

"Years. It ... it will likely take years."

Years. Phanessa turned, too overcome with emotion to keep looking at her friend's face. Her best friend, her first friend, her mentor and her sister, who was leaving her. It was hard enough knowing that Damika would no longer be at the temple to talk to, to train with, to spend her days with. She thought she would have at least a few years of visits, before the wizard came, before she had to set out and disappoint her. She had thought they had more time.

Warmth drew against her back as Damika's arms snaked around her shoulders.

"Please don't be mad at me, Nessa." Damika whispered. "If you ..."

"What?" Phanessa demanded, turning back around.

"If you wait to do your Trial, I might be back by then. If you wait until you're 23, or 24..."

Phanessa frowned. "I don't plan to take the Trial!" Noticing the shock in Damika's eyes she quickly added, "until I'm at least 25." She had nearly confessed her secret! "I wasn't thinking about taking the Trial until I was older. We both know I could use the practice."

Damika squeezed her shoulders, then pulled her in for a tight hug. Phanessa clung to her and let her tears fall. Her friend rocked her, holding her patiently until she was spent. Only then did she pull away, offering her a handkerchief. Phanessa blew her nose and laughed ruefully.

"I must look a mess," she said. Damika wiped a stray tear off her left cheek.

"Nah," she replied. "You always look beautiful."

Her fingers lingered on her cheek, and they were standing so very close. The night was dark, the noise of the crowd muffled in the distance, the flowers smelling sweetly in their night bloom. For once, their scent did not offend her. Phanessa's breath caught in her throat as Damika leaned in closer to her, her mouth inches away. Her heart thundered and she didn't know what to do with her hands, but her eyes shut automatically as Damika kissed her gently. Her lips were soft and warm against the cool night and Phanessa became intensely aware of her body, and the strange, not unpleasant tingles that raced up and down her spine and settled in her lower belly. When Damika pulled away, a quiet noise escaped her. Was it confusion, protest? She didn't know, her head was spinning.

Damika took a step back and swallowed hard.

"I should get back, it's my celebration after all." She shifted nervously, not meeting her eyes. Phanessa nodded, speechless.

"Will you ..." Damika hesitated. "Will you say goodbye to me tomorrow morning?"

"Of course!" Phanessa cried, shocked. "You didn't think I'd let you leave without saying goodbye?"

A grin broke over Damika's face, and Phanessa was relieved. That was more fitting of her friend than the uncertain girl before her just a moment ago.

"Good." she replied and lingered another moment before spinning and heading back to the party, her long strides taking her too quickly from view. Phanessa sat back down on the bench and stayed there for a very long time.

Chapter 11

The next morning the girls stood together at the top of the temple steps to say their goodbyes. Far below them at the bottom of the stairs, a small group of soldiers waited, led by the man Phanessa has seen Priestess Adira speaking to the night before. But the young women ignored their presence, focused only on making their farewells to Damika.

Raidea looked a bit worse for wear thanks to the long night prior, and she patted Phanessa's shoulder awkwardly as she dabbed at her own misty eyes. Petra, to everyone's surprise, wept openly, flinging her arms around Damika and wailing something nonsensical into her shoulder. Damika merely rocked her a bit, rubbing soothing circles on her back before dumping her small friend into the arms of Taruka.

As for Phanessa, she stood straight backed and as stoically as she could. She knew how hard leaving was for Damika and she was determined not to make it worse for her. The older girl made her rounds, hugging and kissing her friends with a cheery smile on her face. If it seemed to any of them that the grin did not quite reach her eyes, they made no comment on it, and merely gave her their best strained smiles in return. Finally Damika stood in front of Phanessa, standing on the step directly below hers so that their line of sight almost matched. The other girls backed away a little to give them some privacy.

Phanessa made the first move, wrapping her arms around her friend's neck and squeezing her tight. Damika's arms went around her waist and they stood swaying for a long moment before Damika abruptly pulled away. She framed Nessa's face in her hands and kissed her swiftly, half on her cheek, half on the corner of her mouth before turning and making her way down the long steps. Phanessa lifted her hand to touch the small patch of skin that still tingled from Damika's lips, ignoring the stinging behind her eyes. If Damika looked back, she would not see her crying.

But Damika never looked back.

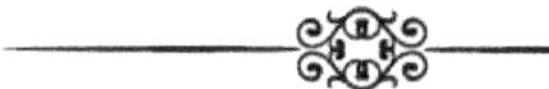

After Damika's departure things changed at the Danrayen Temple. As Petra and Taruka grew closer, Phanessa and Raidea were often left to spend their time together without them. To both of their delight, their friendship grew even stronger than it had been. Phanessa's quiet level-headedness and good-natured patience balanced out Raidea's loud, brash confidence and her often reckless behavior.

While Phanessa had always been content to defer to Damika, Raidea encouraged her to step out of her shadow and become her own person. While Damika and the others took pity on Phanessa's shyness and would order drinks for her, or speak up on her behalf if she was missing a scroll, or if she was given the wrong weapon, Raidea encouraged her to speak for herself instead. She often asked her for her opinions on a matter of subjects, and even made her spend a particularly painful afternoon in Pelgar with two of the local boys. After it was clear that Phanessa had been incredibly uncomfortable, Raidea never asked it of her again, but often teased her about her lack of interest in men.

The truth was, Phanessa wasn't sure she was completely uninterested in the opposite sex. She just wasn't particularly *interested*. But when she thought about the other girls at the temple, her Danrayen sisters, she was equally unmoved. The fact was that she hadn't experienced any sort of interest in anyone, male or female, except for Damika. She didn't know what that meant, and wasn't inclined to examine it too deeply. After all, she was destined for other things, and was fairly certain that the Flowers wouldn't take kindly to her shirking her responsibilities for anything as silly as romance. In any case, had she wanted to explore her feelings further she couldn't anyway, as Damika was no longer there.

When Phanessa and Raidea were not busy working around the temple grounds they spent time in their own endeavors. Raidea joined Petra and Taruka whenever she could so that they could all train for their Trials, something Phanessa refused to do. It pained her to think that the other girls might view her reticence as cowardice, but she simply could not bring herself to pretend that the Trial was something she would ever be able to attempt. As much as she loved her life within the Danrayen walls, she had never forgotten that she was not truly one of them, and could never hold that honor.

Instead of training with her friends, Phanessa found herself filling her free hours by tutoring some of the younger initiates, just as Damika had done for her. She was surprised, and well-pleased to learn she was no longer the least experienced Danrayen trainee, and that moreover her own past struggles gave her a unique insight on how to best advise others on ways to improve. The younger girls looked up to her and her friends, and often spoke about how formidable a group they made.

Phanessa would have been amazed to learn that they held her in the same regard as her older Danrayen peers.

It took nearly two years after Damika's departure for Taruka and Petra to attempt The Trial of Danray. They decided on it together, and took theirs at twenty-one and twenty-two, respectively, less than a month from each other. They had a joint celebration and left for parts unknown together soon after. None of Taruka's family was in attendance at their commemoration, but Petra's father and six brothers were all invited by the priestesses. As most of the young men needed to stay behind to protect their farmlands from Cassalain raiders, only two of her brothers joined her father for the celebration.

Luckily for Raidea this included the eldest, Dante. She caught one glimpse of his messy brown hair, hazel eyes and farmer's muscles and had disappeared with him for the majority of the evening, much to Petra's exasperation.

It was almost a year after their departure when Raidea sought Phanessa out. She was finishing her run, a practice that she had kept up even after Damika had left. She knew it was silly, but she felt like somehow Damika would know if she wasn't pushing herself, and even though it had been years since she last saw her friend, she still didn't want to disappoint her.

As she jogged towards the baths, she ran into Raidea who was seated on a bench outside them. She slowed, still panting, and wiped the dripping sweat off her brow.

"Hola," she greeted her friend, flopping down on the floor in front of her to stretch. "Were you waiting for me?"

Raidea smiled at her, but looked troubled. Phanessa reached out and touched her knee.

"What is it?" she asked her nervously.

"Nessa," Raidea started, covering her hand with her own. "Nessa, I have to tell you something." Phanessa popped up off the floor and sat next to Raidea.

"What's wrong?" she asked her, growing more concerned.

"Nothing's wrong, exactly, it's just," Raidea met her eyes and took a deep breath. "Nessa, I'm ready to take the Trial."

Several emotions assailed her at once. Pride, of course. Apprehension and worry, as the Trials were never easy. Sadness at the thought of losing her last close friend.

And fear. Fear because the time was passing far too quickly, and soon she too would have to leave the safety of the temple in hopes of finding the unnamed prince and delivering him to the Flowers of Prophecy for the Naming. It was almost laughable, if it weren't so terrifying.

Phanessa made herself focus on her first emotion, pride. Her heart thundered in her chest but the smile she gave Raidea was a real one.

"Well of course you are," she squeezed her hand. "I'm surprised you've waited this long!" she teased her.

Raidea looked down. "I thought, well. I thought if I waited long enough, you'd realize that you're ready too." Phanessa carefully extracted her hand from Raidea's.

"Dee ..." she started.

"Damn it Nessa, you're ready! I know you're scared, I'm scared too, but we can't stay here forever. If we both take the Trial we can leave together, like Taruka and Petra."

Nessa gave her a look, and Raidea's lips twitched.

"Well," she amended. "Maybe not *quite* like Taruka and Petra." They both snorted, their giggles lifting the mood a little.

"But we can find them. Maybe we can even find Damika too." Phanessa's heart clenched at the thought. "We can do what we always said we would, travel the realm together. The five of us, 'Daughters of Danray,' remember?"

Nessa smiled. She did remember. But she also remembered why it was an impossible dream for her. Carefully, she twisted to look her friend in the eye. She didn't want to lie to her, but how could she tell her the truth?

"Dee. I don't plan on staying in the temple forever. I promise you." She frowned, choosing her words carefully. "I know that I will leave, and I will do great things." She smiled ruefully. "Well, I will try, in any case."

"Of course you will!" Raidea shot at her with a swift punch to her upper arm, making Nessa yelp. Her chest warmed at her friend's faith in her.

"But," she continued, "not yet. I'm sorry Dee," she held up her hand before Raidea could interrupt her. "Not just yet."

Raidea was quiet for a long while.

"Do you want me to wait for you?" she finally asked Phanessa.

Si! Nessa thought, desperately. *Don't leave me alone!*

"Of course not, tonta," she made herself say lightly. "You're ready now. You should take the Trial now."

Raidea smiled forlornly at her, and Phanessa's heart twisted.

"Don't look so sad!" she demanded. "This is a good thing. A wonderful thing! A cause for celebration." Raidea's face brightened a little, and this time her smile was warmer.

"Thank you. I'd hug you but..." she wrinkled her nose. "You stink!"

Phanessa launched herself at her friend, rubbing her sweat-soaked face against her as Raidea squealed and tried to shove her off. They ended up on the ground, their wrestling kicking up small puffs of dirt. In the end, both girls ended up taking baths, their hearts much lighter than they had been before.

Raidea's Trial was held less than a month after that night. Phanessa rose early with her, as they had done for Damika, Petra and Taruka before. She noted the tension in Raidea's body, the dull fear behind her eyes and wished there was a way that she could shoulder some of her friend's burden. But it was all a part of the Trial, and it was not hers to share.

She sat meditating with Raidea far past the sunrise, and soon after the other trainees began trickling into the courtyard to join them. Some of the younger girls that Phanessa helped train brought her some food from the kitchens, a rellenito — sweet mashed plantain stuffed with refried beans and chocolate, and some jugo de mango. Touched by the gesture, she forced herself to eat it despite her nerves, the sticky sweetness of the fruit sticking to the roof of her mouth. Finally, after what seemed like an eternity, the priestesses roused Raidea from her trance and escorted her into the inner sanctum.

Outside the minutes, and then the hours crawled forward slowly. After a while, a nervous energy settled among the young women, and Phanessa could hear the rustling of restless limbs, and worried whispers circulating. She willed herself to stay calm, and still, eyes never leaving the sanctum doors. When Tz'ola began to dip her sun crown towards the western sky a small sliver of apprehension managed to slip past her defenses but she mentally shoved it aside.

Just because the other girls Trials took less time doesn't mean that there is anything wrong. No one knows what goes on in the Trials, this could be perfectly normal.

She almost managed to convince herself of it when she noticed Priestess Ianuaria join Mamá in her periphery. The healer was holding a basket of medicinal supplies and both women looked somber.

Phanessa's heart kicked wildly in her chest and her hands became clammy. It wasn't perfectly normal after all — something had gone wrong. Unconsciously she began rocking her body back and forth, her hands opening and closing over her crossed legs. Roaring filled her ears, her blood began to rush and her heart pounded far too rapidly. Raidea needed help. She knew it was forbidden but Phanessa needed to go to her, to go into the sanctum, to join her, to find her, to protect her friend!

She launched herself up and took two staggering steps forward, not sure what she intended to do but knowing that she must do *something* when just then, the inner doors creaked loudly. She stopped in her tracks, a small seed of hope blossoming within her chest. Slowly they were pushed open, until a hunched, bloody figure tumbled out, collapsing motionless on the ground.

Raidea!

Phanessa ran forward, reaching her just as Priestess Ianuaria did. Carefully Raidea's body was turned, and Phanessa recoiled in horror, a strangled cry breaking from her throat. Raidea was still, too still, her clothes were soaked with so much blood that it was difficult to assess the full scale of the damage. From what Phanessa could see, slices marked the sides of her legs and all the way up her arms, and her usually beautiful hair was matted with blood. But worst of all, the reason she had jumped away and had to force a rush of bile back down her throat was Raidea's eyes. The skin around them was distended and puffy, her lids completely swelled shut and rimmed with ugly purple bruises.

"Is she?" Phanessa whispered, afraid to finish her question.

Ianuaria shook her head and summoned a few of the older girls to her side.

"Help me get her to the infirmary," she ordered, and Phanessa stepped forward to help, but a strong pair of arms held her back. It was Mamá, who cuddled Phanessa to her side.

"Ven," she said. "Let them work, we can meet them in the infirmary in a moment." Phanessa watched as they lifted her friend's body and began carrying her away.

"Be careful!" she tried to scream at them, but all that emerged was a hoarse croak. The arm Mamá had wrapped around Phanessa's waist began to shake, and she realized it was her own body that was trembling, and shaking Mamá's with her. She allowed the woman to lead her towards her home, the small cottage sandwiched between two of the larger buildings. Once there Mamá had Phanessa sit next to the fire, which she lit quickly despite it being a warm day. After draping her in a quilt she wrapped the girl's fingers around a glass and made her drink. Phanessa knew her too well to try and argue, but once she had swallowed a few sips, her eyes darted to the door.

"Mamá," she started.

"I will walk you to the infirmary as soon as you settle your nerves," Mamá replied in a tone that bore no argument. "There is nothing that you can do for her that Ianuaria and the others aren't already doing. And you will be of no help to anyone in your state." Shame creeped up the back of Phanessa's neck. What kind of warrior allowed something like nerves to paralyze them in such a way? As if sensing the path her thoughts had gone, Mamá sat down next to her with a sigh, the top of her head reaching just above Nessa's shoulder. Despite her small stature, Phanessa couldn't help feeling like the little girl she once was under Mamá's care.

"When I was an initiate, I had a very dear friend," she began, and Phanessa jerked her head to look at her. Mamá never spoke about her time as a Danrayen trainee.

"I was not as fortunate as you to have such a lovely group, but there was one girl who was particularly kind to me and we became very close." Her eyes softened, as if remembering.

"Her Trial was ... difficult. We had scheduled ours close together, hers a week before my own. When she emerged ..." Phanessa did not interrupt her as she trailed off, simply waited quietly for her to continue.

"It wasn't like Raidea. The scars she held were not any that could be seen with the eye. Instead, her heart was broken, her spirit dimmed. I didn't know what to do, or how to help her. At least, not at first." Her face hardened, and she looked up at Phanessa with a serious expression.

"You think that your love for your friends, your caring, makes you weaker than the others." Phanessa tried ducking her head, but Mamá's fingers tilted her chin up to meet her eyes.

"You're wrong. It is your love that will save them."

Only after Mamá had made sure Phanessa had drank every drop of liquid in the cup, and that she had stopped her trembling, did she allow her to rise. Together they made their way to the infirmary, where Phanessa paced the halls until the Priestess Ianuaria finally emerged, looking exhausted. Phanessa ran to her side.

"She is resting," Ianuaria told her. "She is strong, and will recover, but it will take time. We may need to make a special allowance for her, and grant her leave to stay past the month."

Relief crashed over Phanessa so powerfully that it almost knocked her over. She hugged Mamá, tears slipping from the corners of her eyes. Her friend would live! The initial shock of joy at hearing of Raidea's well-being dimmed somewhat, however, when she realized that there was still a worry that weighed heavily on her mind. Steeling herself, she turned back to the priestess.

"Will she," her voice wavered, but she willed herself to continue. "Will she ... be blind?"

The hard lines on Priestess Ianuaria's face softened slightly, and she offered Phanessa a kind smile.

"I am a Danrayen Priestess and Healer," she told her, pride in her voice. "One of the best in the realm. I have done everything in my ability, but sometimes the dioses have other plans. I do not believe she will be permanently blinded, but should that be the case, Raidea will still be a Danrayen Warrior." And with that, she patted the girl on the shoulder and turned to stride down the long hallway, leaving Phanessa and Mamá behind.

Once she was sure it was alright, Phanessa left Mamá and crept into Raidea's room quietly. Her friend had been cleaned and bandaged, looking much better without the blood caking her flesh and clothes. Still, the purple bruising and swelling around her eyes was still shocking and ugly, somehow worse with the shiny, sticky salve that coated them. Phanessa had to close her own eyes and take a few deep breaths so as not to burst out crying. Not that there was anything wrong with crying, of course, but she didn't think she could do it quietly enough so as not to disturb her friend.

Later she realized it wouldn't have mattered; Raidea was in such a deep sleep that she didn't stir for days. In fact, she took so long to wake that Phanessa began doubting the kind words and reassurances of the healers, wondering if Ianuaria had been wrong after all, and Raidea's eyes would never open again.

Phanessa stayed by Raidea's side day and night, speaking to her throughout the day, reading to her, retelling stories of their days with Damika, Petra, and Taruka. She helped change her bandages and bathe her, and requested a comb from one of the other girls so she could brush out her long hair. At night she slept on a cot next to her, unwilling to leave in case she woke up.

It took four long days, but Raidea finally woke, able only to open her left eye at first. It took much longer for her body to fully recover, but in a matter of weeks she was taking her first hesitant steps around the temple grounds. By the end of the month she had reverted back to her bubbly, flirtatious self, but Phanessa could see the impish light in her eyes had been dimmed. They never spoke of it, of course, but Phanessa quietly mourned the loss of that lightness.

CHAPTER 12

When Raidea left the temple, Phanessa had never felt more alone in her life. She had lived without the company of family, peers, or friends for many years in the Palace. But back then she had not known what she was missing. Now, she felt it all too well. She missed Taruka's gentleness, Petra's loyalty, and Raidea's fun.

But Damika she missed most of all.

She often hoped that she would come back for a visit, as she had promised, but the years passed without word. Not even a letter found its way to her, and her heart broke with it. Some days she felt as if she would shatter from the loss, that it was almost too much to bear. But bear it she would, for she had not forgotten her path, and her purpose at the Danrayen Temple. She had a mission from the gods, and the wizard would come for her soon.

It was late afternoon near midsummer, not long before her 23rd birthday when Phanessa received a visitor. The High Priestess Adira herself sought her out in the training yards, where she was helping some younger recruits practice their sword holds. The priestess motioned for the children to leave them.

"There is someone here for you," she informed her evenly when they were alone.

Fear trickled down Phanessa's spine. Could it be the wizard? She had grown increasingly aware of the passage of time as of late, knowing that soon enough she too would be leaving the temple, the only place that had ever truly felt like a home, and the people who had truly felt like family. The priestess's eyes betrayed nothing, giving her no hint as to the identity of her visitor. And though they were alone, they were too exposed for them to speak openly.

Was it the Auberon? Would she be leaving? When? She wanted so very badly to ask.

Instead she simply nodded, and let her practice sword fall on the ground, which kicked up a small puff of dust upon its landing.

Adira motioned to the common rooms.

"You will find your guest in the second study."

Phanessa's legs felt stiff and disjointed as she crossed the fields. Her eyes took in every child practicing in the distance, the horses grazing near the stable, and Priestess Ovidia amid the livestock, breaking up a ram fight. She wanted to memorize every window, every statue, every discarded weapon and every blade of grass. If her mysterious visitor was in fact the Archwizard Auberon, it meant that her life as a Danrayen was swiftly coming to an end.

Stepping into the common rooms she stopped at a water basin to quickly wash her arms and face. She patted the remainder of the water into her hair, trying to tamp down the unruly strands that were gritty with dust. She did her breathing exercises, in through her nose, out through her mouth, a few times before her stomach and nerves settled. Finally, she squared her shoulders, and began making her way to the second study. She was no longer a small, frightened child. She was no longer even the Name-Bearer. And she may not be a true Danrayen, but her teachers and friends had ensured that she was a warrior nonetheless. She could handle the wizard. With one last fortifying breath, she opened the study door.

It was not the wizard.

He resembled the wizard, only a little. The man before her was much younger, thirty perhaps, and had a wizard cloak in the color of pewter that draped down to his gray boots, accentuating his tall frame. His black hair was thick and wild, his eyes a light honeyed brown, framed with dark lashes and hooded with even thicker brows. He had a closely cropped mustache and beard framing a top-heavy mouth and pointed chin. Besides his unruly hair, he appeared fastidiously organized, with nary a stain or crease on his clothing. Like the wizard she had met so many years before, he bore necklaces and talismans, but wore only a single ring which boasted a large black sapphire.

So, a wizard then. Just not the *wizard. Curious.*

She entered and shut the door behind her cautiously, and he greeted her with a formal bow.

"Are you," he started, hesitantly. She raised an eyebrow at him, equally unsure.

"That is, you are —" his voice was deep, but uncertain once more. Finally, he cleared his throat and asked; "Do you know the Archwizard Auberon?"

Phanessa considered how to answer. She was still not fully aware of how much danger the outside world posed to her... was she still sought after? Was she still considered a traitor to the realm? She thought quickly, her mind racing. It was certainly around the time that the wizard Auberon had said he would come for her, and the High Priestess Adira had sent her in to meet this man without a word of warning. Phanessa may not know this man to trust him, but she knew and trusted the priestess. Still, she was cautious in replying.

"I knew him, once. Many years ago." He narrowed his eyes at her, consideringly, then nodded, as if making a decision.

"You are her. Very well. I am Alric, the Wizard Auberon's apprentice. He sent me to collect you."

Her breath caught in her throat. So it *was* time. And yet, Phanessa wondered why he had not come himself.

"Where is he?" she asked him. The apprentice winced.

"He has been imprisoned."

"What?" Her heart leapt up to lodge in her throat. Imprisoned? What did that mean for her, and the quest? It was a selfish thought, she realized, to worry more about the implications to herself rather than a man in prison. She had no love for the wizard, but she wished him no ill will either.

"Why?" she demanded, schooling her voice. He regarded her incredulously, as if scarcely believing she could ask such a question.

"He has spent the last ten years garnering support for the Unnamed Prince. It has been a perilous expedition, but many royals and commoners alike believe the will of the Flowers to be far more important than the will of the monarchy. If they say there is another prince, a prince who will bring us peace, they are willing to support him instead, if found." Alric rubbed his mouth and sighed.

"But not everyone embraces change. Some are too deeply embedded in the old ways, and loyal to the crown. Word of his efforts reached the wrong ears, and he has been imprisoned for treason."

Phanessa crossed to an armchair and sat. Any other time she would have been too shy to be alone in a room with a man, let alone address him, but the news had driven any semblance of embarrassment from her body.

"What did he tell you of me?" she asked, having to angle her neck up to see his face.

"Everything." He crossed to her, and with an elegant motion swished his cloak out behind him before seating himself on a stool in front of her.

"He sent me to help."

"To help?"

"To help you find the unnamed prince."

Phanessa stared at him unabashedly. So, he did indeed know everything, then. She had never thought too much on how she and the wizard would find the child, but she had faith that he, as one of the most powerful men in the realm, would surely lead them. She knew nothing of this apprentice, of this Alric, and yet she was meant to help bring peace to the kingdom with him?

Not to mention that her experience with mages had not been a positive one. First, Auberon had played with her life as if she were a disposable piece to be moved about on a table game. Then Kichka had used her magia against her, and she had been powerless to stop her. The experiences had left her wary of those with magia. But if this man, Alric, knew of how they could achieve the task of finding the child, then she supposed she would have to at least accept his aid, if not fully trust him.

She rubbed her forehead, thinking.

"What have you learned?" she finally asked him. "Do you know where the boy is?"

He fidgeted a little on the short stool and cleared his throat once again.

"We know the last known location of King Enrique before he crossed into the Cassalan. He was in Lloronday."

"And?" Phanessa urged, confused. Alric looked deeply uncomfortable.

"Well, if he spent some time there, there may have been young ladies nearby. Perhaps in a nearby town. Or there are traveling groups of young women, who, erm, visit troops and offer them, some, well, entertainment." A blush was creeping up his collar and on to his cheeks. "Perhaps, the king visited one of these ladies, and ..."

"Are you trying to say," Phanessa interrupted him "that you believe the late King Enrique had an affair before his passing, and that it resulted in a child?"

Alric nodded, looking relieved. She nearly scoffed at him. Did he think she did not know what passed between two people who had attraction to one another? Or was perhaps unaware of how children came to be? *He should spend ten years with adolescent young women,* she thought. *Then he may learn that they are not nearly as innocent as he believes!*

"And if that child was born early, he could have been born the same day as Prince Frederico," the apprentice continued. Phanessa raised an eyebrow at him.

"It is what Queen Issalia named her son. Or rather what the palace scholars banded together and decided would be proper. It means —"

"'Ruler'. Yes, I know." Realizing something, she narrowed her eyes at him. "So does Alric."

He waved his hand dismissively. "A fitting name for a prince, but ill-suited for a mage and scholar, I'm afraid. How did you know this?" She made a face at him.

"Ah. Of course, my apologies, Name-Bearer." Phanessa jumped up, as if struck.

"Don't call me that!" Her voice trembled, with fear, rage or something else entirely, she was not certain. He had stood when she did and offered her another bow.

"My apologies once more. I am told you were known as something different here. What shall I call you?"

She opened her mouth to answer, and then shut it, swallowing hard. She had been Phanessa for nearly ten years. She had loved being Phanessa. But she could be her no longer. Phanessa was a Danrayen, an initiate training for the Trial of Danray. Phanessa belonged to a sisterhood, and had friends, wonderful friends who shared a common goal. But outside of the Danrayen Temple she did not exist, and she could not drag her out into that world. Phanessa's path was no longer her own. Once again, she needed to be someone new.

"Nova," she told him after a brief pause. "You may call me Nova."

He nodded. "A pleasure, Nova."

"And I know who Prince Frederico is," she snapped at him. "The priestesses train us on all relevant political matters. How else are we to serve the realm as Weapons of Danray if we do not know of the state of the outside world?" She was so insulted that he could think she was ignorant that for a moment she forgot she was not truly Danrayen.

"It's simply, well ..." it was her turn to fidget. She did not want to offend him, but, "after ten years, is chasing after camp followers the best you have come up with? And what if there were many women, and several had children? How will we know which one is the true prince?"

He nodded at her, and she was relieved to see that he did not look offended or annoyed. He began rolling up his right sleeve, uncovering a bandage about the width of her palm. He pulled it down, and there, on his forearm was a tattoo of a Flower of Prophecy.

"It has become a symbol for support of the Unnamed Prince, and a new royal line," he explained to her. "It is a dangerous mark to have, but mine is special."

"Special, how?" It was a lovely tattoo, but it seemed just that. A pretty drawing.

"The ink was mixed with pollen from the Flowers."

She sat down, hard.

"You —" her voice croaked in horror. "You *harvested pollen* from the Flowers?"

"My Lord Auberon did, yes." She stared open-mouthed at him, aghast. He shifted restlessly at her accusatory gaze.

"Yes, well. It was a risk, to be sure. But Auberon was sure he could find a way to spell the ink so that it would glow in the presence of the true prince."

"Glow..." she repeated, still shocked.

"Yes. It really is quite ingenious, you see, the pollen is what the bees eat, and they are the ones who find special children in the realm. They find the Name-Bearers, after all. Even you, though Auberon redirected them, they still were able to find who they were looking for. Now, using the pollen and modifying a spell from the Zocunsti Text he was able to -"

She raised a hand to stop him. She had little interest in magia.

"Will it work?" That was all she needed to know.

She had finally managed to offend his pride. He drew himself up taller, and the muscles in his forehead pulled down, drawing a sharp line between his brows. "Of course it will work."

"So that's our plan, then, to make our way to the king's last known location, and search for a woman whom he may have lain with, ten years ago? And hope that your marking glows in the presence of her child?"

"It is a start."

"I suppose it must be."

They agreed to begin their journey early the next morning, giving her a chance to pack her meager belongings. Their plans were laid out hastily, and he managed to bow to her at least twice more before she could slip out of the study. She wasn't sure whether to be amused or annoyed by his awkward motions. After leaving his company, she took a long, slow walk around the temple, lost in her thoughts.

She realized that while leaving at first light made sense for their journey, the young apprentice might also have wanted to give her the extra time to say her goodbyes. However, it was something that she simply could not do. If she let anyone know of her plans to leave, they would assume she was abandoning the path of Danray and would attempt to convince her to stay. As it stood, as soon as her disappearance was discovered come morning, all the Sisterhood would believe she had abdicated from the path. Only Priestess Adira would know the truth, but it was a truth that she could not share. There would be whispers and speculation, anger and pity.

Her departure would confirm what she had felt from the moment she had set foot in the temple ... that she was not strong enough to be a Danrayen Warrior. That she did not belong. Knowing that this day would come did little to dampen the feeling of regret and sorrow at leaving the home she had known and loved for the last ten years.

When she finally made her way back to her quarters, she found a satchel and bag by her bed, along with a water skin and some bundles that she assumed were food. The other girls were all out riding, or in lessons, so she had time to pack in peace. As she did she found there were also several of the small throwing knives that she preferred set out for her. Fingering their sharp edges her mind drifted to Damika and her endless hours of training, honing her one passable skill with a weapon. Damika would find her gone whenever she returned, with no explanation as to why she had left.

She would be so disappointed in her.

Lifting a large scrap of fabric next to the blades, her breath caught in her throat. Her mysterious benefactor, Priestess Adira, she could only assume, had also left her a traditional Danrayen blade, *La Espada*. Espadas were only to be used by Trial-endured Danrayen Warriors; they were an honor bestowed upon them only after they had proved their worth. The girls had trained with them, of course, but to have one of her own ... it felt wrong. Disrespectful. Almost sacrilegious.

Tentatively she pulled the blade from its sheath. The hilt was fashioned to resemble a butterfly, the body and antennae making up the solid grip with the open wings making up the guards on either side. The blade had a long cutting edge with a tapered point, and was impossibly sharp. Each Espada is meticulously constructed by the greatest Danrayen bladesmiths who imbue it with all the strength and power of the Danrayen order.

Phanessa gave it a tentative swing and the blade cutting through the air made a satisfying *swoosh*. She placed it back in its scabbard and set it aside for later. At this point in her life she had broken enough rules that she didn't imagine one more would matter too greatly to any gods who might be watching her. Besides, it was a gift, and she would not turn down such an honor.

Her eyes burning with unshed tears, she finished packing, placing her wool breeches and leather tunic on top of her bag to change into in the morning. They were her best garments, after all, and would be useful for the long journey ahead.

Stuffing everything underneath her bed, lest the other girls guess her intentions, she made her way outside. She may have not been able to say a proper goodbye, but there were those she wished to see before leaving for good. She spent a little time with Priestess Ianuaria, who had bandaged her wounds and healed her breaks over the years.

She had gotten to know the women a bit better after Raidea's Trial, and found she liked her easy way of being. She was always calm and serene, no matter how much chaos reigned around her. When she had first met the priestess, she had wondered how someone with such a gentle nature could have ever been a young warrior taking her Trial, but she was quickly dissuaded from that thought the first time she saw the strength she possessed, calming hysterical girls lost to their pain, setting broken bones, or holding down struggling patients. Then she could see the warrior within her clearly.

After, she continued to the outer fields where the livestock, and Priestess Ovidia, could be found. Her face had the same red-orange tinge as her wild mass of her curly hair, a result of staying out in the sun for too long with her fair complexion. It made Phanessa smile to see it, it was so familiar. She helped her to roll out a large hay bale for the horses, cows and llamas, an activity that left her damp with sweat, and covered in prickly tufts of hay. By then most of the young women had returned from the evening ride, and she joined them in the baths, washing the day's grime off her body while listening to the mindless but comforting chatter. She found she wasn't hungry, but made herself attend dinner, if only to soak up every last moment in the Sisterhood that she could.

After dinner she played a table game with Mamá, who, if noticed that Phanessa was quieter and more reserved than usual, made no mention of it. And if, when saying goodnight, she held onto her a little longer than their usual hugs were, well then, Mamá simply squeezed her a little tighter. That was her way, knowing sometimes better than the girls what they needed in the moment.

She didn't sleep that night, but lay awake, listening to the deep tranquil breaths and the occasional soft snores of the trainees, staring up at the ceiling until the faintest whispers of dawn could be seen through the window. Then she stealthily slipped from the room with her bundle, changing in the hallway so as not to make too much noise. Finally, she padded softly down the steps and out of the building, leaving behind the temple grounds for good. She understood then why Damika had not looked back, all those years ago. She didn't look back either. She didn't think she'd have the strength to continue if she looked back.

CHAPTER 13

Alric was waiting for her at the edge of the forest, a heavy-looking pack on his back and a carved walking staff in his right hand. She reached him just as Tz'ola's crown began rising over the neighboring hills. Nova approached him hesitantly. She may not have had time for embarrassment the day prior, but reality had set in during her sleepless night. She was about to embark on a journey, for goddess-knows how long, with a *man*.

Nova had never spent much time in the company of men. A few of her instructors in the palace had been male, scholars and professors, but that felt like a lifetime ago. And she had never been as bold as the others when they were in Pelgar, chatting with would-be suitors. What did one *say* to men? She rubbed her left leg with her right foot, anxiously, not meeting his eyes.

"Have you eaten?" his voice was raspy, as if he had very recently woken. She shook her head, and he frowned at her. "You don't look like you slept much either."

She shrugged.

"We have a long journey ahead; we won't have time to stop to nap or rest if you are too fatigued to continue. We must make good time."

With those words she was finally able to meet his eyes, gaping at him incredulously. How *dare* he!

"I may not be a true Danrayen," she growled at him through clenched teeth, "but I am no mere maiden either! I can keep up with a pampered palace mage well enough!" She stalked past him through the clearing in the woods.

"It's that way," Alric called after her, gesturing to her left. She squinted at him, an embarrassed flush creeping up her cheeks. She knew that! And if he hadn't made her so mad, she would have remembered. Raising her chin defiantly, she altered her course. As she had her back to him, she failed to notice a small, smug smile pull the corner of the mage's mouth. In her anger, she had forgotten her nerves at being alone with him. Whistling softly, he followed her.

The longer they walked, the more Nova forgot to be either nervous or angry. When she had joined the Danrayens she learned just how much she valued being outside, and their first day took them farther than she had ever explored on her regular excursions. When Alric noticed her bending to pick a few herbs or pocket some nuts or seeds he began questioning her, and she happily explained the medicinal uses of the various plants and how to spot them.

From there the conversation extended to the rest of her Danrayen training and she realized he was very much a scholar, peppering her with inquiries on the customs and practices of the priestesses and trainees. At one point, when describing to him a particularly disastrous episode involving her spear and General Alessia's trousers, he roared with laughter and had to stop to wipe the tears streaming from his eyes. Her stomach had jerked with the oddest sensation, and she was delighted to find that he was not as difficult to spend time with as she had feared. In fact, he was quite easy to talk to, and a good travel companion.

When the sun was high above them in the sky, he removed two rolls from one of his bags, passing one to her. Smelling it, Nova realized that last night's dinner was well forgotten and that she was starved. The roll was stuffed with cheese, herbs, bits of sausage and was utterly delicious. She ate every crumb and would have had another, but was too shy to ask. Instead, she nibbled on the nuts and seeds she had found along the way, offering some to Alric as well, which he took, more out of politeness, she thought, than genuine interest.

Despite his earlier protests they did stop to rest several times and refilled their water skins in a spring they found along the way. Before she knew it, the first day had passed and they were setting up camp for the night.

Nova gathered firewood while Alric removed a long, rolled up string from a pouch. It was the color of twine but more delicate, not quite as thin as sewing thread, resembling more a small ball of yarn. For a very confused moment Nova wondered if he meant to sit and knit? He didn't appear to be someone who would enjoy that particular pastime, but she knew better than most not to judge others on their appearance. Instead of pulling out knitting needles, however, Alric began unraveling the string and laying it down on the forest floor, forming a large circle around their camp with it.

"What are you doing?" she asked curiously.

"I'm warding our camp; nothing will be able to pass the boundaries without my express permission," he explained. She began lighting the fire but peeked at him under her lashes as he folded his long body down, sitting cross legged in front of where the two ends of the string met. He began muttering unfamiliar words, and a reddish tinge began marking his arms, neck and face where his skin was exposed. The color seemed to trace the pattern of his veins and flowed down to his fingertips where he grasped the string.

It was unnerving, and Nova wondered if the rest of his body also bore the strange red flow of magia. She flushed at the realization that she was picturing what was underneath his clothes, and shook her head to dislodge the image. The magia that Alric was pouring into the string traveled across its length counterclockwise, creeping across it like flame over alcohol.

Finally, the red sparks circled back around to the start where the mage's tapered fingers were grasping the ends of the string. Once it made a perfect circle, the power met, combining between his hands with a crackling hiss. A red transparent veil of energy shot up from every part of the string, bending towards each other and meeting once more above their heads, forming a perfectly domed shield around them. As soon as it had flashed, the light was gone, as if nothing had ever happened.

Alric pulled a stone from his inside breast pocket. It looked like black onyx but with added flecks and swirls of red, orange and gold. He sat still for a moment, clasping it between both palms. The red tint that marked his flesh faded into the stone, as if he were pouring the magia into it somehow.

"Que es eso?" Nova asked him, a little breathlessly, when he was finished. She hadn't dared speak to him during the spell, as her experiences with magia had left her wary of it. She had known Alric was a mage, of course, but she hadn't seen him perform magia until that moment. It left her uneasy and more than a bit uncomfortable.

"Just part of the spell," he replied, rolling out a bed mat. She was relieved when he placed it a few feet away from her own, not too close so as to make her feel uncomfortable. "We will be safe within the circle. It will allow you to leave and reenter if you need to relieve yourself at night, but I would suggest you hurry back. There have been strange tales about these woods."

She glanced suspiciously at the string. No echo of the unnerving magia was visible, and she wondered if she would feel anything crossing that boundary. Shivering, she decided that she would rather wait until morning if she had to relieve herself rather than pass through the magical barrier. Turning, she was about to ask Alric to let her know next time before completing the spell but noticed that he had instantly fallen asleep. She could tell by the slow rise and fall of his chest, and his parted lips.

Shaking her head, she laid down and tried to relax. She would let him know, and also ask him about these "strange tales" he had mentioned in the morning.

The next day was so beautiful Nova quite forgot her questions of the night before. Wordlessly they broke down their camp and shared some tortillas and cheese before continuing. Their path would take them deep within the Andalan rainforest, through the farmlands of Holencia before reaching the Great Mountains of the Cassalan border.

The journey would have taken more than a week on horseback, using the main roads, but they could not travel that way, Alric explained. The path was most often used by the Andalan army and the merchants who traveled in large numbers and hired armed guards for protection.

With the kingdom's soldiers and knights fighting the war in the north, there was little protection in Andala against bandits, flesh peddlers, and worse. Nova was well aware of this, and while many Danrayens chose to travel north to join the war after their Trials, many stayed to protect the realm for that very reason. Since the unsavory individuals tended to target the common roads, travel through the forest was preferable, but would take them weeks to reach the border, if not longer.

The brush was too dense for horses or ponies, and so they would have to walk the many miles on foot. Luckily the Andalan forest was nowhere near the Night Wood in the east, or they would have Night Wood creatures to worry about as well.

Nova thought the threat of bandits and flesh peddlers was quite enough risk.

Intent on their mission and their journey, time began passing surprisingly swiftly. Despite her initial reticence to Alric's warding, Nova was pleased to learn that their magical night barrier also helped to keep out the howling winds and the few bouts of rainfall that they encountered. They were lucky that they were traveling during their realm's dry season, had it been the rainy season they would have been soaked with rain more often than not. While she continued to be wary of magia, she grew more accustomed to it, and to the mage, when it was clear that he was not intent on harming her with it.

The days passed in amiable companionship, learning about and adapting to what made them both unique. While Alric was not too fond of the nuts and seeds that Nova continually picked (squirrel food, he called it) he did enjoy cui cui stew, and Nova began setting snares in the evenings before he'd erect the barrier and checked them in the morning to see if they had caught any of the small rodents, which they often did. Alric learned that she got easily cold at night and made sure to set his bedroll further from the fire so that she would feel more comfortable moving closer to it.

Alric learned how skilled she was at tracking prey, and navigating the sometimes overwhelmingly thick underbrush of the rainforest. Several times, when he would have cast a spell to direct them, she found their path instead by examining the shadows cast by the sun, or the direction of growing moss.

Nova found that Alric was easy to talk to, and they shared stories of their upbringing. It was difficult for her at first, having diligently trained herself to keep her past a secret, but as there was no need to conceal her identity to Alric she slowly began opening up to the mage. They spoke of the palace, and she was happy to learn that although he was not familiar with Rosa Maria, he was well acquainted with la señora Awaq, who was still the head palace seamstress.

"Do you know that she still pinches me in fittings?" he asked her, aghast. Nova burst out laughing at the look of disgust on his face. "Imagínate, at my age, being pinched for fidgeting!" She enjoyed these conversations far more than the ones regarding the scandal she had left at her escape.

"But it really wasn't my fault," she insisted to him one day, scooping to grab a fallen pitahaya. "Truly, the Flowers would not name him."

"I believe you," he told her earnestly. "I would not have helped Auberon all these years had I not believed that to be true. They are the Flowers of Prophecy, after all, and their prophecy is always true."

Nova frowned. "Then why —"

"The Queen Issalia, Falcon of Frost was born into royalty, lived in royalty and wed into royalty. She was told, her entire life, that she would deliver a royal heir. After losing King Enrique to the war, all she had to hold on to was that she would bear his child and continue the royal line. When she heard of the Flower's prophecy ... well. It was easier to blame a thirteen-year-old girl than accept that they would not name him."

Nova had never thought of it that way. Explained like that, she almost felt sorry for the queen. Then she remembered the fate that awaited her if anyone were to discover that she was the Name-Bearer. *Almost.*

She turned to him to ask about Princess Zerlina, the Queen's daughter who had been born a few years after the prince, to see if he had any guesses as to her mystery father, when out of the wood behind Alric emerged a creature the likes of which she had never seen.

It appeared quickly, breaking through a clump of bushes and barreling forward into the small clearing that marked their path. Nova hadn't noticed anything strange, or heard any sounds to give her pause. The Great Andalan Rainforest was full of animals big and small, and the rustling of leaves or movement in bushes was hardly ever a cause for concern. But the thing that emerged was no ordinary forest creature.

It was tall, taller than Alric, and his frame was well over six feet. It appeared somewhat like a large dog standing on its hind legs, but instead of fur its body was covered in a coarse leather hide. And its face ... its face was *wrong*. It had sunken-in eyes that drooped down into gaunt cheeks, which sloped in before jutting out aggressively into a protruding snout. When it saw them, it opened its mouth to reveal several rows of sharpened teeth and a rolling tongue which dribbled spittle onto the forest floor.

With a wild cry, something between a bleat and a screech, the creature lunged at them, approaching Alric who was the closest. The mage barely had time to turn around before it was nearly upon him.

Nova didn't hesitate. All semblance of thought, or worry, or fear evaporated and she acted on pure instinct and muscle memory alone. Her Danrayen training kicked in and she crossed her arms, pulling two throwing knives from their leather holsters on her sides. Bending her arms at the elbows she extended rapidly, releasing them from her grip with exacting precision, aiming for the creature's face. One hit the beast's open mouth, breaking off several teeth but doing little damage. The other embedded itself deeply in the thing's left eye. It reared back and screeched, forgetting Alric in its pain.

The mage stumbled backwards awkwardly, managing to half trip over his own staff. Before he could right himself, Nova unleashed her Danrayen sword and leapt in front of him, swinging the blade in a wide arc and slicing open the thing's stomach, dropping its contents in a foul-smelling, steaming pile on the grass.

The creature fell on top of its innards, instantly dead.

Panting and shaking with the fear-shock still coursing through their veins, Alric and Nova stood, staring horrified at the remnants of whatever had attacked them. Pinpricks of energy coursed through Nova's arms and legs, bringing her mind back to her tense body. She found herself acutely aware of everything, the light wind against the raised hair on her forearms, the bead of sweat trickling from her scalp down the back of her neck. Birds twittered and chirped, either uncaring or unaware of the danger that had been so close to them. And horribly, of the heady scent emanating from the fallen body at her feet, like sour milk, rotting fruit, and death.

Alric was the first to recover, turning to her.

"Thank you," he said softly, startling her out of her shock.

"What?"

"Thank you," he repeated, and crossed to envelope her in his arms. "You saved my life."

He pulled away quickly, but the contact had been long enough to make her already thundering heart jump up to her throat. The years with her Danrayen sisters had taught her to be more accustomed to touch, but she had never been held by a man before. The sensation was ... strange. She didn't like it, but she didn't dislike it either.

You saved my life.

So she had. It surprised her. She imagined her friends would have been quite proud of her, finally putting her training to the test. She glanced over at the thing again.

"What is it?" she asked him.

Alric approached the carcass slowly, holding a handkerchief over his nose and mouth to muffle the stench.

"I've never seen anything like it, it looks like a beast of the Night Wood."

"The Night Wood?" The thought alone was appalling. "This far out? They never venture too far past its edge; they cannot survive that long out of its shade. For something to have made it all this way ... it's impossible!" she resolved adamantly. The alternative was too grim to ponder. So absorbed in analyzing the creature, Alric barely heard her.

"I have heard stories..." he mumbled, using a branch to lift the thing's head. Nova shuddered and looked away. She knew that she should remove the dagger from its eye, part of her training included not leaving usable weapons behind. She thought of how Petra would have strode straight to it, planted a heavy foot on its skull, and yanked the dagger out without a second thought. But she couldn't bear to touch it. Instead she crossed to pick up the dagger not lodged within the creature, and swapped out a spare from her pack into her side holster.

"Perhaps it was a rabid dog?" she asked without conviction. Alric didn't even bother acknowledging her. They both knew it was no dog.

When he finally straightened and moved away from the creature his mouth was set in a hard line, and there were shadows behind his eyes.

"You'd best tell me about these stories, then," she told him as they moved to continue their journey.

CHAPTER 14

The Night Wood had bordered the Andalan realm, and others, on the east for as long as anyone could remember. The Wood stretched from the sandy coasts at the southernmost point of Andala, creeping up its length like tangling vines encompassing the side of a house, and even climbed the towering mountains that separated their realm from Cassalan.

From what Nova understood, the Wood was no better on their enemy's soil, and created an effective eastern border for them as well. In Andala the division between their land and the Wood was clear, grass or healthy rolling fields turn instantly to damp, dark earth, and the gnarled, twisting branches of the Night Wood's trees cast an unholy shadow which clearly divides safety from darkness, and death. It was unclear if the Wood continued into the north where the northern tribes lived, for so rarely did anyone venture to or from their harsh lands.

What *was* known about the Wood was that terrible, nightmarish creatures lived within it, and no one who strayed under its canopy had even returned. People did not enter often on their own volition, for tales of the Wood were recited to each citizen of the realm as bedtime stories since they were children. They were cautionary tales meant to keep them safe. The stories seemed more like the stuff of legend and myth, meant only to keep unruly children in line, but the truth was that the horrors which lay within the Wood were very real and did not need any embellishment to be frightening.

Every now and again some of the creatures would venture from their lands and cross into Andalan territory, terrorizing the towns closest to its borders. Las Salta-Sombras, or Shadow-Jumpers, were the most dangerous. They were beings that could hop from shadow to shadow in the blink of an eye, pulling unsuspecting villagers into their murky depths with inky black tentacles. Their foul limbs spring out from the shade like the cracking of a whip, snatching people away in an instant to be lost to the darkness forever. They only strike in the shadows of night when Tz'ola's protective rays are no longer visible in the sky. But they are dangerous, for Salta-Sombras are indistinguishable from regular shadows, and the reason why many villagers refuse to let their children out of doors after dark.

Because of the threat they pose, fires are also a recurring problem within those villages, due to the high number of oil lanterns that are lit and used nightly to ward off the dangers. Any hard gust of wind could knock one over, lighting simple wooden houses in an instant, engulfing several homes in flames before being spent. And yet, even the threat of a horrible and gruesome death by fire was preferable to falling victim to creatures of the Night Wood.

Ghouls and orcuyos are also a problem that need to be dealt with regularly, by the soldiers stationed on the rim of the wood, and the occasional traveling Danrayen.

The only solace that the people have is that beings from the Night Wood cannot survive outside of its boundaries for very long. If they do not return, they wither away and turn to ash within hours. That is why the insinuation that the beast they had just fought was a creature from the Night Wood was so alarming; they were days from its borders. It should have been impossible

As they walked Alric explained that in the capitol they had heard whispers of creatures that were wandering from the wood and surviving days, even weeks outside of its protection. They were dismissed as rumors, bedtime stories used to scare children into good behavior. Alric himself had not truly believed it either but was too sensible to dismiss them altogether.

"If it is merely a rumor, or a story to scare children, it is a cruel one," Nova grumbled. "Why would parents want to scare their children so horribly? Aren't the creatures of the Night Wood fearsome enough, without adding that they can now travel greater distances?"

"To keep them safe, of course. Parents will go to any lengths to keep their children safe," he replied pragmatically.

Nova's mouth twisted in an uncomfortable grimace. She did not know what parents would do to protect their children, as hers had handed her away. Logically she understood that they wouldn't have had any choice, but that knowledge made her abandonment no less painful.

"Besides," Alric continued. "We now know it was likely more than a rumor."

Nova didn't know what to believe. She had grown up hearing the same stories of the Night Wood for decades. To have the rules change now, after centuries of irrefutable stability, was a shift too incredible to fathom. Especially so soon after another once-in-a-lifetime event that she was a witness to herself; the Flowers of Prophecy refusing a Naming. Things were changing, shifting, and that scared her. What did it mean, and what part did she have to play in it?

After that day they agreed to begin their travel the moment the sun rose, and built a fire before dark whenever they could, making sure it burned throughout the night. Alric was confident in his protection spell and assured her that not even creatures from the Night Wood could penetrate it, but Nova slept better as far from shadow as possible.

The seasons slowly began changing and Nova realized that almost an entire month had passed since first setting out with Alric. It seemed almost a lifetime ago, and indeed in many ways it was; she had been a different person when they had first met. A Danrayen Trainee, with sisters, friends, a home and a different name. There she was Phanessa, Daughter of Danray.

Here in the Great Forest she was Nova, hunter, gatherer, adventurer. She felt a great communion with the plants and animals of the rainforest and enjoyed the almost serene task of their steadfast travel. Her skin browned and her hair, once a deep auburn, lightened to a more reddish tint in the sunlight. She felt a different sort of companionship with Alric than she had ever experienced before, one of intellectual connection and mutual respect. That was not to say that she had not experienced deep kinship with her friends at the Sisterhood, but there she was at times suffocated with the weight of her lies, and the unbearable fear that she would be found out. Her friends were loyal to Danray and to the realm, and as much as she loved them she could not be sure that their sense of duty would not have won over their bond of friendship.

With Alric, she could simply *be*. She had no need to prove herself or hide who she truly was. He knew of her past and was keen to learn about her very recent present. And despite the insurmountable task that lay before them, the dangers of discovery and the threat of the Night Wood, for a time, she was content.

One morning they awoke and found a light frost had covered the ground as they had slept. Their encampment was clear, of course, thanks to Alric's warding spell, but the chill in the air made Nova grateful that they were only a week away from their destination. Once they were in Lloronday they would most likely be able to buy winter coats, boots, and gear for their journey back. If they were successful in finding the prince, of course.

It was most likely the frost that saved them that day. They were walking quietly, as they did most mornings. Nova had realized very early on in their quest that the mage was not at his best in the moments right after waking, and learned to allow him to begin their conversations. If not, his mood was sullen and snappish, which would then turn remorseful. Which was silly. Some people were just not morning folk. No one dared speak to Petra before their morning meal, not even Taruka. There was no reason to feel guilty over what you were or how you were built. Nova smiled ruefully to herself at the thought. She had never felt anything *but* wary about who she was, and it was nice to know that others sometimes struggled as well.

She was yanked from her thoughts as apprehension slammed into her belly and she swung her arm out wide to stop the mage, bringing her other hand to her mouth to motion silence. He froze instantly, trusting her training and instinct. After a moment, she thought that she had overreacted and was about to apologize to him, embarrassed, when the tell-tale crunching of boots on icy grass echoed in the quiet glade. They dashed behind the trunk of a particularly wide ceiba as a blur of green and brown darted past them, leaping up into the branches of another tree adjacent to theirs.

It was a person, the hood of their moss-colored cloak pulled up to conceal their face. They swung a large bow forward and pointed it towards something behind Nova and Alric. Nova peeked around the trunk, her eyes widening in horror. Barreling through the forest were not one, but two of the same creatures which had attacked her and Alric weeks prior, the *things* from the Night Wood.

The archer let loose arrow after arrow, striking the lead monster's leathery flesh in rapid succession. Unfettered it pressed forward, seemingly unaffected. Neither the beasts nor the mysterious archer had yet noticed Nova or Alric, giving them an advantage. Nova reached for her blades, but the mage caught her arm, shaking his head. He motioned to their right, silently, indicating that they could slip away undetected. Her mouth dropped open in shock. Clearly he couldn't mean for them to run away and leave the single soul in the tree to the creatures? She ripped her arm from his grasp.

"Our task is more important!" he hissed. "I am meant to be protecting *you*." Without pausing to consider his words, she spun from behind their hiding spot and yelled;

"*Aim for the eyes!*"

If the archer was surprised at her call or by her sudden appearance they did not betray it. They launched two arrows, instantly striking one of the creatures in the left eye. Nova released her daggers, slicing the other across the nose and brow. Both beasts roared in pain and rage, but Nova didn't hesitate. Sending a quick prayer that the archer would not hit her by mistake, she pulled her Espada from her back and swung, aiming for the belly as she had with the first monster she had slain.

This time she struck too hard and the sword became deeply embedded within its flesh, and she had to abandon it to move out of range of its swiping claws. She ducked under the second creature's reach, rolling on the springy wet moss and pulling more daggers from her boots in one fluid movement. From her low position on the floor she managed to land a throw to its neck, but the other flew wide.

The creature, gurgling and spouting blood from its open wound, staggered towards her when more arrows pierced its torso, again and again and again, until it stopped, swayed, and landed in a heap near her.

Nova had not forgotten about the second beast, her blade still in its belly, but it was faster than she thought and one of its claws hit its mark, gouging her left bicep. Red electricity crackled in the air, hitting the thing, marking its skin with spider web red blotches. It stiffened and convulsed, giving Nova enough time to grasp the handle of her blade and wrench it out with all her might, spilling its innards on the forest floor.

It, too, fell at her feet.

Panting, she turned to see Alric pulling out his strange crystal from his breast pocket, a sickly ruddy tinge seeping from his skin into the stone.

"Estas bien?" he croaked. She nodded at him.

"Thank you," she said, a little breathless from the battle. Together, they both turned to look up at the mysterious figure in the tree, catching their breath.

"It is safe enough now," Nova called up to them.

They were crouched on a thick branch, the deep green leaves obscuring part of their form. Turning to face them, the archer swept back their hood to reveal the face of the most attractive man Nova had ever seen in person. His hair reminded her of the sunflowers that would occasionally decorate the palace, darker towards the roots and then tumbling into light golden waves that he tossed back from green, almond shaped eyes. His skin was tanned and flushed from exertion, and there was a smattering of brown freckles over his nose and cheeks.

A strong jaw was lightly brushed with a dark stubble which traveled down from under sharp cheekbones to stop just above his neck. Meeting Nova's eyes, his full mouth pulled into a roguish grin.

Raidea would swoon.

"Earth gods …" he muttered in an unfamiliar accent, gazing at her with clear admiration that made her stomach twist.

"Are you Danrayen?" he asked as he leaped down from the branch and began crossing to them. Alric shifted to stand in front of her, and she scowled at his back. Hadn't she just proven that she could take care of herself?

"Not exactly," she replied, stepping sideways to better see the handsome stranger. Alric pulled himself up taller, but didn't move to block her again. In any case, the new man seemed either unaware or unimpressed with the mage's bewildering show of bravado.

"What does that mean, 'not exactly?'" he asked, stopping a few steps short of the two. Nova realized that while tall, he was still shorter than the angry mage in front of him and seemed a few years younger as well. Perhaps in his late twenties. Up close she could see his bow was as impressive as his aim had been, and almost as tall as he was.

"It means I'm not," she replied, her tone dry.

"You sure? Because you move like a Danrayen. O tal vez eres una diosa, some sort of minor goddess who makes it a habit of rescuing helpless men?" He swept down into a bow, managing to wink at her at the same time. She blushed, and Alric bristled. *What is wrong with him?* Nova wondered.

"I was trained by them, but I am not a Danrayen."

"You left the sisterhood? Or were you kicked out?"

It was Nova's turn for irritation. Even if she *could* tell him her story, she had no intention of explaining herself to a stranger, no matter how handsome he might be. She rolled her eyes at him and motioned to

Alric for them to leave, which he seemed more than eager to do. The archer quickly threw up his hands to stop them.

"Alright, alright, none of my business." His tone was apologetic. "But you've saved my life and in doing so have earned my trust and loyalty. Two things not to be taken lightly."

Alric snorted derisively. The man glanced at him but continued.

"My name is Rawl. Come, I'll take you to my village where you will have food, drink and rest. My people will ensure that your bellies are full, beds are warm, and packs stocked by mañana."

"There isn't a village nearby," Alric finally spoke, his mouth pressed into a tight line under his mustache, and his voice dripping with suspicion. Rawl simply grinned.

"Isn't there?"

Nova grasped the hem of Alric's tunic and pulled him to the side, out of hearing range of the man — Rawl. He looked down at her, brows pinching together in concern.

"Are you alright?" he asked, his voice softening. Gingerly, he rolled up her sleeve to check her wound. She let out a hiss as the material pulled at the matting blood.

"I'll live," she replied. "But I could use some equipment, needle and thread, bandages, and herbs to keep infection at bay. And we could use replenishments of food, water... Lloronday is still quite a ways away, with no villages that we know of in between. We should accept his help."

Alric frowned. "I don't trust him," he glanced back at the archer, who was leaning against a tree, watching them through hooded eyes.

"Why don't you like him? We know nothing about him!"

"Only bandits live in the woods. What else could his people be?"

She swayed, slightly, on her feet. How much blood had she lost?

Noticing, Alric's face set in grim determination.

"But we are a mage and a Danrayen-trained warrior!" he declared, overly boastful, to make her smile, no doubt. It worked. "What have we to fear?" Nova knew it was his concern for her wellbeing more than a belief in his own words that had changed his mind, but she was feeling fainter by the moment and was grateful. Bandits or not, if they had medicines and food, she would welcome their company. Not all of them were bad; most were just ordinary, tired people who had lost their homes.

The never-ending war against Cassalan had required rations taken from hard working farmers, portions of their crops, their cattle and livestock which was their livelihood. Not to mention the war tax. Many families could not keep up with the demands of the battles and had lost their homes. It was true that some turned to a life of violence and crime in response, but many only stole from the rich caravans of nobles or, if they were bolder, the army supply runs to the Cassalan border. Besides, they had no proof that Rawl's people were even bandits in the first place.

Decided, she nodded at Alric and accepted his arm as support. Together they faced the archer once more.

"Very well. Take us to your village."

CHAPTER 15

Alric was correct when he said that there was no village near them. No formal village, at least, not one that would have been shown on an official map or scroll. But Rawl led them through a complicated maze of twists and turns that took them deep within the forest and made both Alric and Nova more and more nervous about their destination, and more importantly if they would be able to find their way out unassisted if they needed to. Less than an hour later, however, they broke through a densely clumped cluster of trees and emerged at an open grove that had both of their mouths dropping open with awe.

Trees and vegetation had been cut back to form a long oval glade, where tents and hutches were erected in rows, leading to a larger tent at its far end. The area was divided in two, with an open circle in the center where there was a roaring fire and spit. Many people were gathered there, dressed much as Rawl was, in long forest-colored tunics and hooded robes. There were men and women of varying ages, and even children scampering around the adults and playing games near the trees together. The appetizing smell of cooking meat wafted its way towards them.

"Who are you?" Alric asked Rawl, his eyes narrowing. Rawl grinned at him and clapped him on his shoulder, which the mage promptly shrugged off. If the action offended him, Rawl made no indication of it. Instead, he threw open his arms to gesture to the camp and said,

"Welcome to the Company of Padir."

Before Alric could question him further, Nova collapsed, the mage barely managing to catch her before she hit the ground. The men worked in swift, silent agreement, Alric scooping her up and following Rawl through a throng of people and into a green tent. Inside stood a woman perhaps twenty years their senior with pin-straight black hair that fell to the backs of her knees. Seeing Nova, she instantly cleared a cot, motioned for her to be placed upon it, and shooed both men outside once more.

"Vete, vete!" She flapped her wrist at them, tutting. "No use hovering over me while I work. I'll make sure la nena is well."

The men stared at the cloth door for a long moment, both unsure on how to proceed. Finally, Rawl scratched the back of his head and cleared his throat.

"Una cerveza?" he asked the mage.

Alric kept staring at the tent where his friend lay, concern etched on his brow. Finally, realizing there was nothing more to be done at the moment, he sighed and gave the archer a short nod. They moved away and Rawl grabbed a small boy by the back of his cloak as he was running past.

"Mijo, grab us two pints of ale, andale," he told the boy, who scurried off with a wide grin, showcasing his missing two front teeth. Rawl led the mage to some leveled tree trunks where they sat, stiffly. The two men waited in awkward silence until the boy returned, carefully balancing two large tankards of the fermented drink, one in each hand, his little face scrunched with careful concern for his task. They both accepted it from him, Rawl rustling the boy's hair and slipping him a bright orange from somewhere up his sleeve. The child beamed at his prize for a job well done and scampered off to meet his friends across the way.

Alric wondered where the archer had found the fruit, as it was still early in the season for them. Then again, the frost has come earlier this year, perhaps the citrus had yielded earlier as well.

Uneasy and distrustful, he frowned down at the beverage in his hand. Rawl pulled a long sip from his own cup and motioned to the other man's untouched drink.

"As you can see, mage, you are vastly outnumbered here. Had I wanted to kill you, I would not need to choose poison. You may be powerful, but I doubt even you could handle 30 men. And the women can be just as fierce." He grinned, and Alric noticed the man had a dimple in his right cheek. For some reason, it irked him, but he took a sip of his ale.

"Eso, mago," Rawl said, clapping him on the back and making the mage spill some of his drink over his trousers. Glaring, Alric attempted to mop up the mess with his pocket handkerchief.

"You said you are the Company of Padir."

"Yes."

"Are you bandits?" he asked outright.

"Do we look like bandits?"

"Yes," he replied honestly, taking another sip gingerly. Rawl laughed.

"We are not bandits; we follow the path of Padir." Alric frowned.

"I have never heard of Padir," he confessed. Wary as he was about the archer and his company, it was not his intention to cause offense. Luckily, it didn't seem that Rawl took any.

"Padir is a forgotten god, by most, but not by us. He was a traveler, and a trickster. He did not stay in one area for too long. His moods and temper were mercurial, and our people tend to be the same. Despite it he was fair, other than causing the occasional mischief, which we are wont to do on occasion ourselves." His green eyes met Alric's, twinkling over the campfire. "We go from town to town, bartering, performing, trading game for what we may need. We move often, but have several camps spread in the north of Andala, stretching from here to the sea."

Alric, ever the scholar, was fascinated, but tried not to seem overeager. Schooling his voice to casual nonchalance, he asked,

"And you are free to tell me this? It breaks no code?"

Rawl ran his tongue over his upper lip and laughed.

"We have many codes, many rules, but our existence is no secret. Our camps are well protected and difficult to find if you are not of the Company. If you have not heard of us, then I gather you must be from the south."

Alric drank from his ale, avoiding the question. The stranger might have piqued his curiosity, but he had still not earned his trust. Nor had he forgotten why they were there. He glanced behind them at the long row of tents, his concern for Nova clearly evident on his face.

"Rojya will be just fine." Rawl spoke softly, placing a comforting hand on the other man's forearm before quickly removing it.

"Rojya?" the mage asked, confused. The archer's dimple flashed again.

"A small, fox-like animal with a patch of red fur at the tops of their heads. Stronger than they look. It seemed apt, for your redheaded friend." Alric snorted, but when he didn't disagree, Rawl continued.

"Reselda is a cunning hand at the healing arts. Touched by the hand of Ixchel, she is," he continued, referring to the Great Goddess of Healing. For some reason, perhaps due to his exhaustion, the ale, or the easy comfort offered by the man besides him, Alric relaxed.

"Besides, it seems to me the girl can take care of herself. The way she handled those creatures... I've been meaning to ask, what *were* those things, anyway?" Alric raised a brow in his direction.

"You don't know?" the mage asked him.

"It's not the first run-in we've had with one of the monstros. Though I've never seen two at once" the archer explained. "But I still could not tell you what sort of nightmare spawn it was. Un demonio?"

"Do you know where they come from?" Alric pressed.

"Come from? They just appear!"

"Which way do they usually appear from?"

Rawl studied the mage's face intently.

"You're asking me if I've noticed that they come from the east. You can't be asking — you don't think that they are coming from the Night Wood? Its borders are days from here, a week, at least! Nothing from the Wood could last that long or make it this far!"

Alric did not answer, and Rawl grew quiet in contemplation. They sipped their ale, staring into the curling smoke from the bonfire. After some time, long after their mugs were empty, Reselda found them. Alric sprang up to greet her.

"La nena esta bien, she's fine," she told him with a cheery smile. "Strong one, she is. She's resting now, but wouldn't let me dose her with a sleeping draft. Says she needs to see you first." Impulsively, Alric grabbed her hand and kissed it before striding back in the direction of the medicine tent. Reselda lifted the hand to her chest.

"He's trouble," she told Rawl, fanning herself coquettishly. He shot her a flirtatious look.

"More trouble than me?" he asked, grabbing her other hand and planting a loud, exaggerated kiss on it. She laughed.

"A different sort of trouble," she replied, tweaking his nose. Then her face grew somber. "Mijo, Leader wants to speak to you. About your guests, I'm sure." Rawl nodded. He had expected as much.

"Take care," she warned him. "I like them."

"You know, I do too," he remarked thoughtfully, kissing her cheek and turning to follow the mage.

When he reached the tent, he found Nova sitting upright, her color much improved. Alric was sitting at the foot of her cot, and their heads were close together in discussion. They both jolted apart when he entered.

"Feeling better then?" he asked her, crossing his arms and leaning against one of the wooden poles. She nodded shyly.

"Much, gracias. Reselda is very skilled, and very kind."

Alric rose. "Thank you for helping her. I know that you offered us shelter for the night, and we will gladly accept, but we must continue our journey at first light."

"Our leader wishes to meet with you." Rawl told them. "It is a formality. No guests may be allowed in our camp overnight without Leader's permission."

Alric and Nova exchanged a glance. This was the first they were hearing of it. She lifted her brows, and the mage exhaled loudly through his nose.

"Very well, we shall meet this leader of yours. Where is he?"

"Leader is not he." Rawl corrected him.

"My apologies, where is she?"

"Leader is not she either." Alric glanced back at Nova, who shrugged.

"Then —"

"Leader is simply Leader," Rawl explained. "If you are feeling well enough, we should meet them sooner rather than later Rojya."

Nova glanced at Alric curiously at the last word, but the mage simply rolled his eyes.

"I'll explain later," he told her.

They exited the tent together, Alric stepping between Nova and Rawl. He led them down the long row of tents, around the raging bonfire and towards the large structure they had seen when first entering the camp. While the other tents were made up of wooden poles and loosely draped panels of decorated fabrics in bright colors, this one had thicker beams and pieces of thinly stretched leather to form the walls. The leather pieces, stitched together as they were, formed a patchwork tapestry in different shades of tan and browns. Two men guarding the entrance nodded at Rawl as he walked by. One of them lifted the fabric at the doorway to usher them inside.

The interior looked even bigger than it had appeared on the outside, with long, slender benches and pillows decorating its sides. There was a table littered with parchment paper and maps, and a thick fat candle slowly dripping globs of wax down onto its wooden surface. There was also a large tray with fruit, cheeses, and cuts of meat. Nearby, a large pitcher perched precariously on the edge of a small stool, and by the purple ring around its base Nova could guess it was filled with wine.

At the far end of the enclosure was a large chair, and on it, the person Nova could only presume was "Leader." She then understood why they were neither male, nor female, for Leader was somehow both and neither. Their face boasted liquid gold eyes framed with delicate lashes, which sat over the highest cheekbones she had ever seen. Their jawline was sharp, their chin long and pointed and their hair straight and unbound, flowing down past their shoulders in the same, strange honeyed-gold as their eyes, like a lion or lioness. They had an otherworldly beauty that was both delicate and devastating. The hands that perched on the armrests had nails painted in black and were adorned with several golden rings. At the foot of their chair sprawled two of the largest hounds Nova had ever seen.

All in all, Leader was an imposing sight.

Nova's court training kicked in, and she curtsied, despite not wearing a dress, and when that did not feel quite right, she straightened and saluted them with a Danrayen bow, right arm crossed to left shoulder, left forearm parallel to the floor, palm up. Alric followed her lead and bowed deeply. Leader motioned for them to approach.

"What have you brought me, young Rawl?" they asked the archer with an even voice, both melodic as a song and as sharp as a newly-honed blade.

Rawl plucked a grape from the silver tray and tossed it up, catching it in the air with his mouth.

"They saved my life," he confessed.

"Oh?" Leader cocked their head, eyes never leaving their guests. Slowly, Rawl explained the events of his day, how he had been tracking a fawn through the forest, and had stumbled across not one, but two of the accursed beasts that they had faced before. He had fled, with little hope of outrunning them, but found a high branch where he might pick them off with his arrows. But they had proved too tough for his weapons, and he feared that they would climb up the tree after him or knock the entire thing down to finish him off.

"But then, a voice rang out in the wood, clear as day, *'Aim for the eyes!'*" he said.

Nova blushed as she realized that the guards at the door, as well as several others, had made their way into the tent to hear Rawl's story. She had to admit he told it compellingly, though she felt he embellished her skills a bit.

"With a great pull she unstuck her sword, and the monstro died, groaning at her very feet," he finished, and applause rang through the tent. She ducked her head lower, hiding her flushed cheeks.

Leader smiled at her, not unfriendly. "Are you Danrayen?" they asked her. She couldn't help it; a loud sigh escaped her chest.

"She was trained by them but is not Danrayen," Rawl replied for her. "Seems to be a bit of a touchy subject," he added, and she scowled at him.

"There is nothing to be ashamed of, child," Leader addressed her. "Amparo, here, was a Danrayen, but did not pass her Trial." They motioned to a large woman in the corner who had come in with some of the throng to hear the story. Nova met her eyes with surprise, and the woman nodded at her in acknowledgment. She lifted her left sleeve, and on her enormous bicep was a fierce-looking butterfly tattoo. No, not a butterfly, but a moth. Close enough to the Danrayen symbol, but clearly distinct. Nova was impressed.

"Now she walks a different path, and there is no shame in it." Leader continued.

Leader regarded them with interest and a marked hush fell upon them. Nova resisted the urge to fidget. Alric stood tall, meeting Leader's gaze straight on, and she took comfort in his presence, solid and true besides her.

"You are not in these lands by chance." It was not a question. "A former Danrayen trainee, and a university educated mage. You are both a long way from the south. What brings you to these parts?"

Nova stiffened but attempted to conceal it. Alric shifted beside her, but she dared not meet his eye.

"We are searching for my brother." Alric told them, with not a hint of deception in his voice. She was impressed, as her history proved that she wasn't the most skilled at lies. Concealing her secret seemed to take up all her ability for misdirection, leaving none for everyday falsehoods. But Alric lied brilliantly.

"He is the youngest and was the pride of our mother. My family comes from a long line of soldiers, and as the oldest it was always my destiny to join the Andalan army. But when it was clear at a young age that I was gifted with magia, my education and training were provided for and he took my place as a soldier in the front lines of Cassalan. We have not heard from him in many years, and it was my mother's dying wish that I should find him, or at least what had become of him. We head to the border where his last correspondence was sent."

Leader's eyes shifted to Nova's. She did her best to appear nonchalant.

"And the girl?"

Alric didn't falter. "I may be a powerful mage, but there are many dangers for one traveling these lands alone. I hired her for my protection."

It was then that Nova was sure their ruse would fail. Trained by Danrayens or not she was no true warrior, these people would surely see that no one in their right mind would hire her for their protection! Especially not a full-fledged wizard who stood a head and a half taller than she! But Leader simply nodded, accepting the story, a long-tapered finger tapping on their lower lip pensively. Finally, they seemed to come to a decision. Meeting Rawl's eyes, they spoke.

"Rawl will take you to our second camp. There resides a seer, one with the unveiled sight. She will help you in your journey."

"She has true unveiled sight?" Alric asked, his tone surprised.

"I said as much, did I not?"

"My apologies, Leader." Alric bowed to them again. "It is simply that the Unveiled Sight is so exceedingly rare, I myself have never met a true seer. Nor have I heard of one living in my lifetime."

"Sarakshi is a secret. Her family has no desire to have her taken to the palace as an entertainment, or to the mage university to become a weapon of war. If our codes were not clear, I would have not told you about her existence at all. Once you have received her aid, our debt will be settled to you and you will forget of her existence."

Alric nodded seriously, but Nova could tell he was itching to ask about the codes. What code would cause these people to entrust them with such a secret?

"You have our word," Alric swore solemnly, and Nova nodded.

Leader lifted a hand, and just like that they were dismissed. Rawl escorted them outside of the tent. Alric and Nova both took deep breaths, and stole a glance at each other. Nova bit her lip, fighting against the desire to burst into hysterical giggles. What a strange day it had been!

Rawl began leading them away again, and with no other option, they followed.

"The seer's name is Sarakshi?" Nova asked the archer when they were a few steps away, the fall air turning crisper as nightfall approached. He nodded.

"Was that her given name, or what they call her?"

"Why do you ask?" He cocked his head at her curiously, casting a golden curl over his left eye. Something about the motion made Nova blush. Perhaps it was her distraction that caused her to answer, carelessly,

"Oh, well Sarakshi means 'good sight'. Quite fitting if that were her given name, wouldn't it be?"

As soon as the words left her mouth, she saw Alric widen his eyes behind Rawl with concern.

"How do you know that?" Rawl asked her, teasingly. "What are you, the Name-Bearer or something?"

"What! Of course not!" she blurted, panic lacing her voice. "There hasn't been a Name-Bearer in years!"

"Not since the betrayal," he agreed, unknowing of how much those words hurt her.

"Right," she agreed with him dejectedly as they made their way towards the bonfire.

"Do you think she really did it?" he asked them.

"Did what?" she replied, sniffing the air. The cooking meat which she had noticed before collapsing made her stomach grumble.

"Offended the Flowers? Betrayed the realm? Maybe the queen just didn't like the name and wanted someone to blame," he continued.

She was shocked at how close to the truth he was getting, and she could tell by the frantic look in his eyes that Alric was growing increasingly uncomfortable as well. Luckily, they had approached a small cluster of people who were indeed roasting a small doe over the fire. As introductions were made and food was shared, the topic, for the moment at least, was thankfully laid to rest. After their meal, Nova was finally able to pull Alric aside. He indicated for her to be silent and made a few motions in the air with his hands.

She shivered, recognizing the signs of a spell and he shot her an apologetic look. He knew she didn't like being so close to magia. When he was done, he tapped his crystal quickly and put it back in his pocket.

"No one will hear us now, if we're quiet."

Nova blinked. "They won't hear anything at all?"

"If they try to listen, they will hear the noises of a muffled conversation that they just can't make out. But we can speak freely."

"Que vamos hacer?" she asked him. "What do we do? We need to continue; how do we reject their offer and be on our way?" He sucked his lower lip between his teeth, brows furrowed. Finally, he shook his head.

"I don't think we do. Reject it, that is."

"You can't seriously mean to go meet this seer?" she hissed at him.

"She has the unveiled sight! I cannot even tell you ... this is a once in a generation occurrence if that!"

"So, you would rather satisfy your intellectual curiosity than continue our quest? Para que? You do understand that I will be an outcast and traitor until my fate is fulfilled, and you will be too, if you are found with me. Your mentor is in a palace cell, but you want to delay us to meet a girl from a child's story?"

"Think about it, Nova!" He placed his hand on her uninjured shoulder. It was heavy, and warm despite the cold. "She can give us direction to the unnamed prince." Her eyes widened. *Could she?*

"But how?"

"We allow them to believe we are going to ask about my brother. But when we arrive, we seek her council to find the boy. Then, we make our escape. Immediately."

"And if she tells everyone where we have gone? Of our mission?" He thought quietly for a moment.

"I don't think that these people concern themselves with royal matters. They say "the south" like it is a different realm altogether. They may exchange the information to some Andalan soldiers, but by then we will be far ahead of them. It's our best chance at finding the boy."

The truth was, they could use any advantage given to them. If they suddenly had access to a seer, a *true* seer, it couldn't be a mere twist of fate. Perhaps this was their path. Nova looked up at Alric and nodded. He smiled at her, relieved, and gave her shoulder a squeeze before releasing it. It was decided.

CHAPTER 16

The camp started early the next morning, with a fine breakfast shared by any and all who wished to partake in it. Nova particularly liked their oat and honey cake and had two heavy pieces, honey dripping from her fingers which she lapped up greedily. Alric, quiet because it was far too early for him, noticed and shook his head at her in exasperation, like one would to a small child. She merely stuck out a sticky tongue at him which drew out the tiniest of smiles despite the early hour.

When she looked away, he slipped his own cake into a handkerchief to surprise her with later. He shuddered to think how sticky the cloth would be after, but her delight would be worth the inconvenience.

Nova was able to find thick winter cloaks for both Alric and herself, although due to his height, the mage's would not hang far past his knees, and left much of his forearms exposed. Still, it was warm and would be needed, as the weather would get cooler as they approached the mountainous border, so he accepted it without too much complaint over the indignity.

That morning they also learned that they would not be the only ones heading to the second camp. A family of four, a husband, wife, and two young children were joining them on the trail. They had an elder daughter, they explained, that lived in the camp with her betrothed. The young couple had sent word that they had found a holy man to perform their marriage ceremony, and the family was to join them for the festivities.

They set themselves up near Alric and Nova, introducing themselves and chatting softly with the mage about the upcoming nuptials, their faces beaming with happiness and pride. Their children were two small girls of five and seven, and they stared openly at Nova in awe. During her time at the Danrayen Temple, Nova had learned that she quite liked children, and was very good with them, so she was surprised that when she smiled and waved at them they ran to hide behind their mother's skirts. She looked at Nova apologetically.

"Our women are quite fierce, but they haven't seen many Danrayen trained warriors. Only Amparo, and she isn't exactly the friendly sort."

Nova smiled and nodded, pretending that her feelings weren't hurt. Alric subtly reached for her hand and briefly squeezed her fingers, which helped.

Rawl found them soon after, looking earthen and golden and as cheery as Alric was dark and moody. Clearly the early mornings did not affect him! Once again Nova was dazzled by his good looks and sunny nature, her cheeks heating when he bent to kiss her hand in greeting. The couple received a firm handshake and a kiss for the mother, and the girls were tossed in the air and tickled mercilessly which drew delighted peals of laughter.

Rawl attempted to shake Alric's hand as well, but the mage turned, acting as if he hadn't seen him. Rawl's jaw twitched slightly, Nova noticed, but he hid it quickly, handing them packs with fresh food, bread, skins full of water and a small pack of medicinal equipment for Nova's injury.

He refused any payment from either herself or Alric, insisting that the code was clear. He was to deliver them to the hidden camp as payment for the life they rescued. Together they made their way out of the encampment, something which took far longer than it should have with the amount of people who stopped to see them off, give the Padir family hugs, or pull Rawl aside for last minute counsel.

When they finally found themselves in the thick underbrush once more, Alric seemed to be wrestling with himself about something. Nova was well attuned to his moods and was fairly certain that he was debating his dislike of the archer against his desire to learn more about him and his people. She whistled cheerily, hiding a grin. She knew which side of him would eventually win.

She didn't have to wait long. Not an hour into their journey Alric turned to Rawl and blurted,

"What are your codes? And why would you risk the safety of this seer for us?"

Rawl exchanged a look with the Padir father, whose name was Polo, they had found. His wife was Fernanda, and their girls were Zuri and Brianna. Polo and Rawl both looked at the mage, amusement lighting their faces.

"They are the codes of Padir," Rawl explained, patiently. "Padir is, as I explained, a lesser god, and a nomad. As are we." He angled his head at Polo. "Polo is our cuentacuentos! Why don't you tell them the story of Padir?"

"Si, Papa!"

"Please Papa!" the girls cried out, and Polo blushed charmingly at the attention. He nodded and took a sip from his water skin before starting.

"Once, long ago, the Goddess of the Wind and the God of Rivers met on a long stretch of earth. Instantly delighted with one another, the Goddess of Wind pushed herself over the River God's surface, creating rushes and ripples as they moved together. They danced in this way, swirling and playing and cutting across the land for many, many miles, and for many, many years until exhausted and sated, both went on their way. Neither god was a stagnant god after all, as it was in their natures to travel and touch every part of the earth, exploring every inch of space available to them. So, they parted happily, and as friends.

During their dance, however, the Wind Goddess had splashed droplets of the River God's surface onto the banks beside him. Without either of them noticing, the droplets mixed and tangled with the very earth and from the ground sprung the god Padir."

Polo paused his story only long enough to swing young Brianna to sit on his shoulders, who squealed with glee. Ignoring the plump hands that gripped his hair, he continued.

"Padir was the son of two traveling gods, resulting from their glorious play. And in that fashion he was a traveler himself, never meant to stay in one place for too long. And because his birth came from such a joyous union, he was also a mischievous god, quick to pull tricks and pranks.

Padir walked for many seasons, learning the ways of nature, the sun, and the stars. He made friends with the other minor gods and gods of the forest, who taught him how to hunt and ride upon the backs of wild stallions. He made wine from ripe fruit, swam with the spirits of the lakes, and danced with the starlight, living the new life he had been brought into.

One day Padir came upon a small village full of people. He had never encountered people before, having spent all his time with animals and the other lesser gods of the wild. Curious about what they might be like, he watched from a distance and came to develop an interest in one man in particular. Padir noticed that the man's profession seemed to include finding and catching wild horses, taking them back to his home to be trained.

Being a clever god, Padir came up with a plan to examine the people and their village more closely. He went out to a nearby field where wild horses roamed, and transformed himself into a beautiful, painted stallion. He became so lost in the thrill of running with his new friends, his strong, fast legs and the feeling of his white mane rippling in the wind that he forgot his plan, luxuriating in the sensation of living like a horse.

However, a few days later the man came out to the field and Padir remembered his goal. He saw the man take note of him, surprised at the new addition to the herd, and set his sights on capturing him. Padir gave him a good chase, for a thing well fought for is a thing well appreciated, but eventually let the man lead him home, a strong rope around his neck.

Padir lived with the man and his family for some time, allowing the man to train him. He spoke to the other horses in the man's care and found that the man was fair and just to them, treating them well with friendship and kindness.

But Padir's story is not always a happy story, for the god had lessons to learn. And one day bandits came to the small village, finding the home where the man lived with his family. Coveting what he owned they ransacked his house and attempted to steal his horses. When the horses spooked and rebelled, and proved too wild for them to steal (for in that moment they remembered the wildness in their blood) the bandits tried to burn them and their home to the ground instead. They set fire to the stables, leaving the horses, and Padir, trapped inside.

But the man was a good man and ran to the stables, rushing into the flames to open each stall door, letting all the horses go free. Before he could escape himself, however, the man fell from the heady smoke in his lungs.

Padir, having watched the man risk his life for the lives of himself and the other horses in his care, rode back into the stable and the flames and dragged the man out of the fire. Padir was very burned in the process, but such was the price to pay for someone who would risk their life for yours.

Padir stayed with the man and his family as they made their way across the land, seeking aid from their troubles. The first home that they came across drove the family away, shouting and yelling at them to get off their land. In anger, Padir snuck behind their home and stole a sack of grain, carrying it away between his horse teeth.

The second home was much the same, driving the family away from their land, and from them Padir was able to steal a basket of apples from the orchard, which the family then shared with him.

But at the third house the family was welcomed warmly, and plans were made to have them stay and build a new life. Padir, knowing that the man and his kin would be well cared for decided to take his leave, and left for them a braided lock of his white mane, which turned into pure gold once sheared off his horse head. And so, Padir's time with people came to an end."

There was a hushed quiet as the story ended, each person still lost in the picture Polo had painted. They walked a few more steps when Rawl broke the silence.

"When one travels as much as we do, codes are important. The first of which is to treat strangers the way you would want your family treated. The second is if you are treated poorly, that person is forfeit to their goods. Third, if someone saves your life, you repay them in the most thorough way that you can."

"Tell the rest of the story, Papa!" Brianna demanded, her chubby fingers slapping her fathers forehead with excitement. He winced good-naturedly.

"Please finish the story Papa!" Zuri agreed. With a smile, Polo continued.

"Well, after Padir left the family, he wandered the earth once more, still in horse form. You see, his injuries from the fire were so severe that he was worried that he would not be able to return to his god-body. Days turned to weeks, weeks to months, and months to years. Padir traveled so long and so far, he often forgot that he was not truly a horse.

One day in his travels, many years later, he happened upon a stunning mare the color of sunshine on a clear day. As she approached him he became embarrassed by the scars that marred his flesh, and turned to run. But the mare caught up to him instantly, as if moving over the grass fields by magia. When she reached him she ran her nose across Padir's injuries and they disappeared, revealing smooth horse flesh underneath

Then, in a sudden burst of light, the mare transformed into the form of a beautiful young woman.

'I am Eponine, horse goddess.' she said to him. 'I know who you are, God-son Padir. And I know how you have lived and loved my people, treating my children with kindness. For this, you have my thanks, and shall always call me friend.' Padir was so enamored by the vision before him that he remembered his true nature and body, and quickly transformed himself back into his god form. Once he was man again he took the goddess's hand, kissing it.

'I would rather call you wife,' he told her. With a smile as dazzling as all the stars in the night sky, Eponine agreed, and they roam together to this very day."

The girls cheered at the happy ending, and Nova noticed that even Alric had a small smile on his face.

They stopped for lunch not long after that, and Nova sat herself by a cluster of daisies. She began painstakingly weaving each individual flower together to form a chain, which could then be wrapped and shaped into a crown. Taruka had taught her how to do it, many years before, on a warm spring morning after training. She was not particularly skilled at it, but she was determined to win over the two little girls.

Seeing that it was fall, however, and that the frost had arrived early, the daisies were quickly dying, and she was not sure that she would have enough to finish both crowns. She was so focused on her task that at first she didn't notice the youngest girl, Brianna, slowly inch her way towards her. When she did her head shot up in surprise, making Brianna jump a step back, but the girl stayed close.

"Are those coronitas bonitas?" she asked Nova, timidly. Nova twisted the half-formed circlet on her lap.

"My friend called them 'Spring Rings,'" she told the girl. "She's the one who taught me to make them."

"Reyna used to make them for us." the girl told her, crouching low on her heels. "She said they were coronitas bonitas."

Nova smiled. The name Reyna meant "queen", and she found it quite charming that someone with that name would have made the girls "pretty crowns."

"Is that your eldest sister?" she asked her, and Brianna nodded.

"We're going to see her," she confided. Just then, Zuri joined them, clutching a small cluster of daisies nervously in her right fist.

"I — I found these over there," she said, pointing beyond a cluster of trees. Her voice was quieter and less self-assured than Brianna's.

"That's wonderful!" Nova cried, reaching out her hand. "Now I can finish one for each of you!"

Zuri observed her outstretched hand and hesitated, shifting on her feet. She was clearly still afraid of her. Nova's heart squeezed a little in her chest, but she kept the smile on her face so as not to discourage the child.

Brianna solved the problem for all of them, jumping up from her crouch, grabbing the flowers from her sister and crossing to press them into Nova's hand. Instead of moving back to her original position, she sat right next to Nova, pressing against her side to peek at her work.

"Will you show me?" she asked, her big brown eyes looking up at Nova without a trace of fear. She had won one of them over, at least! Nova smiled and smoothed her hand over the back of Brianna's copper hair.

"Of course!" she replied happily.

When they all packed up to continue their journey, both children had a bright coronita adorning their shiny hair, and Nova's heart felt much lighter.

That evening Alric unraveled a longer piece of string to create a larger encampment for their group. Polo and Fernanda were particularly impressed and grateful. Traveling a large distance with two young children was already difficult enough, and Nova could understand their appreciation for any added safety that could be provided. Still, she wondered if she was the only one who was put off by magia, and the strange tint of it that lingered in her friend's skin directly after casting it.

While Fernanda and Polo began setting up the camp the mage sat to rest, and the girls were climbing all over him within minutes. During their walk he had assured them that he could show them trucos de magia when they stopped for the evening and they demanded that he fulfill his promise. Nova lingered away from the group for a moment, watching in amusement as Alric began performing his "magia," which was in truth cleverly practiced sleight of hand. The girls, knowing no different, sat captivated by the show. Nova smiled, watching.

He's very good with them.

He was a university trained and powerful wizard, but the girls clearly had no fear of *him*, unlike their initial hesitation with her. But she didn't think it with any malice, as the girls seemed quite taken with her now as well, so she couldn't be resentful of their affection towards the mage. She watched as Alric removed an acorn from behind Brianna's ear, which prompted howls of laughter, the girl cupping her ear and tilting her head to see if any more treasures fell out. She was giggling herself when Rawl approached her, holding two sticks and string.

"There was a creek not far back," he reminded her. "Shall we find dinner?" Her laughter fell away as she shyly accepted the makeshift fishing rod and followed him. She waved at Alric as she passed, pointing to the rod in her hand. He glanced at her, his brow furrowed, a trick half-formed between his fingers, but she smiled at him with as much reassurance as she could and shook her head. When would he learn that she could take care of herself?

"Don't worry," she mouthed at him, and followed Rawl into the forest.

They chose a spot at the widest end of the creek in their view and settled down quietly. Nova tried not to fidget, keeping her eyes on the running water rather than on the handsome man beside her. She had just become accustomed to Alric, but he was, well, he was just Alric.

Rawl was ... different. He was mysterious and charming, and perhaps even a little dangerous. He knew nothing of her, who she was, or of their mission. He was dangerous because she wasn't sure that they could trust him, dangerous because despite that, she desperately wanted to. She was just relaxing into the lulling task of waiting for a bite when he broke the silence.

"I don't think that magician of yours likes me," he remarked plainly. She glanced over at him sharply.

"He is a wizard, no mere magician." She snapped; the irony of her words not lost on her. When they left him, he had been performing street illusions, after all.

"Just because he can perform tricks does not mean he is not well educated in true magia, and spell work." She shifted uneasily.

"Besides, he is not *my* anything."

"No?" Rawl asked, his voice a little too nonchalant. "Are you sure that *he* knows that?" His eyes met hers, and she watched as the corner of his lips pulled into a slow, teasing grin. She looked away, blushing furiously. What exactly was he implying?

"We have become friends. Nothing more." She was unsure why she felt the need to clarify the nature of her relationship with Alric, and it made her uncomfortable to do so. The green-eyed archer was far too adept at making her feel awkward and uncertain. Thankfully in that moment something caught at his line, and in the following moments that particular line of questioning was abandoned in favor of securing their supper.

Their meal was delicious, the fish flavored with herbs and spices neatly bound in cloth packets that Fernanda brought out for cooking. Polo cut thick chunks of bread, baked fresh that morning, and the newly formed group ate happily, scraping the juices of the fish off their plates with their crusts. After a quick argument about whether they still needed to schedule watch shifts for the night — Alric nearly purple with indignation that the effectiveness of his ward could be questioned by an *ignorant forest rat* — they settled down for the night.

Nova was impressed by Rawl's restraint, at the insult his eyes had merely flashed with ill-concealed amusement and he had thrown up his hands, claiming that "there was no use in arguing with the pompousness of uppity scholars." He had shown remarkable self-control, as in the Danrayen Temple furious fights had been started for much less. She couldn't help but remember all of the brawls that Petra and Raidea would get into, and she drifted off to sleep with a small smile playing on her lips.

CHAPTER 17

Many miles away

Damika sat in front of the campfire, a thick fur strewn across her lap to ward off the evening chill. In her hands she twirled a small item, watching the light of the flames glint off of its reflective surface. Her mind, and her heart, were far away.

"Dami," Taruka called softly, stepping out from a cluster of trees as quietly as smoke over water. She glided just as gracefully towards their camp, a couple of wild fowls clutched in one hand, her bow in the other. The fowls were thin, winter had hit much quicker in this part of the tierra, and game had been scarce for weeks. But thanks to Taru's skill with a bow, their party had not gone hungry.

Yet.

Taruka elegantly folded her long frame and sat next to Damika, placing her catch on a wooden stump but keeping her bow close. Night had fallen, and the dark had become even more dangerous as of late.

"Why don't you try to get some rest?" Taruka asked her, motioning to the small tents where Petra was already asleep. "I'll take watch for a while."

Damika clutched the item in her hand harder, its sharp edges digging into her palm. The pain pulled her from her stupor, sharpening her wits. She shook her head.

"No, it's alright. I'm not tired. You get some rest. Leave those birds; I'll prepare them for tomorrow."

Taruka nodded, but made no move to leave. They sat together in silence, watching the tendrils of smoke lift and dance through the cold night air. The air was clear and crisp, and the stars shone brightly above their heads like a canopy of fine jewels. A little to the south, the constellation Danray was visible, her sword held high in the night sky.

After a little while, Damika's shoulders relaxed, though she hadn't even noticed how tense they had been to begin with. She knew that this was Taruka's way. She wouldn't push, wouldn't intrude, but was simply there for you until you felt comfortable enough to unburden your mind.

Damika sighed.

"It's been years, Taru. Years, and we're no closer than when we started."

"You don't know that. We receive new information all the time, and we follow it to its source. One day, it will lead us to where we need to be."

"What if it doesn't?" It was Damika's greatest fear. "What if these years have been for naught? What if I pulled you and Petra away from accomplishing great deeds for this, some foolish quest?"

Taruka placed a gentle hand over Damika's clenched fist.

"Petra and I chose to come with you. We were delighted when you sent for us. There is nowhere we would rather be. If Raidea's Trial hadn't been so difficult, I'm sure she would have joined us as well. And once Nessa —"

Damika shifted her hand from under Taru's, looking away. Taru didn't continue. Damika rarely wanted to speak about Nessa, and with Petra's soft snores reaching them across the campfire, she understood why. Her heart ached with it.

"We will find what we came for," Taru assured her friend. "We knew it wouldn't be simple, that it would take time. At least we three are together now. We'll all be together again some day, I'm sure of it."

Bracing herself on Damika's shoulder, Taruka rose once again, and crossed to the tent she shared with Petra. Adjusting herself into the small space she lay down and gathered Petra close to her, sniffing back her tears. Petra, who hadn't so much as shifted when Taru had entered, was instantly awake at the sound. She turned in her arms, cupping Taru's face between her strong, calloused hands.

"Are you crying?" she demanded, running her thumbs beneath her eyes. "Why are you crying, mi amor? Tell me who to kill." Taruka responded with a watery chuckle, clasping one of Petra's hands in her own and moving it down her face to kiss her palm.

"I'm just so grateful that we're together," she confessed, and felt a twinge of guilt that she had so much when so many others didn't.

Petra relaxed and pulled Taru close to plant a gentle kiss on her lips.

"We'll always be together."

"Do you think we'll *all* be together again?"

Petra glanced out towards the fire, and Damika, knowing exactly what Taru was asking. She pulled her back down into her arms, tracing soothing patterns on her love's back. Taruka relaxed into her embrace.

"The Goddess Danray will see us all together again. You'll see amor, you'll see."

As they drifted to sleep in the comfort of one another, Damika sat outside alone, between her fingers the small amber butterfly pendant, twirling around and around in the firelight.

CHAPTER 18

The next morning, Nova was delighted to find that after washing, the girls insisted on wearing their flower crowns for the journey, and that Brianna even snuggled into her lap for their morning meal, still sleepy and warm.

"Today's journey will be a bit more difficult than yesterday." Rawl warned them. He pointed to a looming cliff in the distance. "We must climb that to descend the other side."

Both Nova and Alric looked at the cliff's steep face with concern. It was high and sharp, no doubt with treacherous loose rocks and stones that would make their climb difficult. Not to mention they had no way of knowing what was on the other side of it, or if it was more perilous than the part they could see. Nova's arm tightened slightly around Brianna, who she held against her, the heavy-eyed girl playing quietly with the leather laces of her shirt.

"The children?"

Polo and Rawl took out two large strips of embroidered cloth, and with Fernanda's help showed them how they could be fashioned into slings which could bear the girls on their backs. Nova was still uneasy, and she could tell that Alric was as well, but the Padirs insisted that they would be fine. But Rawl was not finished yet.

"There is more. On the ridge of the cliff there is, well, a carriage of sorts."

"A carriage on a mountain?" Alric asked suspiciously. When he glanced at Nova she simply shrugged. It made no sense to her either.

"It is a carriage attached to a pulley system. The ropes extend across the canyon on the other side of the cliff and will make our descent far easier."

Nova and Alric exchanged another worried look, but they nodded. Both were educated people, and they understood the mechanics of such a contraption, even if neither had seen one in person. Nova never thought that she had an issue with heights, but the idea of being suspended over a precipitous drop made her stomach churn. But if that was the way to the camp, and the seer, then that was the way that they would go.

Working together they all made quick work of breaking down the camp and began walking once more. For much of the journey Zuri walked side by side with her mother, but Brianna chose to stay tight to Nova's side, her little legs moving quickly to keep up with the long-legged strides of the adults. Still, she never once complained, and talked Nova's ear off about her friends back at the Padir camp, about her sister Reyna's upcoming nuptials, the dress she might wear for the celebration, and more.

When she realized that Nova would lean down to scoop up certain fallen nuts and fruits off the jungle floor, she began scanning the ground herself, helping her to collect them. At a certain point, when Alric was well entertained by peppering Polo and Fernanda with more questions about the Padir people, Rawl dropped back to walk by Nova.

"You've quite the shadow there," he remarked, ruffling Brianna's hair. The girl wordlessly lifted her arms and he scooped her up without question. She tucked her head underneath his chin and shut her eyes, the exertion of the day catching up to her.

"I like children," Nova admitted, smiling at the picture they painted.

"Planning on having a litter of your own then?" he asked her, and she gaped at him. Children of her own?

"I — I suppose I never thought about it," she confessed, a bit dumbfounded by the prospect. She never had the luxury of imagining a normal life, at least not for very long. But if they found the true prince, and returned him to the palace ... if there was truly peace to come in Andala ...

But no. Those were dangerous thoughts. Fanciful, even. It was best to only consider the next foot forward. Right now, her mission was to find the boy and to keep him safe. Whatever she may want, the type of life she may wish to lead, well, that would simply have to wait. A thought occurred to her.

"Do *you* have children?" she asked him.

"No, though I intend to, later in life. Several, if I can. There are so many children left orphaned by the war. If I can settle down long enough, if I can find the right partner, I would like to take some in."

It surprised her. She hadn't thought that a man would think of such things, providing homes to children in need. It made her like him a little bit better. Perhaps that was the reason why she began telling him of the young children that join the Danrayens, the fierce little girls that choose a warrior's path and work every day to achieve their goal. He questioned her about her life with the Sisterhood, and when he avoided asking her about her departure from their sect, she relaxed into their comfortable exchange.

He told her about his own upbringing and the nomadic way of the Padir, how his mother raised him and his younger sister alone.

He explained that he and the other Padir children of his group would perform acrobatic tricks in towns they frequented for spare change. They were laughing — quietly as Brianna had fallen asleep in his arms — about a particular "failed" tumble that had knocked him into a nobleman, and how that nobleman had left that day with a missing purse, when she noticed Alric scowling at them. Rawl sighed.

"Your mage is still not warming up to me." She shot him a warning look and he smiled ruefully.

"My apologies. *The* mage is not warming up to me."

"He just doesn't know you yet."

Nova watched Rawl's face as he regarded Alric. His lips were pressed into a tight line, and he almost looked disappointed. But then he caught her eye and the look fell away, his signature grin back on his lips.

"But I can survive his dislike as long as you and I are friends, Rojya!" He bumped her arm with his elbow, and she turned the color of his nickname for her, which made him laugh. His company and stories had made quick work of the long walk, and before she knew it, it was midday and they had reached the base of the cliff. Brianna woke up full of renewed energy, and they all sat in the shade of a large tree to have a quick, light meal before ascending.

Nova was relieved to see that there was a narrow path that looped upwards and would provide surer footing than hiking alone. When they were finished, Fernanda helped Zuri and Brianna into their slings, Brianna with her father and Zuri with Rawl, since "Rawl already carried Brianna all morning and it wasn't fair" according to the older girl. It seemed his charm extended to all ages.

Then, together, they began to climb.

There was little time or energy for idle conversation, as every moment was spent ensuring their balance and slow, steady progression up the cliff. Twice, Nova's heart leaped into her throat, once when Alric tripped in front of her, the other when Polo's leg slipped off the side of the rock face. He was able to grasp a thick root to keep from toppling over the edge, but Brianna's startled shriek was enough to tighten the muscles in her neck and shoulders painfully and cause her blood to rush to her ears in a frantic drumbeat.

By the time they reached the peak Nova had a newfound respect for the Padir family. She had been training every day of her life for the past ten years and even her legs were burning from the exertion, but they, and Rawl, seemed fine. In wordless agreement they moved away from the precipice and sprawled out on the dry ground, drinking deeply from their water skins.

The girls were released from their slings and ran about, far more rested than the adults. Nova's ego was slightly mollified to see that Alric was in worse shape than she was, his face red and blotchy and his legs shaking slightly. After a few minutes he began to look around the clifftop, which was a large plateau of mostly rock with a patch of tall trees to their right.

"I see no 'carriage,'" he said. Rawl nodded, and pointed to the opposite precipice, several yards from where they were seated.

"It is on the other side of the ledge, with an overhang to conceal it. Though anyone walking nearby could see the ropes."

"That doesn't seem —" but whatever Alric was about to say was drowned out by Fernanda, who gasped and sprang up from her seated position, grabbing at Zuri and Brianna. The rest of the group swung around to see what had caught her attention, and Nova's blood ran cold. Out of the covering of the cluster of trees to their right, men began to emerge, all of them holding weapons, and chains.

Flesh peddlers.

Polo and Fernanda scrambled up grabbing their things, Rawl stringing his bow, Nova unsheathing her blade and Alric raising his staff.

"Hurry!" Polo cried to them, swinging Zuri over his shoulder and sprinting towards the cliff's edge where Fernanda was already heading, Brianna in tow. "If we reach the carriage, they won't be able to stop us!"

Men continued to stream out of the woods, yelling words to each other that were swallowed up by the roaring wind of the clifftop. Rawl released arrow after arrow, hitting several men as he ran backwards towards Polo. Nova grabbed the back of his tunic and guided him, so he could continue firing as they moved.

"Help the family!" she yelled to Alric, and had to repeat herself over the wind. He hesitated only a moment, and then dashed to where they had disappeared over the edge. By then one of the bandits had reached her and Rawl, coming up on their side where the archer had no clear shot. Still holding on to him she swung her Espada high and quickly, cutting the bandit's neck before he even realized that she was holding a weapon.

Her stomach turned and she had to swallow back bile - there was no time to consider the first human life she had taken.

They reached the edge, Rawl still dropping men with his exacting aim. She looked down and saw a ledge where a vessel of sorts was attached to ropes leading down and away from the cliff over a long canyon. Polo was lifting Brianna inside of it to join her mother and Zuri, but the girl was crying and struggling. Her wails were loud enough that even Nova could hear her.

"My crown! Mi coronita bonita!" she was crying. Out of the corner of her eye, Nova could see the twisted flower garland trembling in the wind, caught between two large boulders. Polo hopped in afterwards, and she motioned for Alric to do the same. Rawl cursed and dropped to his knees, his bow knocked out of his hands by the bandit's archer.

"Lucky shot," he grumbled as she gripped him under his arm and hauled him up. She shoved him towards the carriage where Alric and Polo helped draw him over the wooden slats. In the commotion, no one noticed little Brianna squeezing through the wood and rushing to grab her flower crown. Fernanda screamed and when Nova turned, three men had jumped down to their ledge, and one had caught Brianna in his dirty, meaty hands.

Rage engulfed Nova, burning her from inside out.

She abandoned her blade for fear of accidentally striking the child. She leapt instead, extending her leg to kick the bandit closest to her in the stomach. As he bent over, gasping in pain she used his own momentum against him, careening him over the ledge. She whirled to face the one who had Brianna and extended her same leg, breaking his shin.

When he fell to his knees, she wrenched the girl out of his hands and spun back to her group, shoving her at Polo who was half out of the carriage and staining his arms out towards her.

The bandit who had escaped injury grabbed her from behind, but at least Polo had Brianna back. She watched in horror as two more men jumped down to their ledge and made their way towards her group, and noticed Alric and Rawl attempting to leave the confines of the carriage to reach her.

Looking up she could see there were at least five more bandits ready to join their brethren, her group was far too outnumbered to survive. Alric and Rawl would be killed, Polo sold into slave labor, and Fernanda and the girls ... they would face a worse fate.

Nova screened the contraption quickly, searching — and then found it. The rope keeping it perched on the ledge.

She slammed her head backwards, breaking her assailant's nose. His grip loosened long enough for her to grab the dagger hidden in her boot. She exhaled and threw it forward, splitting the rope in a single motion. The carriage lurched and began propelling her friends down the hill.

One of the men struck her on the back of her head, making her pitch, her legs wobbly. She would have fallen off the edge herself had rough hands not prevented her. She was hoisted back up to the plateau where more men were crowded.

"Apúrense! Restrain her!" one cried out.

"The girls —"

"Forget the girls! You see that sword? That's Danrayen. We've caught ourselves a Danrayen!"

There were murmurs of interest and awe. She didn't bother correcting them. Woozy, Nova realized that they must have brought up her blade as well. Glancing around she saw it was being held by a large man with stringy, greasy hair and a missing front tooth. If only she could reach it ... but her vision was blurry, and her limbs felt weak.

"Little girls fetch a pretty penny, but there are some who will pay even more for a pet killer."

Killer! She railed internally, throwing a few wild kicks in their direction. *Danrayens are warriors, battling for the honor and glory of Danray! They are no mere soldiers, or paid assassins.* Nova felt a quick burst of pleasure when she heard one of her captors gasp and drop to his knees. Her foot had met its mark at a particularly vulnerable piece of his anatomy.

Her satisfaction was short-lived, however, as her punishment was a sharp backhand to her face. Gritting her teeth, she panted against the stinging pain in her right cheekbone and eye. The pain in her head intensified and her vision faded in and out. Even so, she continued to struggle against her bindings as best she could.

"Some men even like a woman who will put up a struggle in the bed chambers," one of the cucarachas professed, reaching towards her to brush some hair off her face. She snapped her jaws at him, a mere inch away from sinking her teeth into the soft flesh off his hand. He pulled away quickly as his companions laughed uproariously.

"Of course, I love my anatomy a little too much for that risk," he continued unaffected, with a repulsive grin. The group laughed again as Nova seethed. If any one of them attempted to lay a hand on her ...

But her hands had been bound behind her, attached by a chain to shackles placed around her ankles. If she hadn't been so angry and frightened, she might have been flattered at the level of precaution they had taken with her. She was hauled up to her feet, and with continual shoves was made to shuffle forward, following the rest of the company.

"Throw her in with the savage," the man with the missing tooth said. Nova thought he might be the leader. "Can't have her too close to the goods."

They broke through the cluster of trees and into a small wood atop the cliff. As they continued walking, Nova realized that it extended for far longer than it would appear on the rocky part of the plateau. She was unsure how long they had been traveling before they stopped, as her head injury blurred both her vision and her awareness, but they finally reached its right-most edge. An entire slope of the hill had been cleared of trees, and ropes had been attached from stump to stump for an easier climbing path. At its bottom she could see the faint curling wisps of campfire smoke, and large wooden enclosures that were unmistakable even from a distance.

Slave-carriages. It was a full bandit camp. How long had it been since the Padir people had used this particular route? Clearly not for many months if they had not noticed an entire bandit camp set up at the cliff's base.

Nova was not aware of just how she made it down the hill. She was most likely carried, as she began to fade in and out of consciousness. The next thing she could remember clearly was that she was inside one of the cages.

She opened her eyes slowly, blinking heavily to clear her hazy vision. Her head pounded, making her feel like her very skull was expanding with every beat. Her bruised cheek stung, and the pain was not aided by the fact that the injured side of her face was pressed against old and splintering wood that smelled of damp rot. She was sprawled out face down just inside the door as if someone had tossed her in, leaving her where she landed.

Slowly, very slowly, she shifted her arms in front of her and braced them, pushing herself up into a half-seated position. She took a few unsteady breaths before raising her head and looking around her enclosure. There, in the corner, muscular arms crossed around his knees, was a large man with warm, dark skin, like the bark of a tree bathed in sunlight, smooth and rich. Her eyes met his, and she was reminded of a forest pool at midnight.

Though she was locked in a small space with him she did not immediately feel threatened or defensive, everything about him felt deeply rooted to the earth. That is, until she sat up fully and was able to view him more completely. With a sinking feeling she realized that he was wearing the underclothes of a soldier's armor, but not in Andalan colors.

While their soldiers wore purple, he wore red.

He was a member of the Cassalain army.

CHAPTER 19

lric was half out of the carriage before Rawl could grab him and haul him back in, the wizard nearly propelling them both to the canyon floor in the effort.

"Are you insane, mago? You'll plummet to your death!" he yelled, both to be heard over the rushing of the wind as they descended and out of sheer fury. He had the mage's upper arms gripped tight and gave him a hard shake for good measure. "What are you going to do, scale the ropes back up the mountain?"

"I must do something!" Alric roared back, desperation making his voice crack. His eyes were fixed on the top of the summit, straining to see anything, but it only got smaller and smaller as they fell away.

"We will get her back," Rawl growled, shaking him again. "Mirame, mago. *Look at me!*" Alric reluctantly tore his eyes away and twisted his head to peer into the earnest green ones in front of him.

"We will get her back." Rawl repeated. Alric stared at him miserably for a moment, searching. Whatever he saw in Rawl's gaze convinced him, and he nodded dejectedly. Rawl, convinced that the wizard was not about to throw himself off their transport, released his hold on his arms. Behind them, Polo and Fernanda were trying to comfort the wailing Zuri and Brianna. It was their terror, more than anything that made the mage collect his wits and accept that there was nothing to be done at the moment.

"No lloren, don't worry," Alric told them, his voice cracking once more. He cleared his throat and tried again. "Don't worry about Nova, she is a warrior, remember? She will take care of herself." He wasn't sure if he was trying to convince them, or himself, but he met Rawl's eyes once again, as if daring the archer to defy him. "And we *will* bring her back."

The rest of their descent was quiet, save the whimpers and sniffles of the girls and the wind, which dissipated the closer they got to the canyon floor. Alric continued to glance back at the summit, as if somehow, he could see something that would assure him that Nova was unharmed. After a few tense minutes they finally reached the bottom.

The carriage dragged along the ground for a few feet, kicking up a cloud of dust and making each of them cough and reach for their water skins. Together they exited and regrouped a few yards away, at the start of a hidden, winding dirt path. Rawl, Polo and Fernanda clustered together, conferring, eventually agreeing that the family would continue their way to the Padir camp on their own. The encounter with the bandits had left them frightened and wary, but ultimately it was better to keep moving towards the safety of the camp rather than stay and wait for the others to return to where they were. And although no one wanted to say it, they all knew that their return was not guaranteed.

Alric and Rawl watched the family set off in the direction of the camp, then together, the archer and the mage turned and began the long journey back to rescue their friend.

The quickest path was to cross the canyon directly and find a way to scale the rock face back up to the top. But the distance that was crossed in mere minutes inside the transport would take a full day on foot, and it was already getting late. Camping overnight in the open was never a good idea, but even if there was a safer way, neither man would have heard of it, for they both wanted to reach Nova as soon as possible. As it stood, their urgency aided them in making good time, resting when only absolutely necessary. They made it almost halfway across the distance before darkness began to fall, Rawl insisting that they stop for the night. No doubt that they had a battle ahead of them, and they would be of no use to anyone if they arrived weak and exhausted. And moreover, who knew what creatures waited for the cover of darkness to strike?

Alric was hesitant but understood the logic behind the suggestion and reluctantly agreed. They chose a spot by two large boulders which could shelter them from behind and leave them less exposed. Alric added an extra protective layer to his warding spell that would allow them to light a fire without allowing the light or smoke to be detected by anything or anyone outside of their circle.

Rawl had not said anything while Alric warded their camp, but he could feel the archer watching him closely. It made the mage uncomfortable, so much so that he had stumbled over the ritual, much to his chagrin. He dismissed it as the strain of the concentration it took to add the reinforced warding, and his concern over Nova. He missed her quiet humming as she stoked the fire or readied their super. She always took care to not watch as he performed magia, and he had grown accustomed to doing so in peace. But the archer observed him both openly and intently.

If Rawl realized that the extra protection was more than a simple addition to the spell, or that it seemed to tire the man out more than the regular warding, he made no mention of it. But during supper the larger piece of cooked meat found its way onto the mage's plate, along with some extra slices of potato.

They ate without speaking, blowing on their food to cool it, Alric refusing a wordless offer of the archer's wineskin with a shake of his head. Nor did they speak when they cleaned up or rolled out their sleeping mats and prepared themselves for bed. They lay still for a long while, one on either side of the fire.

Alric wondered about Nova, where she was, if she was unharmed. He knew, better than most, how well she could care for herself, but it is one thing to defend yourself against an enemy in battle, another quite entirely to be captured by slave traders. As a woman, and an attractive young woman at that, she was at risk for more than mistreatment. Flesh peddlers had been known to "sample their wares" before selling them to the highest bidder, and he sent up a prayer to Pachamama that they could make it to her in time.

Then, considering, he added a prayer to the Goddess Danray, as he thought she might be endeared to Nova, even if she wasn't a true Danrayen.

Hold on Nova. We are coming. Alric wouldn't have thought that he was capable of sleep that night, but after the tension of the day's exertion, his body began to respond to take care of itself. He had just begun to relax into sleep when a voice startled him awake.

"Tell me about your brother."

Alric glanced in Rawl's direction, surprised that the man had broken the silence. His green eyes were bright in the light of their fire, and intent on his. Alric rolled away from his gaze, which saw too much, and on to his back, observing the night sky.

"I know you're hiding something, you and Rojya. But I also know that when you spoke of your brother that your tale was true."

Alric swallowed hard, immobile. He lay like that, still, watching the hazy stars until the patient, undemanding silence coaxed him into speaking.

"He was six years my junior," he started, voice thick with repressed emotion. "His name was Lionel. A constant shadow, following me round every part of the house. I could never be rid of him." He paused, but when Rawl made no move to hurry him or interrupt, he continued.

"Lionel was two when our father died. A soldier in the war. He crossed into Cassalan, and like so many others, had his blood spilled on a land not his own. He died, lejos de casa y de su familia. Even before we learned I had magia; I had no wish to join him in a needless war. To die a senseless death."

"You don't strike me as a coward." The words were said without malice or accusation. Alric shrugged, as much as one can manage a shrug while laying down.

"Perhaps I was, then. Perhaps I am even now. For I still have no taste for battle, for war. But Lionel, Lionel was different. He was too young to remember our papa, the man, and our mother painted his memory as our papa, the hero. He wanted to be just like him."

"Fierce little man?"

"Oh yes," Alric replied, rolling over and bending his elbow under him to prop his head on his hand. He met the archer's gaze across the fire, the tiniest flicker of mirth dancing behind his eyes.

"Always dragging around a practice sword, or a plain stick before that. Whacking away at invisible enemies, breaking things, un travieso. A regular little hellion." His lips turned up at the memory.

"If he wasn't following me, he was generally running amuck and getting into trouble."

The smile melted off his face. "Which is exactly what he did. Ran off and joined the army, first chance he could, and got into trouble."

"You speak as if you believe him dead."

Alric laid back down and turned away from the archer, who made him say too much with his sympathetic eyes and easy manner.

"It is the young who die in war."

They rose with Tz'ola and broke their camp at record speed. Alric was grateful for the cloak Nova had managed to find for him, even if it was too small. The canyon was cold and dark upon waking but would quickly heat up as the sun climbed the sky. Until then, the cloak was a Goddess-send. As the men walked, they discussed how they would make it back up the cliff.

"Is there a spell that could bring us both to the top?" Rawl asked him. "Or one that could help, somehow?" Alric pondered for a few moments, fiddling with the ring on his finger.

"Posiblemente, but it would take extraordinary amounts of power to do so. I do not have the means to harness that energy with me. And if I did, well, I would be useless once we got to the top. I would need days of rest, if not a full week."

Rawl nodded, disappointed, but not surprised. Magia was a tricky business, which is why there were so few true wizards in existence. And why, when they were discovered, were so often recruited to the University and encouraged to serve the realm.

"But," Alric continued, his expression pensive; "I could charm the bottoms of our shoes, for sure-footing. We would be less likely to slip or trip."

It was better than nothing. They continued walking and it soon grew warm enough to remove their outer clothing. The canyon was dry and arid, stretching flat and bare for many miles, a stark contrast to the lush woods on either side of its expanse. It cut through the forest like a dusty red river, and was no less perilous to cross than if it were a rushing stream. Even so, their second day was far less eventful than the first, with neither bandits nor battles to delay them.

Rawl did have to shoot a few wild predators that saw them as an easy meal, but with his aim they were easily picked off at a distance before they could strike. It pained him to leave their carcasses behind, as at another time they would have been skinned and cut, their pelts saved for the leather workers of his tribe, the meat used to feed them, and with the rest of the animal returned to Tierramadri, nothing going to waste. There was no time for that, however, as the longer Rojya remained with her captors the more likely she was to be harmed. He didn't care to entertain those sorts of thoughts for very long.

Rawl snuck a glance at Alric. The mage's brow was so creased with worry that the grooves on his forehead looked like deep canyons, and his eyes were filled with sorrow. Rawl could only imagine what the man was feeling, he had only known Nova for a few days but he recognized a kind soul, gentle heart and fiercely protective spirit.

She was exactly the type of person one would want in their corner, and as their friend. If he was this distraught at having lost her, how must the mage be feeling? Determined to distract them both, even if just for a moment, the archer turned to something that had always brought him comfort.

Rawl began to sing.

He had quite a pleasant voice, clear and melodic with tones that could pick up a jaunty tune and encourage dancing and laughter, or deepen and lower for more poignant ballads, which could occasionally reduce even grown men to tears. He chose a merry children's tune about a love-sick squirrel and the acorns he would find for his beloved, and her many spurns and rejections.

When he began, Alric shot him a look that clearly indicated he believed him mad, but Rawl ignored it and unabashedly belted out the chorus. He was growing used to the sullen mage's disapproval, and his prickly moodiness was almost endearing at this point.

"She wrinkled her nose and turned her tail,

Leaving him in the shadow cold.

For what she longed for more than nuts

Were monedas of pure gold!

The squirrel was bereft and sad,

For riches he had none

So, he made his way to the magic owl

To see what could be done."

"Why would a squirrel have need for gold?" Alric interrupted, grumpily. "The song doesn't make any sense."

Rawl burst into a wide grin, showing off his dimples. He had managed to shift the mages thoughts.

"It's a children's song, it need not make sense. And, well, she liked the look of pretty things I imagine."

"It's a silly song."

"If it makes you feel any better, the magic owl turns two of the squirrel's acorns into pure gold, to return to the lady squirrel. She stores them in her cheeks for winter, but then drowns in the river from their weight."

"Dioses!" Alric exclaimed, horrified. "This is a children's song?"

Rawl nodded.

"He finds another lady squirrel that appreciates nuts, seeds, and his efforts. They survive the winter and live happily together having many little ones. It teaches our children that family, food, and security are more important than seeking gold and riches."

"Bit of a harsh lesson, if you ask me," Alric grumbled.

Rawl simply chuckled and continued singing. By the time he reached the end of the last verse he noticed a small smile under the mage's dark mustache, but he was far too clever to mention it. Instead, he launched into another song, one with themes far more explicit than the last, involving a traveling circus, their strong-man and the mayor's precocious daughter.

At one point Alric burst out laughing and Rawl was delighted to find it an unrestrained and cheerful sound, albeit a short lived one. The mage immediately looked guilty, as if he couldn't believe that he was even *capable* of laughter while his friend was being held against her will, but Rawl was undeterred.

Once the song was complete, they slowly fell into casual conversation, Alric inquiring the archer about his upbringing, the Padir people, and even answering some of Rawl's questions about himself. When they stopped, briefly, for their noon meal he even accepted some of Rawl's wineskin. By then the day was hot and dust clung to their sweat-soaked bodies.

Alric wet a worn-out but clean handkerchief in water and used it to mop up his face and the back of his neck. He abandoned his shirt for a moment to cool off, exposing a dark spattering of hair across his surprisingly broad chest. Finger-shaped bruises marred the light skin of his upper arms, where Rawl had gripped to keep him from throwing himself off the carriage, and the archer flushed slightly upon seeing them.

Hesitantly, Alric offered him a second, clean rag, and though he accepted it to wipe his face and neck, his shirt stayed on. By then the side of the cliff was clearly within sight, and their brief reprieve from fear and worry began to dissipate the closer they got to its base. By the time they reached it they were both silent once more, their thoughts focused on the perilous trek ahead. They stopped to have a final, quick rest, and then looked up.

It was time to climb.

CHAPTER 20

Nova blinked heavily at the man in front of her, the soldier, not fully comprehending what she was seeing. How could a Cassalain soldier be a captured slave on Andalan soil? Had he been a spy, apprehended by misfortune by bandits and flesh peddlers? Noticing that she watched him, he leaned forward in her direction.

Instinctively she recoiled, hitting her back against the metal bars of their cage.

"Are you alright?" he asked, his voice heavy with an indiscernible accent and laden with concern. "They tossed you in here pretty hard, and you've been unconscious for a while. I would have checked on you, but —" his voice trailed off as he raised his arms. His wrists were shackled and attached to the floor of their enclosure with heavy chains. He wouldn't be able to move very far from the corner he was in.

She relaxed, only a little.

"Your head?" he asked, motioning to her. Gingerly she touched the back of her scalp and found her hair sticky and matted with blood. No wonder she had felt so woozy, head wounds were always dangerous.

"How do you feel?" he asked again. Nova jerked her head up defiantly, ignoring the sharp dagger of pain that resulted from the motion.

"I do not need your concern, Cassalain!" she spat at him, shifting to her knees. She noted a quick flash of emotion behind his dark eyes, one that looked a lot like hurt, and she was almost sorry for her words. But he was a Cassalain, and they were the sworn enemies of Andala. In any case she might have imagined it because his mood quickly turned to anger.

"I am a healer," he snarled. "But I will keep my *concern* and my aid to myself then, Andalan."

Her mouth dropped open and she stared at him incredulously.

"You're a killer!"

"Says the Danrayen!" he shot back. "I heard these dogs talking when they brought you in. They said you killed at least three of their party. So be careful who you call a killer, niñita!"

Nova abruptly turned her back at him, seething in anger. Ordinarily, she would have never turned her back on an enemy, but she was fairly certain that he was well confined by his bindings and besides, the chains were loud enough that she would hear him approach if he tried to attack her.

Both her jaw and hands were clenched tight, the tension in her body only serving to further aggravate her headache. Which only made her more angry. It was the Cassalain's fault that she needed to spend precious minutes controlling her rage rather than finding a way out of her mess.

Slowly, she repeated the lessons she had learned in the Danrayen Temple, breathing deeply through her nose and expelling low, slow breaths from her mouth. It took her a bit longer than usual to calm her racing heart, mostly because every time the anger began to dissipate, fear would creep in instead. She would rather hold on to the anger, at least for a little while longer.

Finally, she calmed herself enough to relax her fists, noting the small crescent moon indentations in her palms left from her fingernails. Absently she rubbed her hands and began observing her surroundings.

A portion of the Great Andalan Rainforest had been stripped of the trees that once grew there, just like the cliff's slope. Slave cages and wagons formed a large half circle around the base of the cleared cliff path, and a campfire blazed in its middle.

Her heart sank as she saw at least thirty bandits around the man-made glade, and she had no way of knowing how many more were inside the caravans or on patrol, or hiding in wait to ambush unsuspecting civilians, as her group had been.

Hesitantly, she shifted her attention to the cages.

It was so much worse than she imagined.

Women and children were crammed into the space, with barely any room to move, let alone lay down or stretch out. She noted a tall barrel in one of the corners of each cage and judging by the smell that was coming from the one in the corner across from the Cassalain, they were meant as privies to relieve oneself.

The children weren't crying, but all had numb, forlorn expressions on their little faces, their mothers a gaunt, haunted look. Tears burned in Nova's eyes. Slave trading was a dirty, disgusting problem in Andala due to poverty from supporting a war, but this was the first time she had experienced it firsthand.

She wanted to scream, to wail, to beat her fists against the rotting wooden planks at the bottom of her cage, to tear their iron bars open and cut down every person responsible for the atrocity.

But first she needed to escape.

The first thing to do was to check the door, of course. The likelihood that the bandits had simply forgotten to lock it after tossing her inside was, of course, highly unlikely, but she had been taught to exhaust every avenue, no matter how slim the chances.

It was, as expected, locked. She thought that she heard the Cassalain chuckle behind her, but she ignored him. Next, she checked the integrity of the iron bars. The wood beneath them was damp and rotting, so maybe the bars were wobbly or insecure in their slats.

She moved around the cage checking each bar except those near the soldier, not willing to approach him too closely. In any case, every one that she examined was sadly well fitted and sturdy, so it was unlikely that the ones behind him were any different.

Finally, she began checking the wood beneath her feet. Perhaps there was a section weak enough to break through. Kneeling, she crawled forward, inspecting every inch beneath her fingers.

She didn't look up to see him, but she could tell that the Cassalain was watching her. She continued meticulously, section by section, wooden beam by beam. About a foot away from one of the sides of the cage was a particularly rotted out piece.

Nova glanced around quickly to see if any of the bandits were watching her. They weren't. She popped up quickly, instantly regretting the action as a throbbing pain pulsed at her temple. She ignored it, slamming her right heel down on the weakened piece of wood, one, two, three times in quick succession. She felt it splinter and give with a quiet crack, and she knelt down to pry up what she could with her fingertips.

She pulled, feeling splinters dig into the pads of her fingers, but straining she was able to peel a piece up ... lifting to reveal more metal beams reinforcing the bottom of the cart.

Defeated, Nova sank back on her heels and hung her head. There would be no stealthy escape. If she was going to make her way back to her friends, she would have to fight her way out. Using her right hand, she gripped the piece of wooden beam she had been able to pry up and using her heel once again she kicked down, snapping it off, leaving her a slightly pointed chunk about the size of her right hand. The Cassalain shook his head.

"I wouldn't recommend that, unless you want to end up like me." She glanced over at him, disgust wrinkling her face, and he lifted his shackled hands again in demonstration. Nova curled her lip and looked away. Surely she could fare better than a Cassalain soldier. But deep down, she wasn't convinced. Even so, she hid the piece of wood as best she could in between her boot and pant leg for easy access. The next time one of her captors opened the door, she would be ready.

She didn't have to wait long. As darkness began to fall, a few of the bandits began making their way from the campfire to the slave cages carrying trays of food. She knew it was not kindness or courtesy that inspired the action; gaunt, weak-looking slaves sold for less coin than healthy-looking ones.

She gritted her jaw, biding her time. When two finally approached their enclosure, she dragged the leg that held her makeshift weapon closer to her body and tensed, waiting. One slaver held a water skin and a heavy set of keys, the other had two trays. The captive's supper, presumably. Climbing the steps up to the wagon, the one with the keys met her eye and jerked his chin at her.

"Move away," he growled at her. She scooted back, only a little. It seemed to do. She didn't recognize either man, and if they didn't see her as a threat, they were most likely not on the cliff when she had killed several of their companions.

All the better for her.

Out of the corner of her eye she thought she could see the Cassalain shaking his head in her direction, but she had no intention of heeding the advice of an enemy. Both men crossed in and the second that they were both within reach, she struck.

Swiftly she pulled the wood out of its hiding spot, gripping the thick part up top, leaving the longer shard pointing down. She rocked back on her heels and sprang up, swinging her elbow in an upward motion to upend both trays over the second bandit. Before either could react, she slammed the piece of wood into the key-holders neck. Keys and plates clanged on the floor as he brought both of his hands up, trying to contain the blood sputtering out of the wound.

She turned and ran to the open cage door.

"No, *don't*!" she heard the Cassalain yell, but it was too late. She slammed into an invisible barrier with such force that it bounced her back, like releasing a slingshot, and she crashed into the bars on the opposite end of the wagon, knocking the breath out of her. Her vision swam again, the blow aggravating her already painful head wound.

"Puta!" the second man screamed at her, dripping in vegetable stew. In a moment the cage was crowded with several more bandits, two dragging their bleeding friend out of the enclosure, another scooping up the fallen keys. Several more, including the one who had yelled at her, approached her angrily and she shrunk into a ball, arms covering her head to protect herself. Kicks landed on her side, her ribs, her stomach.

"Stop it!" she heard someone yell, and suddenly there was a heavy weight draped across her body. She felt it jerk and convulse and peeked open her eyes. The Cassalain had thrown himself over her and was absorbing the brunt of their kicks and strikes. At one point they tried dragging him off her, but as his arms were shackled to the floor, so they couldn't get the right leverage. Eventually they tired themselves out and stormed off, locking the cage behind them with a reverberating clang. The soldier dragged himself off her, collapsing with ragged breaths.

Confused, delirious and injured, Nova wanted to ask him why he had risked himself for her, but before she could open her mouth, darkness swallowed her up once more.

The first thing Nova noticed when she came to was pain. Every inch of her body was numb, on fire, or pounding. And somehow in some places, inexplicably, all three. Without opening her eyes, she did a mental scan, trying to ascertain the extent of her injuries.

Her head was still sore and tender, her thoughts slow and mushy. But she had awoken, which was always a good sign with head injuries. The ribs on her left side, which had been left the most unprotected during the onslaught were particularly painful. She drew in a deep breath, relieved to find that she could do so. Nothing had pierced her lungs then. They were bruised, possibly cracked, but not broken. In a moment she would try to sit up and move her legs, but given that she was able to wiggle her toes she wasn't too concerned.

The second thing that Nova had noticed was that her head was laying on a hard surface which she had initially assumed was the wooden ground. But as she began to think more clearly, she realized that it was in fact slightly elevated, and that the surface was also very warm.

And then, it shifted.

She jerked up, shoving her arms in front of her to back away from whatever it was, eyes flying open to land on the dark brown ones of the Cassalain soldier. Her stomach rolled with a sickening lurch as she realized that *she had been sleeping with her head on his lap!*

"Easy!" he said, raising a calloused hand to steady her. "I managed to stop the bleeding, but that head wound of yours is worrisome; you need to take things slowly."

Nova reached around to touch the back of her head and found that it had been bound by some cloth. Ripped from the sleeve of her shirt, by the look of it. Then she remembered; the fight with the bandits, the magical barrier on the cage door, and how the soldier had thrown himself over her to protect her from their blows.

She was fairly certain that she had no cause to fear him, that he wouldn't have risked himself for her or taken the time to bandage her injuries if he meant to do her harm, but even so she backed up and leaned against the metal bars across from him.

"Why?" she asked. He nodded, understanding her question.

"I made the same mistake when I first arrived," he confided with a shrug that made his chains jingle. "Fought my way through, only to get blasted by that spell."

She said nothing. A part of her wanted to thank him, as he had helped her after all. But another part still held the deep-rooted belief that she had been exposed to since childhood, *Cassalains are the enemy*. Instead, she gave him a small nod, which he returned to her.

"How long was I out?" she asked.

"Half a day. You lost consciousness last night and it's about mediodia now, best I can figure." He scanned the position of the sun in the sky. "But if you're worried about having missed meals, don't. After what you just did, I doubt that they will think to feed us for quite a while."

She scowled at him even as guilt inched her way up to her throat. It wasn't his fault that she had killed one of their captors; he needn't be punished along with her. She reminded herself that he was a Cassalain soldier, and that were he to die of starvation it would be no great loss. Somehow it didn't relieve any of the guilt.

She spent the remainder of the day in and out of sleep, her body clearly needing to repair itself. The first time she needed to use the barrel to relieve herself she had flushed head to toe in embarrassment, but to his credit the soldier looked away and hummed quietly to himself to give her privacy. A courtesy she repeated whenever it was his turn. It was almost nightfall when the bandits returned, this time with the greasy leader she had met at the cliff top. She noted that the others called him "Jefe" and nearly laughed despite her precarious situation.

"So, you killed another one of my men, Danrayen," he spat at her, and she assumed he meant the man she had attacked with the broken wood. So he had not survived his injuries, then. Nova couldn't make herself feel sorry for it. She turned her head as much as she could without losing her view on his pale face, pretending to ignore him.

Internally, she quivered.

"What shall we do about it, amigos?" he asked, watching her intently. The men began throwing out suggestions, each worse than the last, and the blood drained from her face as they described horrors she could never have imagined. It was probably best that there was nothing in her stomach, or else she might have embarrassed herself and emptied it all in front of them at their descriptions.

Finally, their leader held up his hand and the conversation stopped.

"All fine suggestions" he replied, mocking amusement coloring his voice. "But I think we let loose the Cassalain on her, what do you think?" Raucous laughter rang loudly in the clearing. Clearly it was a popular suggestion.

"Did you wonder to think how we got an enemy soldier in our little group?" he asked her, wrapping his dirty fingers around the iron bars and leaning in. His rancid breath struck her and she recoiled, making the men laugh even louder. He crooked his finger at her, as if he was inclined to let her in on a secret.

"His fellow soldiers sold him to us!" he cackled. Nova's eyes flickered to the Cassalain, who was looking forward defiantly, his mouth pressed into a thin line.

"Now what do you think a man has got to do to be betrayed and discarded by his own, barbarous people?"

She couldn't fathom it. The Cassalains were a horrible, monstrous group that wanted to invade her land and kill her people. What would make them cast away one of their own?

"He's been a prisoner for quite a while now, and a soldier for even longer. Must have been a good while since he's last been this close to a woman." Her heart sank. She understood what they were implying.

"Maybe we unlock those chains tonight, see what happens in the cover of night? My guess?" he waited until she turned and met his eyes. "My guess is we'll be hearing your screams." Laughing, they walked away, leaving Nova sick and shaking.

There was a long stretch of uncomfortable, uninterrupted silence before the Cassalain spoke.

"I would never —" he started.

"*I would never let you!*" Her words dripped with venom and her lip curled up into a fierce snarl. "I would *die* first."

"So would I!" he shot back. A part of her wanted to believe him, but

...

"Is it true?" she asked him. "Did your own people sell you to flesh peddlers?" He looked away.

"Why?" she demanded.

He didn't answer for a long time. Instead, he sat, taking slow, shuddering breaths until he was more composed. When he was finally ready, he drew himself up and began his story, his eyes never leaving a spot on the ground.

"I was, am, was, one of the soldiers of the Mountain Pass group. Stationed between our two realms. I have always been a good soldier, a strong fighter, and an able healer, so I moved up our ranks quickly. But —" he hesitated.

She made no move to interrupt him but watched him intently. Eventually he continued with a small shrug.

"Cassalan has had problems with the Northern Tribes. They are constantly at battle with each other, but they are united in their hate for Cassalan. Lately some have even banded together to attack us more often than themselves. In this way, we are often fighting a battle on both fronts. Andala in the south, the tribes in the north."

It was interesting information, and she understood why he had hesitated to tell her. It was information that could give Andala a tactical advantage.

"What does this have to do with why you are being held captive in Andala?"

"My father was Cassalain. My mother is Condori."

That would explain it. The Condori were a small tribe in the north, not far from where Taruka's ancestors had lived. Nova didn't know much about them or their people, but she did understand how quickly those in war could turn on each other if they believed that they were threatened. If the Cassalains were having problems with the northern tribes and her cellmate was half-northern, it could be enough. She nodded, indicating she understood.

"It wasn't all of them," he said, lifting his eyes to meet hers. "My captain is a good man; he wouldn't have allowed it. And I still have friends… but there were some that didn't trust me. When we stumbled across these *animales* crossing from our borders to yours, we should have killed them all and released their captives on the spot. Instead, some of our soldiers struck a bargain. They attacked me, bound me ... and handed me over to them. They told them that if they took me far from my unit and the Cassalain border, they would allow them safe passage." He spit, as if even saying the words left a sour taste on his tongue.

"They agreed, of course."

She sat quietly, thinking about his story. It didn't seem like something someone would make up. Why would they? In fact, it sounded precisely like the sort of thing that happens when scared, stupid people are at war for too long.

Nova sighed. She could understand why Damika had never wanted any part of it. She also remembered Taruka's tale from so long ago, when she claimed her abuelitos were aided by friendly supporters on both sides of the borders, Andalan and Cassalain alike. Perhaps there were less evil Cassalains. She couldn't quite convince herself that they were any good, but at the very least she suspected that the one in front of her had no intention of harming her.

She couldn't trust him, of course, not ever, but she believed his sorry tale.

"Very well, Cassalain," she said tiredly, her body beginning to ache once more.

"My name is Axchel."

She snorted loudly. Axchel meant "man of peace." If there was any man more ill-named then he, she had not met them. Briefly, she considered that giving her his name had perhaps been an offer of peace between them, but she disregarded it. She may not believe he meant to do her harm, but she still wanted no peace with a Cassalain soldier.

She wouldn't use his name. Not ever. There is a power in names, as well she had learned, and she refused to give any to the likes of him.

"Cassalain suits me fine," she retorted. His eyes narrowed at her.

"Very well, *Andalan*," he replied sarcastically, turning away from her once more.

CHAPTER 21

Night came faster than she cared for, and soon enough some of the bandits returned to loiter outside of their cell, leering at them both. They did their best to ignore them, but that proved to be impossible once their leader returned, sporting the same heavy set of keys Nova had seen the day prior.

On the man that she had killed.

This time she met him eye to eye, angling up her chin to stare him down. She would not show him any fear. *It is they who should fear me.* But inside, her heart galloped in her chest.

"Jefe" met her gaze unflinchingly, and a long tense moment stretched out before them, with Nova terrified that she would break from the weight of it. But she dug her nails into her palms, the pain helping to center her, and did not waiver. Finally, he broke the silence.

"I still intend to let the barbarian loose on you," he told her, a chilling smile creeping up his lips. "But I think I'll have you first."

Nova jumped up and backed away to the far end of the cage, barely registering Axchel leaping up and straining against his chains. Jefe stepped up to the door, his people cheering and whooping behind him, the Cassalain yelling and swearing, but all of it was drowned out by the blood rushing in Nova's ears. She was trapped; there was nowhere she could run, no way to fight him, how could she escape?

He tossed the keys back down to one of his men and moved to cross to her. She braced her legs and brought up her fists in a defensive stance, ready to fight to her last breath, when — with a quick whoosh and a sickening squelch, an arrow protruded from Jefe's left eye socket.

He blinked at her with his remaining good eye, confused, before collapsing to the ground, dead.

More arrows flew by their cage, meeting their marks, bandits dropping left and right with startled yelps or painful cries. Then, streaks of reddish orange electricity crackled in the air, striking at her captors who were running furiously in every direction.

Rawl emerged out of nowhere, hopping effortlessly into her cage and scooping her up in his arms. He turned to run through the door and Nova cried out,

"Wait —" but they were already through, no magical barrier to offer them resistance. Rawl ran, depositing her next to a thick tree trunk that would protect her back. He handed her several throwing daggers, Alric must have told him that she favored them.

"Are you alright?" he shouted to be overheard over the chaos. She nodded and gave him a quick shove, motioning that he should get back into the fray. He didn't hesitate but turned, notching his bow and continuing his onslaught of arrows. She threw a dagger at a bandit trying to escape, the blade deeply embedding itself between his shoulder blades. It made him stumble, toppling him into the fire.

She saw Alric, magia vibrating from his skin, burnt orange streaks coursing through his arms like veins. In his right hand he held his staff which he used to aim bolts of electricity, or to occasionally whack people over the head with.

Rawl whistled in admiration as the mage spun, leveraging his staff low to the ground to sweep one of their enemies off their feet. When the man was down, Alric tapped him with the staff's tip, shocking him with the electric magia and making him convulse on the forest floor. With a last, lingering screech, the battle ended. The bandits were all killed.

"Didn't think you had it in you, mago!" the archer chuckled.

"What? You didn't think I simply carried this for show, did you?" Alric replied, spinning the staff between his hands.

"I just assumed it was some pompous wizard thing," Rawl shot at him with a grin. "Glad to see you're more than your pretty looks, mage." They looked around, surveying the damage. Nova dragged herself up stiffly; she had dropped to her knees for her last throw, and slowly approached the slave cages. The prisoners all stood, wide-eyed, having watched the entire massacre. None of them spoke, clearly trying to figure out if Nova and her group were their saviors, or an even worse evil. With a grimace, she checked the bodies of several fallen bandits, scooping up the keys when she found them. Then she crossed to the cages and opened the three that held captives.

"Go," she croaked, her voice hoarse from exertion and emotion. "You're free."

They began pouring out of the slave wagons, slowly and stiffly and her eyes burned to see them. She turned to an older woman who seemed to be directing things, and asked,

"Is there somewhere you can go?"

The woman nodded to her.

"I lived near these woods my entire life, I can find my way through, even in the dark. I will take them to my village, where we will be cared for."

"In the dark? That is too dangerous, you best make camp for the night. They're all dead, they cannot harm you anymore."

The woman met her eyes, repressed fury burning within them.

"We would rather risk the perils of the night than stay another minute in this camp."

Nova understood, and couldn't blame any of them. She watched for a moment as they straggled away, and then made her way back to her friends, fully intending on giving them both a long, grateful hug.

She never got the chance.

As she approached, she knew right away that something was wrong. Alric was still glowing the orangish-red tint of his magia, and it seemed to be pulsing from him in quick, electric waves. He was on his knees, his hands clenching the soil beneath him. She took a step back, terrified of the unrestrained magia.

Rawl was crawling on the ground, searching for something.

"His stone!" he yelled at her when he noticed her. "Help me find his stone!"

She stayed where she was, feet firmly rooted to the ground, eyes wide with horror. The electric magia began humming, zapping away from Alric in wild bolts. His head lifted and she met his eyes ...

They were completely red. His lips pulled back and he bared his teeth at her in a snarl, magia crackling behind his eyes, between his lips, pulsing from his arms. The electricity stretched in her direction and she yelped, stumbling backwards. Out of instinct she grabbed her last dagger, the magia frightening her so fiercely that she was already half-prepared to use it.

The realization shamed her, and guilt curdled in her belly. Alric was her friend, her companion, how could she be so quick to turn against him? But just as she began lowering the blade, more of the red electric bolts burst from him, narrowly missing her but setting a patch of grass beside her ablaze with its power.

"Alric!" she yelled at him. "Alric, stop!"

He seemed unable to hear her, his body convulsing with wracking shudders that spit more and more magia from his flesh. More of the forest floor was catching fire, and she was afraid that the next wild bolts of magia would hit her, or Rawl. She raised her knife once more, tears streaming from her eyes.

"Please, Alric, " she begged, but she saw no recognition in his blood red eyes.

"Por favor!" she screamed at him. "Please don't make me kill you!"

He made a motion to move towards her, the magia stretching even further. With a choked sob she drew her hand back, ready to release, when she heard Rawl yell.

"Wait! Wait! I found it!" He appeared over Alric's left shoulder and shouted to get the man's attention.

"Look at me! Look at me, mage!" Alric turned abruptly, a burst of magia striking Rawl in the face. His cheek bled, heavy drops of dark red dripping down his face, but he ignored it, lifting Alric's strange black and red stone high. He took a careful step forward, and then another. Alric's gaze was fixed on the stone in an all-consuming gaze.

Finally, Rawl reached him and knelt in front of him, wrapping the mage's hand around the strange rock. Nova winced at the sizzling sound their hands made on contact, Rawl must be in so much pain, but he ignored it, whispering quietly into Alric's ear.

She watched, numb with terror as the nasty orange-red tinge began bleeding off Alric's body and into the stone, which seemed to absorb it. His eyes still glowed red and sweat rained from his skin.

"What's happening?" she whispered to Rawl, her eyes not leaving the mage for fear of him snapping again.

"It's Mage Madness."

"What?"

"Mage Madness. Mages, they pull magia from the energy of the world around them, but it poisons their blood to do so. The more they use, the bigger the spell or the effort, the more poison that is created. They have to redirect the contamination somewhere, which is why they wear so many stones and talismans. To help with the poisoning."

"He, — it's a poison?"

"Where did you think the saying 'there's madness in all mages' comes from?"

"I assumed it was just a figure of speech! Because they are so often, well, odd."

"It's more than that."

"Clearly!" she snapped back, finally tearing her gaze away from her friend. "I don't know much about magia, or mages. It was never taught, in the palace or the temple." As soon as she said the words, she winced, and her eyes shifted away from Rawl's. He didn't know about her palace life, and her slip of the tongue could endanger them all.

Luckily the man was too consumed with his concern over Alric to notice her slip up, his brow was tightly furrowed and he roughly jerked a hand through his wild hair. Her words didn't seem to have registered with him.

"It wouldn't be." Rawl and Nova twisted their view to look down at a panting Alric, who was beginning to regain his normal coloring. Even so, Nova instinctively took half step back, and immediately regretted the action when she saw the flash of hurt behind his eyes.

"Take it slow, mago," Rawl said softly, his hands still cradling Alric's around the pulsing stone. Slowly, Alric's breathing leveled out, and the wildly flashing lights within the stone dimmed to muted flickers.

"You wouldn't have been taught any of it at *the temple*." Alric repeated when he was able to speak. So, even in his state he had caught her slip. Nova flushed slightly, but he didn't meet her eye, instead stared intently at the stone in his hand.

"There are different types of magia-users, some more rare than others. Mages have more power than most, and are rare, so the extent of our abilities — as well as our limitations — are kept a secret."

Nova sucked in her bottom lip between her teeth, a deep crease etched between her brows.

"What do you mean there are different types of magia users?" she asked him.

"The most common are those born with Affinities."

"Affinities?" Alric nodded and shifted to sit more comfortably on the ground, Rawl helping him with a steady hand. He was clearly still recovering from the aftereffects of whatever had just occurred.

"Those with natural magia, for a lack of a better term. Those who have an Affinity for healing, for instance, are gifted with what others call a 'healing touch.' So, when they create poultices or medicines, they are more powerful and effective than those of others. When they perform surgeries, their hands are steadier, and a natural healing energy aids in their efforts. There are those with Affinities for gardening, or with animals. I read once that there are seafolk of the Western Isles that can swim faster than most men and hold their breaths for twice as long."

As he spoke, Nova began to relax a little. He was beginning to sound more and more like his old, scholarly self, and his voice took on his usual lecturing tone that he often adopted when educating her on something. It eased her tension, just a little.

"Shamanes have an affinity for rituals, and spiritual tasks. They are closer to the ears of the gods and their prayers are more often heard, and granted. The magia of those with Affinities is a blessing from their patron gods and can be so subtle that it is often undetected. But they have no magical abilities outside of their Affinity."

"I wonder if the Priestess Ianuaria has an Affinity" Nova pondered out loud. Or even some of the other priestesses, such as Priestess Ovidia who had a way with livestock and the land that seemed something beyond mere talent or hard work.

Alric finally uncurled his fingers from his strange stone, which continued to flicker with red sparks underneath its smooth surface. He carefully tucked it back away into his breast pocket.

"It is certainly possible," he answered, not meeting her eyes. "Danrayen women often have Affinities for fighting, or for certain weapons or skills in battle. It would not be uncommon."

His answer surprised her, as she had not considered that one could have an Affinity for battle, and her mind briefly wandered to Damika and her many skills. But she quickly dismissed the thought. Sometimes it hurt too much to think about Damika, and recent events had already left her feeling raw and vulnerable.

"What other types of magia users are there?"

"There are brujas y brujos. They are like mages in that they pull magia from the energy around them, but in such small quantities that it does not poison their blood. They can make potions, perform small, practical spells, but they are not much use in battle so the University doesn't actively recruit them. A few apply and join anyway, but their positions upon graduation are more secretarial in nature. They keep the scrolls and archives organized, create useful spells for categorization, that sort of thing. Dreadfully dull, boring work for most, so most of the women tend to keep to themselves and set up their own practices near towns and villages.

Brujas often set up in a cottage in the woods where townspeople can visit in relative privacy for healing drafts, simple potions, even the occasional love spell. Perhaps not a glamorous life, but often more lucrative than working in the University. And the men, brujos, often work near forges, charming blades and weapons for extra strength, durability and the like. Though some take up with bandits such as these, nowadays most large bandit groups have their own hired brujos."

Nova frowned, remembering the nasty shock she had received when trying to exit her cage. She had recognized it as a spell, of course, but now it made more sense.

"Then, there are wizards. Mages. Any gender can hold the title, of course."

"And you can use more magia than brujos y brujas, and perform bigger spells, but it poisons you, so you must purge it somehow. Into those rocks." She was beginning to understand it all a bit better.

Alric nodded at her again.

"Certain stones can hold power. Some work better than others, but they are of course incredibly expensive. The Archwizard Auberon has a ring of a solid Dragonstear, small enough to fit on his pinky, that can instantly absorb even the most elaborate of spells. But they are rare. Mine is a Phoenixeye, which is quite effective, but obviously a lot larger. I don't have the luxury of placing it on a convenient piece of jewelry." He patted his pocket.

"And finally, there are sorcerers, and sorceresses. They are extremely rare, as rare as true seers." he told them. "Sorcerers and sorceresses are mages with an Affinity to magia."

"Huh?" That didn't make sense to Nova. "Wouldn't all mages have an Affinity to magia?"

Alric shook his head, and then winced at the effort.

"No, mages are capable of *using* magia. They have an ability for it, but not an Affinity. That is why it poisons us, if we are not careful. A sorcerer can pull magia from the elements and use it as easily as someone with an Affinity for horses could charm a skittish colt, or one with an Affinity for plants could coax a dying rose bush back to life. It is as natural as breathing to them, and they need not bleed any poison from their spells, for it is not unnatural to them. It doesn't poison them. There are no sorcerers living in this age. At least, none that we know of."

Shakily, he struggled to his feet, and Nova noticed that he accepted Rawl's help unquestioningly, even leaning on him for support for a moment. Whatever they had been through to reach her, the men had clearly resolved their differences. She would have smiled, had she not been so rattled.

"How did you know about Mage Madness?" Alric asked Rawl. The question was more curious than accusatory. Rawl drew himself up and smiled proudly, his eyes losing some of the concern that had been clouding them.

"My sister is a Mage," he told them, practically beaming. Both Alric and Nova were surprised. After all, as Alric mentioned, it was a rare ability.

"What is her name?" Alric asked him. "Perhaps I know her?"

"Filomila. Mila. But I doubt you would have met, she only just started University last year." He dragged a hand through his hair.

"The Padir don't usually settle in one place too long, and we don't tend to travel south, but she insisted. She was excited to go. The entire tribe pooled together to buy her a Griffinstalon stone before she left."

Alric whistled through his teeth, suitably impressed. They were nearly as good as Phoenixeyes, perhaps even better. After that, the conversation abruptly died, and they stood in an awkward sort of triangle, the two men closer at the top of it, and Nova making up the bottom tip. She wasn't sure what they were to do now, Alric had frightened her terribly, but she in turn had almost killed him. She shifted awkwardly, unsure of what to say. Before she could figure it out she noticed Rawl looking past her shoulder, an uncharacteristic frown marring his handsome face.

"What should we do about him?" he asked, jutting out his chin. Nova jolted and did a quick spin; she had completely forgotten the Cassalain in all the excitement. He sat in his usual spot, legs drawn up by his chest, forearms across his knees, shackled hands dangling in front of him. He observed them quietly, his expression cold. Nova sighed.

"We can't leave him here like this." She shook her head. "I suppose we should release him."

"But he's a Cassalain," Alric commented with distaste. Nova couldn't help but sigh deeply once more.

"Si. I don't like it either. But he helped me. I suppose it is only fair."

Together they crossed to the cage, the Cassalain jumping up as they approached. He said nothing but drew his shoulders back and kept his gaze forward, defiantly. He stayed that way as the men climbed the steps up to the cage and only looked down when he heard the jangling of keys that the archer now held. Puzzled, he furrowed his brow at Nova.

"You are releasing me, Andalan?" he asked incredulously.

She jerked her right shoulder up in an aggressive shrug.

"You would prefer to stay as you are, Cassalain?" He pressed his lips into a thin line as Rawl jumped up into the Cage, motioning for his hands. The prisoner hesitated only a moment before lifting them. Rawl unlocked the shackles and hopped back down. The soldier took a few steps forward and paused at the threshold. Nova immediately understood why.

"There is a magical warding on the door, to keep prisoners in," she told Alric, shyly. She still wasn't sure where they stood. "I don't know how Rawl was able to carry me out." The mage shifted his gaze to the Cassalain.

"It if was a brujo's spell, he's long dead. I suspect the spell died with him." The soldier hesitated once again, and then decisively took a step forward. He walked right through without an issue. Nova exhaled heavily. She had no love for the man, but she remembered the shock of the impact and wouldn't have wished it on anyone held captive against their will.

He approached their group slowly and gave them a short bow.

"My name is Axchel. I am in your debt." He bit out the words as if they physically pained him. Nova didn't blame him, she had not liked being indebted to him either.

"I guard the Overpass of the Snow Goat, on the border of Andala and Cassalan. Should you ever need my assistance, I will be forced to provide it."

At his words, tight, burning resentment flamed to life within her chest. Nova spat out short, rueful laughter to dislodge the feeling.

"We would never seek help from a Cassalain, and certainly not from you. I hope to live the rest of my days and never see you again," she choked out. "Even in death, it would be too soon."

The soldier's nostrils flared and the flesh under his left eye twitched at her words and the venom with which she delivered them. Without another word he turned, stopping only to pick up a fallen bandit blade, and stalked out into the woods in the direction of the border. Within moments, he was gone from sight.

Nova turned her head to see a wordless exchange pass between the men, Rawl nodding and moving away from them to give her and Alric some privacy. She wrung her hands, twisting her fingers in front of her. Heat burned in her cheeks from the shame of her reaction to him, and his magia. She knew now that it wasn't his fault. She opened her mouth to apologize, to beg his forgiveness, but he beat her to it.

"Nova, I am so, so sorry." Shocked, she lifted her head to meet his eyes.

"I know I frightened you. You've never liked magia, I know, I can tell. And this, I, what happened … I can't imagine how much I frightened you. I'm so sorry."

"Alric!" She cried. "I'm the one who's sorry! I could have killed you, and I nearly did. I didn't know. I'm so sorry, I should have tried to help." A tear trickled down her cheek. She had nearly lost someone who had quickly become one of her dearest friends.

He didn't answer, but with the slightest hesitation pulled her into his arms. She wept openly, dampening the front of his tunic while he rocked her slightly and stroked her hair. Rawl watched them in the distance, his expression unreadable.

When she finally pulled away, sniffling, Alric pulled out a handkerchief and handed it to her. It was heavy, heavier than a normal handkerchief, and when she pulled it open, she immediately saw why. In its center was an old, and very squashed, oat and honey cake. The kind she had loved at the Padir camp.

Laughing, she embraced the mage, again dissolving into tears. Slowly, her sobs turned into hiccups, and together they made their way over to Rawl, Nova unbearably relieved that they were all well, and together once more.

CHAPTER 22

Like the other prisoners, Nova had no desire to be anywhere near the bandit camp. Even so, it was far too late to climb back up the slope, especially not in the dark. In any case, both she and Alric were in no state for strenuous activity. Instead, they began circling the cliff to the east, and made their own camp about a mile away.

"Circling the cliff will take at least a week," Rawl confided to them. "At its farthest point we come dangerously close to the Night Wood, which is why we chose the climb. Not to mention, it's clearly much faster. If *someone* hadn't decided to butcher the entire mechanism, we could have pulled the carriage back up." He stared pointedly at Nova, who flushed.

"I couldn't risk the girls," she told him. He made a motion as if to ruffle her hair but pulled back when he realized she was still sporting a bandage.

"Come on, let's set up and get you cleaned up."

They built a fire and prepared supper first, Nova eating ravenously after not having been fed for over a full day. Rawl had been smart enough to raid the bandit camp before they left, and was able to find a plethora of deer meat, fingerling potatoes, maize and even a stale husk of bread that they could share.

Once or twice the food threatened to come back up when she re-membered the things that had been said to her, and what was almost done to her, back at the camp. But she did her breathing exercises and waited for the sick feeling to pass. Alric also ate greedily, the heavy expenditure of magia having weakened him. He only protested slightly when Rawl refused to let him set up his warding spell, claiming that he would stay awake and take first watch.

Nova wet a scrap of clothing with a water skin and washed up as best she could, then allowed Alric to clean and rebandage her head wound. Finally, the two of them stretched out on their bed rolls, thick winter cloaks acting as blankets, and immediately fell into a deep sleep.

Hours later Nova awoke choking on a repressed scream, sweat pour-ing from her. She had been back there, in the camp, but this time no one had come to help her. In her dream the men took turns chasing her, hunting her, and she could see each of their faces clearly, every man she had killed. She dragged herself from the sticky, heavy clenches of her nightmare, struggling against her bedclothes, feeling suffocated, trapped.

In a flash Rawl was beside her, cradling her in his lap. She gripped his shirtfront with an iron grasp and stayed in his arms until the wracking shivers finally subsided.

"Do you want to talk about it?" he whispered, his beard tickling her ear. She shook her head. He smoothed a warm hand up and down her back, and she felt him nod against her hair. She realized then that she was the closest that she had ever been to a man, and after her recent experience she would have thought that the proximity would have unnerved her. Instead, she felt warm, and safe, and not at all embarrassed. Even so, she pulled away from his embrace, squeezing his arms to indicate her gratitude.

"Get some rest," she said quietly, and he cocked his head at her.

"You sure?" he asked, and she smiled at him.

"I'm sure. I'm already up and couldn't go back to sleep if you drugged me." Rawl nodded understandingly, and handed her his bow and quiver. Then, he unwrapped a bundle near his feet.

In it was her Espada.

Nova hadn't forgotten her blade, but back at the bandit camp there had been far too much happening for her to think straight. With freeing the prisoners, Alric's brush with Mage Madness and the Cassalain, she hadn't thought to look for the Espada until later, when the adrenaline had worn off and they had already left the camp. Her eyes filled with tears at the sight of it; she hadn't thought she would ever see the Danrayen blade again.

"It was on one of the bandits. I thought you might like it back." With that he stretched out on her mat, falling asleep almost instantly. Nova stayed up, deep in her thoughts, blade on her lap, until morning.

Their progress around the cliff was slow, especially in the beginning. Nova was still recovering from a multitude of injuries and Alric tired alarmingly quickly. She and Rawl refused to let him ward their camp at night and were awakened twice to predators prowling dangerously close.

Once, as they approached the Night Wood border, they encountered one of the beasts that they had fought in the past. Luckily, she and Rawl made quick work of it, and they were able to span the rock face without further issue. Crossing the expanse of the rocky red canyon took them another two days, leaving Nova antsy and uncomfortable at the lack of vegetation around her. It was only then that they allowed Alric to ward their camp, which he was finally able to do without draining too much energy, and Nova was grateful for it.

She wouldn't have believed she'd ever be grateful for magia.

When they finally reached the discarded carriage and pulley at the far end of the canyon, Nova stopped and followed the ropes up with her gaze. They disappeared somewhere near the top of the summit, and she couldn't believe it had only been a little over a week since she had stood there and watched her friends plummet towards the ground without her. So much had passed that it felt like a lifetime ago.

Once they reached the little path where Rawl and Alric had left the Padir family, Nova began to feel much better. Her injuries were healing, Alric was in better spirits, and she felt far more comfortable in the shade of the cheery forest rather than exposed by large stretches of rock. She was able to hunt again, and at night the three of them ate and exchanged stories, or listened to Rawl's many songs. Once, Alric scolded him for singing a particularly crude drinking song in front of Nova, and she had replied by belting out a tune she had learned from her Danrayen sisters — a favorite of Raidea and Petra, in fact, with even filthier lyrics. By the time she was done Rawl was on the ground clutching his side from laughter and Alric was as red as the chiles in their stew.

Before she knew it, their journey had ended, and they were at last at the second Padir camp. If Nova had expected it to look like the first camp, she was seriously mistaken. Instead of long rows of tents adorning an open clearing, the camp was made up of a series of small, interconnected huts, suspended in the very trees.

The huts were built around the trunks of the ceiba trees in wood of the same color, their roofs built up of more of the same planks with woven vines and leaves. They were linked by swinging wood and rope bridges, and narrow walkways that wove between, to and from each massive trunk. The entire camp, she was astonished to find, was an elaborate network of interconnected tree houses.

Nova felt better when she saw Alric's face, his eyes wide and mouth ajar, and laughed when Rawl clucked him under the chin.

"Flies will get in," he teased him. Alric laughed with him. Looking up again, he shook his head.

"It really is something though."

A little yellow and orange blur launched itself out of a cluster of trunks and slammed into Nova's knees, nearly toppling her over.

"Nova! Nova! Nova!" Brianna cried, bouncing up and down. "We were so scared!" she said, raising her arms high to be lifted, which Nova did with a little effort. Her ribs were still a bit sore. Still, she felt a lot better when Brianna threw her arms around her neck and gave her cheek a sticky kiss.

"You missed the wedding! Reyna made us more coronitas bonitas!"

The rest of the family emerged from behind the trees, and Nova realized that there were rungs embedded in the wood to assist them down from the walkways. They greeted each other warmly, with hugs and tears and questions about their horrible ordeal. They met Reyna, Polo and Fernanda's eldest daughter, and her handsome new husband that absolutely beamed with pride whenever he looked at his young bride.

Eventually it was decided the group should come up to the guest quarters to bathe and rest before seeing Sarakshi. Although their trip had already been delayed far longer than they had anticipated, neither she nor Alric complained. The proposition of a warm bath and fresh clothing was too tempting an offer to refuse.

Her room was small but lovely, with a soft bed mat over some springy combination of dry moss and feathers. A wooden tub sat in the corner, already filled with warm water. As Nova bathed, Reyna came to lay fresh clothing on the bed, Brianna close at hand. While the child would have lingered to talk to Nova, her sister shooed her away, grabbing Nova's old garments for washing and mending, though she was fairly certain there was no salvaging her blouse, save for using the scraps as wash rags.

She stayed in the bath happily until the water became cold, and reluctantly stepped out to dry off. She noticed a small jar of something had been left next to the clothing, and upon sniffing it was delighted to find it was a salve for aching muscles and joints. With a grateful smile, Nova applied it liberally to her ribs and the back of her neck, which had been tense from lack of sleep and constant nightmares.

She assumed that they would ebb one day, but for now it was the price she was paying for having killed. The priestesses at the temple had warned them as much. One must always be prepared to defend yourself and others, but there is always a price to pay for violence. Life cannot be taken easily, even when ending the lives of those on a bad path. It was a Danrayen's duty to protect the weak and powerless, however, and as trained warriors they would be the ones to weather the consequences.

Though she wasn't Danrayen, she understood that now. She bore the price of killing every night, but while she was haunted by the faces of those she had killed, the faces of those that she had saved helped drive those ghosts away.

She was just finishing dressing in wool pants and blouse in a lovely shade of lilac and wheat when there was a knock on the door. Crossing, she opened it to find an equally clean and refreshed-looking Alric at her entryway. She motioned for him to enter, smothering a smile when the mage had to duck to cross the threshold.

"How are you feeling?" he asked her, perching on the small desk which was the only other piece of furniture in the room.

"Better than I have in a while," she confessed, running a comb through her hair, which was still wet and unbound. "You look better too."

The tips of his ears turned pink. "Thank you, I am feeling more myself," he said, and the confession lightened her heart.

"I'm glad," she told him truthfully, beaming at him. He coughed and straightened.

"Come on," he told her. "They've prepared a meal for us, and after, we can see the seer."

He must have noticed the look on her face, because he nodded knowingly. "I know, I am anxious to see her as well. But we cannot refuse their hospitality."

Nova dropped her brush back into her pack and nodded.

"Let's go."

They exited her room traveling by the railed, wooden planks that stretched from tree to tree. They spotted Rawl not too far ahead and made their way towards him, weaving around the heavy trunks. He too had bathed and changed, sporting a walnut-colored cloak rather than the deep green one that he had worn throughout their journey. His hair was still damp like Nova's.

When he saw the pair, his dimples flashed with pleasure.

"Come!" he said happily. "Word of how you saved Brianna has already spread throughout the camp, and no doubt my people have prepared a special feast in your honor." Nova flushed but before she could argue she was being led around even more towering trees and to a large, open area creating a flat balcony between a cluster of ceiba trees. A gasp escaped her throat.

The space was utterly charming. Hanging ropes of oil lanterns illuminated a long, wooden table in the middle of the area. It was large enough to seat at least twenty adults and was filled with all sorts of dishes and foods. The seats crowding it were a mish-mash assortment of stools, benches and chairs of varying sizes and colors, no two exactly alike.

As they got closer Nova could see rice, beans, tri-colored corn and tamales. There were tortillas and queso fresco, two full roasted chickens and an entire large trout wrapped in banana leaves. She could see thick tostones, smashed pieces of plantain fried with oil and salt. Inhaling deeply Nova could smell the intoxicating aroma of onion, chile, ajo, aji amarillo, ojas de laurel, and all the blend of spices and flavors of her land. And in the center of it all was an entire roasted pig, complete with an apple in its mouth.

Alric and Nova joined the adults around the table, the children loading up their plates and sitting cross legged on the wooden beams, their backs propped up against the thick trunks of trees. Wine was passed around, as was ron and cerveza. Stories were told, tales exchanged. Nova listened to Fernanda's retelling of her daughter's wedding, with Reyna interjecting with moments her mother had forgotten.

She saw an elder offer Alric ayahuasca and was relieved when he turned it down, as they had more important matters to attend to that evening. Soon a few of the Padir brought out pipes and instruments, and the air became thick with both smoke and the sounds of the traditional flute songs of their people.

Nova was enjoying herself so thoroughly that she was almost surprised when Rawl stood and crossed over to her and Alric, filled with purpose.

"Are you ready to meet Sarakshi?" he asked them, his tone solemn. Alric and Nova glanced at each other, anxious to find the answers to their questions, but both afraid of becoming too hopeful.

"We're ready," Nova said, willing it to be true. She had never met a seer and didn't quite know what to expect, but they had come this far.

With a reassuring smile Rawl beckoned for them to follow him, and led them away from the center platform, across two narrow walkways and over a swinging rope bridge. A few trees over he stopped outside a hut, about twice as large as Nova's had been.

"She is expecting you."

"Are you —" Alric began, flustered. "Are you entering with us?" Rawl shook his head.

"No, your matters are your own."

Alric and Nova exchanged a look of relief. Neither of them wanted to explain that they had lied about their reasons for wanting to meet the seer. Rawl knocked on the door, and then opened it to allow them in.

Inside the room was bright and colorful, curving around the thick center of the tree trunk to form a crescent moon. On the far right, sitting on a cluster of brightly colored pillows on the floor was a young girl, no more than twelve or thirteen. Nova started, looking around the space, but there was no one else in the room.

"I'm sorry, but are you Sarakshi?" she asked the child uncertainly.

The girl's lips curled into a warm smile and she motioned to the empty pillows past the low wooden table that sat in front of her. They both crossed and sank down, Alric having some difficulty folding his legs into a position that didn't make him look like a gangly stick bug. The girl watched him, openly grinning at his struggle.

"I am Sarakshi, and I have the True Sight. It is what you have come here for, is it not?"

Alric and Nova shared a quick glance. How were they to proceed? How much would they tell this girl, and was it safe for them to do so? But they didn't have to decide. Before they could do or say anything,

Sarakshi's hazel eyes clouded to a pale, misty blue, and her posture sharpened with a quick jolt. When she spoke, it was no longer the speech of a young girl, but a deep resonating voice of something beyond their realm.

"You have not come to inquire about your brother, Orange-Fire," the voice boomed. "You seek the lost king." Nova reached out and gripped Alric's knee. Could she tell them the last place their king had been, before being slain? The eerie smoke eyes turned to her, and with a shiver, she realized that the girl had heard her thoughts.

"But he was not slain, Hidden-Name. He lives with a Forest Lady, on once enemy soil. Now, a land he calls his home. He lives, and hides, for love and for family."

An image crashed into their heads, unbidden, of a modest cottage in the middle of an unfamiliar wood. There was a beautiful dark-haired bruja, obvious by the tendrils of light green magia that flickered over her skin. Her arms were around a burly bearded man, his mouth open in laughter. The man looked up, as if staring straight at them —

It was the king. Older, changed, but undoubtedly King Enrique himself. Both Nova and Alric gasped, and he clasped her hand in his. Just as the image began to fade a figure ran up to the couple, throwing his arms around their waists. He was a young boy, of about ten years old, with his mother's dark hair and the same strong brow and bright eyes of the king.

The vision broke suddenly, like the snapping of a string, and Nova and Alric panted heavily as if having run a long way. Sarakshi's eyes slowly returned to their normal coloring, and when they were her usual bright hazel she laid down among her many pillows and promptly fell asleep.

"That was the king," Nova said to no one in particular. "That was King Enrique." Before Alric could respond, a voice sounded from the entrance of the hut.

"The king! The king lives?" They both turned sharply to see Rawl, just inside the door's archway. By the look of shock on his face it was clear that he had seen and heard everything that had transpired.

"If the king lives, you're not looking for your brother," he spoke slowly, as if unraveling a mystery. Nova's heart skipped, for it was dangerous for him to learn the truth. But Rawl was far too clever for them to deceive a second time.

"If the king lives and resides in Cassalan with a bruja as a lover, and has a son ..." he continued, and then realization struck him like one of his arrows. His eyes grew wide, eyebrows shooting up beneath the wild hair over his brow. "You're looking for the Unnamed Prince!"

Nova turned to the Alric, desperately, but Rawl was already moving towards her.

"You *are* her. You *are* the Name-Bearer!" Nova watched, panic and desperation rising within her as the tell-tale rippling of magia trembled on Alric's fingertips. She didn't want anyone to get hurt, but there was too much at stake, and they had come too far to be thwarted now. She could only hope that Alric could contain himself so as not to seriously hurt Rawl, only incapacitate him enough that they could leave without being followed.

"Wait!" Rawl leapt forward and rounded the table to shield the still unconscious Sarakshi. He threw out a hand towards Alric, his eyes pleading. "Wait, please, just wait. Let me show you something."

Rawl began unbuttoning his tunic and Alric's magia froze as he and Nova watched, equally confused. When the shirt was open to his waist, he pulled it off his right shoulder and angled it towards them.

There, on his skin, was tattooed a Flower of Prophecy.

"We are supporters of the Unnamed Prince." he said.

Alric's magia flickered and died completely and his hands dropped to his lap. Nova looked between the two men, no less confused. It was a similar tattoo to the one Alric bore, hidden underneath the wrap on his arm. When he had shown it to her he had mentioned that it was a symbol for support of the Unnamed Prince, and a new royal line. But she had assumed he meant among the nobility, and people within the Andalan capitol.

To find it all the way out here ...

"I don't understand," she said with a frown. Alric's gaze didn't leave Rawl, but he responded.

"Auberon was collecting supporters throughout the realm for the prince, the boy the Flowers told you about. Tales of your prophecy spread, with people far and wide agreeing that the Flowers must have had a reason to deny the Naming. Those people wait for the true prince to find his way to the Flowers, and to the throne." Nova turned to view Rawl, who had pulled his clothing back in place.

"And you are one of these people?" she asked him.

"Many of the Padir are. We believe in the old gods, in the spirits of the earth, and in the Flowers. And —" he waited until she met his eyes. "And in the Name-Bearer."

"Please don't call me that," she pleaded. He nodded at her as if he understood. Perhaps he did.

"But, do you know ... you should know," he stuttered before biting his lower lip. Alric and Nova exchanged a wry look. This was the first time either of them had seen Rawl as anything but unwaveringly self-assured.

"We should know what?" Nova asked him.

His face was grim. "You are being hunted."

"What?" Alric demanded, whirling to face him straight on. "What do you mean, hunted?"

"I mean, well, that is to say, we have heard." He would not meet their eyes. "There is a bounty for anyone who can find the Name-Bearer." He looked at Nova sorrowfully.

"I'm sorry. The contract came in, perhaps a few months ago?" That had been around the time Alric had set out to fetch her, around the time the Wizard Auberon had been imprisoned. "We learned of it because, well, a few of our camp are not supporters, as I am." Nova's head spun. A bounty out on her? Rawl turned back to Alric.

"You were not mentioned, but it seems that whatever plans you made were shared amongst those with sharp ears, or with loose lips."

"The bounty. What were the terms?" His voice was quiet.

Rawl named a sum too large for her to comprehend, and then met her eye.

"Dead or alive."

Alric stood up, but Nova stayed seated, processing the news.

She was surprised to realize that she was not shocked. Not at all, in fact. She had always been hunted, by those in the palace. Now the hunt was simply out in the open, available to all. She found that the development didn't scare her as it once might have.

She had lived most of her life in fear, one way or another. Fear of failing the Naming Rite, and when she did fail it, in a way, fear that she would be found out. She feared living in hiding as a traitor, and in the temple, she feared her secret being discovered. She feared what would happen when the wizard came for her and she would finally venture into the real world. But somewhere along the way in her impossible journey with her new friends, she had lost her fear. Now, all she wanted was to walk the path laid out for her and complete the Flower's prophecy.

"It doesn't matter," she told the men, rising to stand with them. "It changes nothing. We now know where the Unnamed Prince is, and we need to find him."

"You think it's him? The boy in the vision?" Alric asked her.

"The son of an Andalan King and a Cassalain bruja? Who else could it be?"

"But how will we find them in Cassalan?" Rawl asked, and Alric raised an eyebrow at him.

"We?"

"Don't start with me mage, I told you I am a supporter of the Unnamed Prince. I am joining you in this journey. But there is no way that we can cross the border! It's near impossible if you are a soldier, and we are most certainly not soldiers. There is no way, it can't be done."

"We could bribe our way through one of the underpasses, through the mountains," Nova suggested. It was what Taruka's family had done. But Rawl shook his head.

"You would need to bribe both Andalan soldiers on this side, and Cassalain soldiers on the other. With a bounty on your head, it is too risky, and any young women around your age would be held for questioning at the very least."

"What about climbing the mountains, passing them from above?" Alric proposed, directing his question towards Rawl, who clearly knew more about this part of the world than they.

"Not possible. The terrain is far too treacherous. Even if we found a true path there is no guarantee it won't be snowed over, or covered with fresh fallen rocks, or eroded. Besides, even if we did find a pass we would have to sneak by not only the Andalan soldiers on this end, but the inevitable guards on the other side of the mountain. It is impossible."

"That's not exactly true," Alric reminded them, looking pointedly at Nova. "We do know about a particular pass, and someone with access." Rawl gasped, and both men stared at her expectantly, but she couldn't fathom why. Then the realization hit her so abruptly that she nearly lost her breath with the impact of the shock.

"No," she whispered. Alric and Rawl merely held her gaze, though Alric had the decency to look remorseful.

"We can't. I can't! I *won't*!" The two men said nothing.

"Not the *Cassalain*!"

To be continued.

THE FLOWERS OF PROPHECY SERIES WILL RETURN

Preorder Book 2
THE FOLLOWER OF FLOWERS
MAY 2023

Name Pronunciation and Meanings
In order of appearance

Edwin: *Ed-ween* "Rich friend"

Myra: *Mahy-rah* "Sweet-smelling" / "Aristocratic"

Tz'ola: *Ts-oh-la* Goddess; of the sun

Rosa Maria: *Ro-sah-mah-ree-ah* "Beloved rose"

Issalia: *Ee-sah-lee-ah* "Strong willed lioness"

Enrique: *En-ree-ke* "Home-ruler"

Awaq: *Ah-wak* "Weaver"

Alfredo: *Al-freh-doh* "Wise counselor"

Auberon: *Aw-burr-on* "Royal bear"

Jacobo: *Ha-ko-bo* "Supplanter"

Danray: *Dan-ray* Goddess; of battle and transition

Mamajove: *Ma-ma-hoh-veh* Goddess; youngest of the three Caimen sister goddesses of the Great Andalan Rainforest

Mamamedia: *Ma-ma-meh-dee-ah* Goddess; middle of the three Caimen sister goddesses of the Great Andalan Rainforest

Mamavieja: *Ma-ma-vee-eh-hah* Goddess; eldest of the three Caimen sister goddesses of the Great Andalan Rainforest

Adira: *Ah-dee-rah* "Stong, noble, powerful"

Phanessa: *Fah-ness-ah* "Butterfly"

Damika: *Dah-me-kah* "Open-spirited"

Petra: *Peh-trah* "Stone, rock"

Taruka: *Tah-roo-kah* "Doe"

Raidea: *Ray-dee-ah* "Wise goddess"

Ovidia: *Oh-vee-dee-ah* "Shepard"

Mamá: *Ma-ma* "Mother"

Adan: *Ah-dan* "Earth"

Valentina: *Val-en-tee-nah* "Healthy, strong"

Kichka: *Keech-kah* "Thorn"

Alessia: *Ah-less-ee-ah* "Defending warrior"

Azucar: *Ah-soo-kar* "Sugar"

Ianuaria: *Ee-oon-our-ree-ah* "Healer"

Dante: *Dahn-tey* Steadfast, Enduring

Alric: *All-rik* "Regal ruler"

Nova: *No-vah* "New"

Frederico: *Freh-deh-ree-ko* "Peaceful ruler"

Zerlina: *Sehr-lee-nah* "Beautiful Dawn"

Rawl: *Rah-ool* "Wise wolf"

Padir: *Pah-deer* Minor god; nomadic son of the River God and the Goddess of Wind

Rojya: *Row-hyah* Animal; fox-like creature with red fur

Reselda: *Reh-sell-dah* "Healer"

Ixchel: *Eech-chel* Goddess; of midwifery and healing

Amparo: *Am-pah-row* "Refuge or shelter"

Sarakshi: *Sah-rak-shee* "Good sight"

Polo: *Poh-loh* "Brave wanderer"

Fernanda: Fehr-nan-dah "Adventurer"

Zuri: *Soo-ree* "Beautiful"

Brianna: *Bree-yahn-ah* "Strong and honorable"

Eponine: *Eh-poh-neen* Forest Goddess; of horses

Reyna: *Ray-nah* "Queen"

Lionel: *Lee-oh-nell* "Little Lion"

Axchel: *Ahk-shell* "Man of peace"

Filomila: *Fee-low-mee-lah* "Beloved Miracle"

Acknowledgments

A big part of me can't even believe that I am sitting down to write this.

The Name-Bearer, and the entire Flowers of Prophecy series was born from a dream. A very vivid, wild, crystal-clear dream. That dream became a TikTok skit, which became a viral video, which turned into a TT series, and a promise of a full length novel. And now ... this.

I want to thank every single person who commented "write the book!" or "what happens next?" on that video. To everyone who followed me because of my story, who shared it with their family and friends, who encouraged me, motivated me, pushed me, and waited for me to finally deliver a product I felt was worthy of you. I mean it when I say that it's because of YOU that this story exists in the real world, and not as a faded dream in my memory.

A big thanks to my first round of beta readers who received an absolute disaster of a first draft. You somehow managed to take the most emaciated, skeletal outline and still find some good. You all said the same thing ... give us *more!* I truly hope I delivered!

I owe a very special thanks to Cody Von Ruden, one of the loveliest people on the planet. Who knew that a call for beta readers would lead me to meet one of my very best friends? Thank you for diving deep into this world with me, constantly challenging me on the "why" and the "how", and for your never-ending patience as I worked on a single paragraph over and over again until I got it right. I am so glad that part of this journey meant meeting you.

Speaking about making friends through this whole process, I owe a HUGE debt of gratitude to A.K. Mulford. There are so many parts of this industry that don't get talked about enough, and even with copious amounts of research I still felt a little lost, and a lot unsure. The fact that you were willing to sit down with me and answer any and all of my questions, give me suggestions and advice, and just share your breadth of knowledge and experience with a newbie like me means the absolute world. I am so lucky to have found a mentor AND a friend, and I can't thank you enough.

Para mis hermanas, Desayuno Chapin, the great loves of my life, Vanessa and Sophie. Thank you for holding my hand, drying my tears, propping me up and propelling me forward. Thank you for letting me read my entire book OUT LOUD to you, just to "hear the flow." Thank you for never wavering in your conviction that I could do this. Las quiero tanto.

Mami y Papi – gracias. When I told you I was writing a novel, your "por supuesto" attitude was more inspiring than you know. The fact that me finding this path made so much sense to you just reaffirmed that I was meant to be on it. Thank you for always believing that I am capable of anything.

And finally, many thanks to all the incredible authors who have inspired me beyond measure. Aaron H. Aceves who reminded me that "the world needs our stories." Emery Lee and Sonora Reyes, who let me tag along with all the other "real" authors after their joint book launch and made me feel like part of the group. Jonny Garza Villa who promised me that no matter how I chose to publish, it was going to be ok. Aiden Thomas, who met me ONCE and was instantly so supportive, because "we need more queer Latin novels." Steven Salvatore (who I actually haven't met but heard speak at a panel) for saying that "other authors of queer books aren't your competition, they're your community. So write your stories, because we all want to read them."

Thank you.